# HIS MASTER'S PLEASURE

"I must say, my dear, you look most enticing," he observed.

Indeed Esme did look appealing, her cheeks rosy from the bath, her gold-streaked hair tumbling down her shoulders and her figure seductively evident beneath the chiffon folds of the peignoir. Only her stormy gray eyes belied the picture of a mistress awaiting the pleasure of her master.

"Are you sure you still want to return to Mount Street? We could deal very well together," he murmured.

"Of course I do. I resent being held here against my will, sir!" she replied bravely.

"You wound me, Esme. I am quite famed for my expertise in the boudoir. If you would only abandon this pose of virginal shrinking, you might find the experience quite enjoyable," he said mockingly.

Why he found her so arousing he could not fathom, but as he looked at her now, trembling but determined, a tide of hunger overcame whatever lingering hesitation he might have had about her seduction.

With a muttered oath, he pulled her against his chest. His mouth silenced her outcry as he forced a hard, demanding kiss on her soft mouth . . .

# A SCANDALOUS PORTRAIT

## VIOLET HAMILTON

**ZEBRA BOOKS**
**KENSINGTON PUBLISHING CORP.**

ZEBRA BOOKS

are published by

Kensington Publishing Corp.
475 Park Avenue South
New York, NY 10016

First printing: September, 1989

Printed in the United States of America

# Chapter One

"Damn," Hugo Carstairs fumed, frowning at the engraved missive by his breakfast plate. Pushing aside the half-eaten sirloin, he glowered at the summons from the Prince Regent. The peremptory invitation to Carlton House that evening interfered with his plans and caused him great irritation.

Considered a member of the prince's set, Hugo often wished that His Royal Highness did not enjoy his company so much, and this was certainly true this morning. Of course, he could refuse to obey, he thought, but he gave a resigned shrug and decided to accept the inevitable. If he did not accept, Prinny would just pursue him until he did, and then signify his displeasure in some annoying way. Accepting the invitation, however, would mean postponing a party Hugo had planned for this evening. He would now have to bestir himself to make other arrangements. So fatiguing.

Hugo's mood frequently alternated between anger and boredom. He cursed again as his secretary, a thin, balding young man with a diffident manner entered the dining room.

"Well, Charles, you will be delighted to learn that we must cancel the orgy for this evening. Our prince demands my presence at Carlton House, and it seems I must comply," Hugo said, his momentary annoyance now replaced by the languid air he cultivated on occasions. "I am sure that pleases you," he concluded, eyeing his secretary quizzically.

Charles Leigh, accustomed to his employer's foibles, said nothing, reluctant to give Hugo the satisfaction of a sigh of relief. The youngest son of an impoverished vicar, a distant connection of the Carstairs, he appreciated his good fortune in securing this post as secretary to the Duke of Milbourne, although he often disapproved of his master's libertine, frivolous life. He wanted the duke to take an interest in politics, to debate the country's concerns in the House of Lords and to use his great wealth and position to further philanthropic causes. But Charles had long since learned that the duke's inclinations lay in other, less reputable directions. It was such a pity, he thought. Looking at the duke, he wondered how much longer Hugo could continue on this course of idle dissipation, wasting his considerable intellect, when he could be influencing affairs of great moment.

Refusing to be drawn into a donnybrook, Charles stood waiting patiently while the duke toyed with the prince's letter. Hugo Carstairs was unfairly endowed with not only a great fortune, a distinguished lineage and striking good looks, but a fine mind. Men with half his attributes had gained high office while he spurned all efforts to exert himself along the lines Charles favored. Dressed in cream kersey pantaloons and gleaming Hessian top boots with a black Stultz coat of impeccable fit, the duke was beginning to show some of the effects of his chosen life, but for all that he was still a handsome man. Over six feet tall, with a muscular figure and a shock of black hair arranged fashionably in the windswept style, Hugo Carstairs attracted many women. He did nothing to discourage their admiration, although his attentions were far from honorable. Despairing mothers of debutantes had long since given up on the duke, who showed no signs of desiring the married state again. They warned their daughters to avoid him, for his reputation was fearsome. Charles wondered if the duke's earlier experience had permanently soured him on respectable females. Certainly Hugo preferred the muslin set,

6

opera dancers, Cyprians and such demimondaines as Harriette Wilson, whom he had engaged for this evening's entertainment. Charles sighed. He supposed he would have to contact that disreputable woman and make the duke's excuses. It was not a task he relished.

"Do you wish me to inform Miss Wilson of your change in plans?" he asked, striving to keep any hint of disapproval from his voice.

The duke smiled cynically, well aware of his secretary's thoughts. "Not at all, Charles. I would never dream of exposing you to that lady's exceptional charms. I will handle that errand myself, but it's a damn nuisance. You can notify my other guests, if you will," he ordered with a negligent wave of his hand. "Have you any other tedious business at hand, my dear fellow?"

"I was hoping you would make an appearance in the Lords this week. They will be debating the new civil list, and Castelreagh could use your support." Charles hoped that the duke might be intrigued.

"Too, too fatiguing, Charles. You should know better," the duke reproved, rising to his feet. "I would be better employed at Gentleman Jackson's saloon," he said, referring to the pugilist parlor which attracted the more athletic Corinthians.

Charles had to admit that the duke's rackety life did not seem to have any lasting affect on his physique or his stamina. Although the lines around his dark wicked eyes were deepening and his mouth was too often drawn in lines of boredom and disdain, the man had amazing resilience. But it was not his place to dispute his employer's methods of relaxation. It was a hopeless task in any event.

"Have you any other orders, your Grace?" Charles asked.

"When you use my title so chillingly I know I have incurred your disapproval. Such a Puritan, Charles. I am sure I am a trial to you. But there is one matter. Will you see about that Constable I want to buy? It's at the Gorton Gallery, I believe. It will make a nice addition to my collection. The artist is still not too popular and I want to acquire several of his works before he becomes the rage," the duke said decisively. Where pictures were concerned, he had catholic tastes that the Prince Regent, for one, respected. Hugo's passion for art was one of his most admirable qualities, Charles thought.

"No doubt the prince requires your advice on the latest addition to his collection," Charles offered, hoping to dispel some of the duke's annoyance at the invitation.

"No doubt," said the duke carelessly. "But Prinny need not have been so exigent. Do not forget to notify this evening's guests that the party is off," the duke reminded Charles as he prepared to leave. Then he hesitated a moment. "Thank you, Charles, for putting up with my pecadilloes, dear chap," he said as he left the room.

Charles reluctantly smiled. That was the trouble with Hugo Carstairs. He could always charm one out of one's sullens if he wanted. One could not help but be seduced by that engaging manner. Too bad he so seldom exerted himself to please.


Sometime later, driving his matched grays hitched to his curricle through the morning traffic down Picadilly, the duke showed little of his charm. His black look had been noticed by his tiger—his groom—and the young scamp had taken good care to treat his master gingerly. The duke's rages could be awesome, and his staff walked warily when he was annoyed. But the bright, crisp April morning had a beneficent effect on Hugo's mind, and by the time the equipage turned into Argyle Street, the duke had regained a more even humor. He leaped lightly from the curricle when it pulled up before a gray stone-fronted house.

"Walk the horses, Albert. I should not be too long," he ordered, tossing the reins to his tiger.

"I doubt that," Albert muttered to himself as he watched the duke ascend the steps. Even though it was before noon, he suspected that the Duke might dally with the popular Miss

Wilson in the usual way. She was an expensive piece, and most of the bucks in town would give a great deal to have the duke's entree to her salon and to her bed. Oh, well, Albert thought, it was not his place to question the ways of his noble employer. The duke was a hard master, but a fair one, and the tiger would not like to lose his position by some careless remark. Not many men owned so fine a stable, and Albert loved horses more than he did humans.

"I hope I am not too early to be received, Mary," the duke said, relinquishing his beaver hat and driving gloves to the maid.

"Not at all, Your Grace. Miss Wilson has a guest, but their business is nearly completed," the maid answered with a smile. The duke could have a pleasing word for minions when it suited him, and was very generous with his vails. "You may go right up, Your Grace."

As the duke strode up the stairs, he did not at first notice the figure descending—until they met on the landing. Harriette's visitor was a young woman, wearing an enveloping gray silk cloak that hid her figure but could not completely disguise her youth. Seeing the duke approach, the girl tried to scuttle by him, but he would have none of that. Reaching out a hand, he halted her progress, intrigued by her air of mystery.

"What have we here? A new addition to the ranks?" he asked, amused at the girl's look of fearful surprise. Could this be a recent arrival to the Cyprian ranks? She was an uncommon type, he mused, noting her honey gold hair escaping from a careless chignon, her haunting gray eyes and firm chin that accentuated her high cheekbones. She was not exactly a beauty but possessed a certain intriguing quality. She made no concession to fashion, for her face was free of paint and her eyes showed none of the boldness usual in a demimondaine.

"I don't think we have met before. I am Milbourne. And what is your name, and your business with the fair Harriette?" The duke raised her chin with one demanding hand.

9

Trying to shake off his grasp, the girl looked angry rather than pleased at his attentions—not the usual reaction when Hugo introduced himself to a female.

"That is not your business, sir. Unhand me, please," she insisted, apparently disliking the bold look in his hot eyes.

"Why so indignant? Surely you are not averse to the admiration of a man. You could not be long in Harriette's company without knowing what is expected from women of your stamp," the duke drawled in a brutal manner.

"You are insulting, sir. You are not a gentleman to press questions upon me," she replied severely, her wide eyes sparkling with anger.

Amused and challenged, the duke hesitated. Why was he trying to quiz the chit? He had no reason to pursue the matter, but her air of insulted innocence riled him.

"Come now, my dear. This is no way to treat your betters," he scolded, releasing her chin and catching her by the shoulders in a firm grip. "I think you need a lesson in manners."

Before she could understand his intent, he lowered his head and pressed a hard kiss on her unwilling lips.

As the kiss lengthened, the girl felt a warmth rising from within her, and a frightening desire to respond. She quickly quelled it. She struggled free, then gave vent to her fury with a resounding slap across his cheek.

Before he could recover from this most unexpected response to his careless caress, she had scurried past him and run rapidly down the stairs. For a moment, the duke, angry and provoked by her reaction, was tempted to pursue her, but then he shrugged his shoulders, his usual ennui taking over and he continued on his way up the staircase. No doubt the chit hoped he would be intrigued, but he was far too experienced to be taken in by such a gambit. To hell with her.

Harriette Wilson received the duke with a slight raise of the eyebrows. Such an early call was exceptional. She was accustomed to his outré behavior, however, and welcomed him calmly.

At first glance, one found little in Harriette's appearance to reveal she was the most notorious demimondaine of her day with a long list of protectors, which included the most noble names in the land. Far from beautiful, she had dark hair, which she kept simply arranged, a rather long nose, and large dark eyes that sparkled with intelligence. Today she was dressed in a simple blue silk morning dress trimmed with ruching at the modest decolletage and around the hem. Her charm lay in her vivacious manner and her wit as much as in her expertise in the bedroom. She knew how to talk to gentlemen. She had enough experience, and her heart never betrayed her. It was rumored that this green grocer's daughter had only once allowed her emotions to rule her head. She had fallen in love with Lord Ponsonby, and when he abandoned her, she had vowed never again to enter into an alliance where she exposed herself to unhappiness.

Harriette greeted the duke warmly, for he was one of her favorites, a generous and skilled lover who never made inordinate demands.

He bowed over her hand as if she were the most respectable lady in the land and begged her indulgence for the inappropriateness of the call. One of the reasons Harriette had a partiality for Hugo Carstairs was his polished manners, which she knew he could abandon whenever it suited him. She herself had never had cause to complain.

"You are up and about early, Hugo, for such a practiced debaucher," she teased.

"Yes, well, I thought it prudent to make my apologies in person. We must postpone tonight's party. The Prince Regent requires my presence, and although I would prefer to spend the evening in your company, dear Harriette, our prince easily takes unbrage if his demands are not met. I do hope you will not think ill of me for this cavalier treatment," he said suavely, eyeing her with affection.

"Ah, yes, Prinny can be excitable. I will accept your excuses

11

with reluctance, for I was quite looking forward to this evening," Harriette answered with equal aplomb.

"I would far rather be with you, Harriette, as I am sure you know," the duke responded. She smiled.

"Another time, then, Hugo. Pleasures are doubly enjoyed when delayed," she said with a roguish grin. "Now what can Prinny want from you, I wonder?"

"Doubtless some trifling service that will cost me dear. The last time he demanded my advice I ended up losing a nice Lawrence from my collection. It now graces Carlton House," he added ruefully.

"The Prince has impeccable taste, which you share, Hugo, so you should be flattered. You can stand the doings tonight, I am sure."

They chatted for a few more minutes before the duke took his leave of her. As he was turning away toward the door, he paused. "Incidentally, I passed a most fetching chit on the stairs. May I assume that she will join us on our next entertainment?"

"She is not of the sisterhood, Hugo, so leave the poor girl be. As a matter of fact, she is quite a talented artist, of the utmost moral probity, I suspect. She is going to paint my portrait." Harriette confessed this a bit reluctantly.

"A portrait. But surely you would be better served by a Lawrence or Raeburn than some amateur female dauber," the duke remarked.

"She has an intriguing style, and I prefer a woman."

"And what is the name of this paragon?" Hugo asked.

"Ah, Hugo, I recognize that look in your eye, but her identity must remain a secret to you. She is not a proper object for your artistic attentions," Harriette teased, aware that the duke's enqueries about the young woman were not inspired by any interest in her talent, or at least not in the type of talent displayed outside the bedroom.

"You are hard-hearted, my dear Harriette. Of course I am always looking for new artists."

"Well, I promise to let you have the first look at her work," she soothed.

"I assume this mysterious portrait has been commissioned by one of your numerous admirers," he asked, not to be put off so easily.

"No, this is an indulgence of my own. I can well afford it." Harriette looked at him warily. She did not welcome any rivals for his affection.

"I will await the finished product with impatience. And now I must leave you. À bientôt, dear lady," he said with an expert bow.

Harriette laughed and bid him a fond farewell. Hugo was a rogue, she thought, but such an attractive one. They had parted today on amicable terms, but she wondered if he would be content to let the matter of the lovely artist rest there. She was an innocent, Harriette surmised from long experience, and not fitted to cope with the likes of the duke. He would not learn of her identity from Harriette.

A rare frown broke over her smooth brow. The girl was obviously quality, and would be shocked by any overtures from such an established rake as the Duke of Milbourne, no matter how noble his title or handsome his person. Perhaps she ought to warn the girl. But Harriette soon forgot her uneasiness for she rarely worried about the future, being content to enjoy the pleasures of the moment.

*Chapter Two*

Fannie stuck her head in the door of her cousin's retreat. "May I interrupt you, Esme?" she asked timidly, knowing how much Esme cherished her privacy when she was working.

The girl in the painting smock lay down her brushes and turned to welcome the visitor to her studio. "Of course, Fannie. The light is going now, anyway." It was a bare, bleak room, with few furnishings aside from a large easel, some battered cupboards, a shabby sofa, and a couple of out-of-fashion chairs. Esme stepped back from the watercolor resting on her easel and eyed it dubiously. Then with a shrug, she covered the painting with a cloth and signified that she was at Fannie's disposal.

Despite their very different looks and temperaments, the cousins were warm friends. Fannie, the only daughter of the Earl and Countess of Cranford, was a cheerful, plump girl with carrot-colored hair whose only claim to beauty was a wide smile and merry eyes. Her cousin Esme, although not in the fashionable mode, had lovely honey-blond hair and wide, wistful gray eyes, which gave her a fragile appearance belied by her strong chin and sculptured cheekbones. Little could be seen of her slim figure beneath the loose painter's smock, but in truth, Esme was well formed, with an elegance and stature denied to her cousin.

14

"Come sit down, Esme. You must be tired, standing all afternoon before that easel." Fannie patted the sofa beside her.

Esme smiled at her cousin, amused by the girl's confiding air. Although she did not share her cousin's passion for the *on dits* of the Vogue, or her concerns about social success, she was ready to lend a sympathetic ear to Fannie's accounts of her doings.

"Mama sent me to ask you to accompany us to the Lieven's ball tomorrow evening," Fanny said as her cousin joined her on the sofa. Seeing Esme's moue of displeasure, she hurried on persuasively. "Please, Esme, do come! I would so welcome your company, and the parents feel you should not completely ignore fashionable company. You will never find a husband cooped up here with your paints and brushes!"

"But I am not looking for a husband, dear Fannie," Esme protested, sighing. They often engaged in this argument. She realized that her uncle and aunt believed her painting to be merely a ladylike hobby. To them it was a distraction from the real business of fashionable young ladies: to secure their future by attaching themselves to an eligible gentleman. Esme could not persuade the earl and countess that her painting was far more important to her than foolish flirtations and idle conversation about gowns and entertainments.

"So you insist, Esme," Fannie said, "but even a dedicated artist must have some gaiety. Please come with us tomorrow. I want you to meet someone."

Esme smiled. She could not resist her cousin's enthusiasm. She suspected, too, that the girl had involved herself with some unsuitable young man, and wished Esme's aid in persuading her parents of his respectability. Fannie had a penchant for finding gazetted fortune hunters and impecunious younger sons who rarely returned her wide-eyed devotion. She was forever sighing over some young fool, Esme mused, instead of accepting a more reliable partner.

"And who is it this time, Fannie?" she asked.

Fannie gave a melodious sigh. "His name is Algernon

15

French. You will admire him, I know, Esme, for he's a poet, unappreciated as yet, but he has as much ability as Lord Byron, I think," Fannie offered a bit tentatively. "He's so different from most young men. You will find much in common with him, I know." She hesitated a moment. "I suppose once he meets you I will be utterly cast in the shade."

"Don't be such a pea goose, Fannie. You have much to attract the right man," Esme replied stoutly. She doubted if this Algernon French was any more suitable, or any more enamoured of Fannie, than others who had preceded him.

"Aside from his poetic talents, what else does Mr. French have to recommend him, Fannie?" Esme asked. "What are his prospects, for I doubt he could support a wife on his scribblings."

"Oh, Esme, don't be so practical! You sound like the parents. He is of modest estate. I believe his parents are gentry, but that is not important. I find him so unassuming and comfortable. And he is exceptionally kind to me."

"Who wouldn't be kind to you, Fannie? You are so warm-hearted. But surely this young man has not made advances toward you!" she reproved, Esme tried her best to assume a stern air, but she could not help but be amused by Fannie's soulful look. "Has he requested your hand without approaching Uncle Egbert?"

"Well, he hasn't actually asked for me, but I know he likes me," Fannie explained, blushing at some secret memory.

"You have not been meeting him on the sly, Fannie!"

"Only once in the Park, and my maid was with me," Fannie admitted. "He has come to call several times, and has read me his poems. But when he visits, mother scowls and looks disapproving. It is very off-putting. The parents should be happy that any man takes an interest in me!" Fannie tugged at her red curls in despair. Her Season had not produced one respectable offer, despite the generous settlement her father might be prepared to make.

"They only crave your happiness, I am sure," Esme soothed,

16

patting Fannie with a comforting hand.

"Oh, well, you would never understand—you are so attractive yourself. It is such a waste. If you exerted yourself you could have every beau in London at your feet." Fannie looked with envy at her cousin.

"Nonsense, Fannie. And I am not interested in having beaux at my feet. But I will consent to accompany you to the Lieven's ball if that will improve your humor," Esme said, smiling with affection at her cousin. Since she had joined the Cranford household as a grieving young girl, she had been warmed by her cousin's friendship and love. Fannie might have been jealous of this unwanted intrusion into their family but she had always treated Esme as a much-loved sister, and Esme had responded in kind.

The Earl and Countess of Cranford were a rather austere couple. Their inordinate concern with propriety and society's good opinion made Fannie's lot a hard one. They were less interested in Esme's conduct and behaved toward her with something approaching indulgence. They accepted her preoccupation with her painting more than most parents would. So the least she could do was accept their invitation to the Lieven's ball.

If Esme could not wholly love her guardians, she respected them and felt a great deal of gratitude for their hospitality. Her own father, the Countess of Cranford's younger brother, had died of the fever when Esme was twelve. His grieving wife died soon after. If the Cranford's had not taken Esme in, her lot would not have been an easy one, although she had inherited a bit of money upon her twenty-first birthday, now some months past. When she had suggested to the Cranfords it might now be possible for her to set up a studio in some country cottage in order to pursue her art uninterrupted, they had been scandalized. She had not insisted. Esme did her best to accommodate herself to guardians whose interests were totally opposed to her own because she felt obligated to behave in this fashion. Aunt Mildred and Uncle Egbert had enough difficulty in launching the 18-year old Fannie on the marriage market and restraining the more shocking excesses of their son and heir, Viscount Robert Weirs, who was a sore trial with his gambling and wenching. Esme didn't wish to add to their troubles.

Fannie, her purpose accomplished, smiled happily. She began a panegyric upon her latest admirer, not noticing Esme's distracted air. When the two girls left the studio to dress for dinner they were in accord, although Esme saw difficult days ahead.


Carlton House was ablaze with light as Hugo Carstairs entered it that evening, dressed elegantly in black knee britches and pristine white linen. A group of flunkeys lined the entrance hall to take his hat and announce him to the august assembly. The Prince Regent insisted on great formality in his entertainment. As Hugo expected, the reception hall was thronged with a raffish crowd. Prinny received him graciously.

"So kind of you to answer my summons, Carstairs. I want your advice on my latest acquisition after dinner." The large, fat prince, his Hanoverian blue eyes gleaming in his bland face, was well pleased in having gained his ends with Hugo. The prince could sulk nastily if his wishes were balked. Poor Beau Brummel had been banished for making an insulting remark about the prince, a remark not entirely undeserved, Hugo thought. Brummel had jeered to Lord Alvaney, "Who is your fat friend?" and that had ended the relationship that had enabled Beau Brummel to become the fashion arbiter of the day. The prince, who had so long admired Brummel's caustic wit and elegant manner, had abandoned him and Brummel had ended in disgrace and poverty. The Prince could condescend to his friends, even invite intimacy, but a corresponding license was not entertained.

Hugo Carstairs, who cared little for any man's opinion and shared his prince's arrogance, found Prinny amusing, but not even for his future sovereign would he bow in obeisance. Still, if Prinny suspected that the duke was annoyed at his summons to Carlton House, he did not show it.

Like all the Prince's meals, the dinner was interminable and lavish, with twenty courses, each more elaborate than the last. Tonight's dinner in the opulent Gothic dining room, which reflected the style of the gold plate, elaborate silver, and crystal of the table settings, was modest by the Regent's standards. There were only two dozen guests. Still, the event was far too sumptuous and formal for the duke's taste.

Seated on his right was Prinny's matronly mistress, lady Hertford, whose blowsy manner enthralled the Prince. The duke found her dull, recalling Mrs. Fitzherbert, who had been a much more scintillating hostess. Cursing his acceptance of the invitation, Hugo wondered why he had been summoned. He longed to get away, but knew that Prinny would drag out the dinner as long as possible. The Regent was a dedicated trencherman, his appetite formidable. He showed the results— flesh falling in waxy jowls from his chin, his massive stomach, despite his corsets, bulging with excess. Only remnants of the charm which had once made him "Prince Florizel," now remained, but when he wished he could still charm and cajole. Since he craved a favour from the duke, he was at his most beguiling, talking across Lady Hertford to his guest about art and politics, trying to fascinate and almost succeeding.

Finally the meal was over, and Prinny signified he wanted the duke to accompany him for a private audience. Cavalierly, he abandoned his guests and led Hugo to a small anteroom lined with pictures.

"I want your advice on a new painting, Carstairs. I found it in a small gallery and think it has great charm, not at all like the rather coarse stuff that fellow Constable turns out. I can't understand what you see in his daubs," Prinny complained, fearing he had missed some aspect of the artist's talent.

"Constable is unique. He has a strange charm and an uncanny ability to touch the most mundane scenes with his

19

genius," the duke replied shortly.

He looked at several of the canvases with a discerning eye. There were some quite nice miniatures by the prince's friend Richard Conway—an eccentric artist with a rather brittle elegance—and a new Andrew Geddes, an artist who painted Scottish scenes the prince enjoyed. But the regent ignored these additions to his collection and led the duke to a small oil leaning against the wall.

The subject matter was different, wilder and less contrived than most of Prinny's paintings. Outlined against a stormy sky and a gray sea, a young boy was depicted before a craggy coast—a rough fisherman's lad, perhaps. The colors were subtle and unusual, a soft blending of nature's hues, but for the dramatic contrast of the boy's ragged scarlet jersey. And the boy himself looked lost and frightened, his thin, angular face compelling. The painting held a haunting quality that intrigued the duke and reminded him of someone, but he did not know who.

"Who is the artist, sir?" Hugo asked, unable to draw his eyes from the painting.

"That is the question. You can see it is signed only *Arethusa*, an attempt to hide the artist's identity, no doubt. As I recall, Arethusa was a nymph attendant upon the huntress goddess, Artemis, changed by her mistress into a fountain. I think the artist must be a woman," the prince explained, not surprising the duke with his knowledge of Greek mythology. Prinny was a cultured man, despite his gross appetites.

"Where did you discover it, sir?"

"Ah, yes, and it is a find, don't you think Carstairs? I was sure you would be struck by the rare quality of the painting just as I was. I bought it from a small gallery owner—Gorton, I believe. You have found some jewels there yourself, I think, so you must know the proprietor well." The prince chuckled, pleased with the duke's obvious fascination. Then he continued slyly, "It isn't often that I beat you to the post, eh?"

20

"Not at all, sir. Your collection is brilliant and evidences your impeccable taste," Hugo replied. For once, he conceded, his sovereign had stolen a march on him, had discovered a new artist with obvious promise. "I would like to see more of this mysterious artist's work and discover the his or her identity. He looked again at the signature.

"Ah, I hoped I could pique your interest and that you would do a bit of detective work for me," the prince said. "There must be more paintings by Arethusa. I want to add them to my collection."

The duke reluctantly turned away from the painting. "I will certainly try to track down the artist. But I warn you, sir, I will not sacrifice any other gems to you willingly."

The prince laughed, his huge stomach jiggling, and appeared pleased rather than offended. "Capital! Capital! You have endorsed my discovery. I was quite sure, but occasionally I do make mistakes," he admitted modestly.

"Rarely, sir," the duke flattered. "I commend your purchase." Now that the purpose for his invitation had been accomplished, he was eager to begin his investigation. If most of his pleasures were emphemeral and frivolous, Hugo took art seriously, and valued his reputation as a connoisseur.

"Thank you for showing me the painting," he said to the prince. "I am honored that you sought my opinion." Together they left the room. "I will interview the Gorton Gallery man tomorrow. After all, we must be first in the field."

"Don't forget, Carstairs, I am not satisfied with this one example. I command you to find me others!"

The duke made no promise, for he well knew the prince was capable of stealing a find from under his nose, or insisting that Hugo give him an art work he fancied.

Prinny's extravagances were monumental and Hugo wondered if he had yet paid for the picture. The poor artist might be honored to have his painting included in the prince's collection but that would not buy him the necessities of life.

As Hugo left Carlton House, he settled back into his carriage. His mind still full of the painting, he recalled the girl he had seen at Harriette Wilson's. Her image floating hazily in his mind. For some reason that oil had reminded him of Harriette's visitor. She was an artist, too. Could she be Arethusa? It was a disturbing idea, with little foundation, but the duke was impatient to learn more.

## Chapter Three

"Now that you have come out of your nun-like seclusion, at least for one evening, you must promise me two dances tonight," Robert Weirs, the Cranford's heir and only son, demanded in his irrepressible way.

Robert was an engaging young man, fair-haired and somewhat of a dandy with twinkling blue eyes and a careless grin. He and Esme had always been friends, but she suspected he was trying out his charm on her since he had come down from Oxford and joined the Guards. She did not dream of taking him seriously but he amused her, was companionable and a safe distraction.

"I would be delighted, Robert. You are such a skilled partner." Esme smiled at her cousin.

"Is that the only reason?" He sighed lugubriously, implying that she had wounded his amour-propre. "I have to get my bid in early for this rare treat. No doubt you will be besieged by offers now that you have come out of hiding." Robert, like the rest of his family, did not understand Esme's reluctance to join the social set to which her birth and breeding entitled her.

"I doubt if there will be queues," she protested. "You would be better off enjoying the company of this year's crop of debutantes."

"Nonsense. I have looked them over and they are a paltry

23

lot. Not one can hold a candle to you, dear cousin." He spoke gaily, but beneath his insouciant air, Esme sensed a regard that while flattering, was somewhat puzzling. She hoped Robert was not serious in his attentions. But then, Robert probably felt safe with her. She would not be taken in by his cozening ways and expect more than he was prepared to offer. At twenty-five—four years older than she was—Robert should be looking for a wife. Esme knew that his parents were anxious to see him settled with a proper bride and beginning to set up his nursery.

"Really, Robert, you ought to be hanging out for a wife," Esme said in her best severe sisterly manner. "You know that Uncle Egbert and Aunt Mildred are not happy with your rackety ways."

"Ah, but I am not ready to settle down yet! Having too much fun enjoying the delights of London!" he exclaimed, shuddering at the thought of surrendering his freedom.

"And those delights include too many late nights, the gambling halls and worse, I suspect. That was an expensive little charmer I saw in your curricle in the park the other day," Esme reproved. But she was unable to keep the mischief in her eyes from spoiling the effect of her criticism.

"I am shocked, Esme! Proper young women do not notice such things." Robert riposted, not at all displeased that she had noticed his latest bit of muslin.

"Uncle Egbert will not find it too amusing if you end up in dun street, Robert," she continued, determined to make her point. "He is so proud of you, and you don't deserve his approbation, I warrant."

"You are a hard-hearted female, Esme, insisting on hiding away with your paint brushes and then wanting to deny more frivolous souls their light amusements!" he jibed.

But Esme sensed some meaning beneath his banter that troubled her. She hoped he had not delivered himself into the hands of money lenders. That would not sit well with her uncle, who expected prudence in his heir. "I suppose it is my duty to keep an eye on you and lead you from temptation," she said lightly.

"More likely to lead me into it," he muttered, then seemed to regret what he might have revealed. "And how about replacing that scandalous Cyprian in my curricle this afternoon," he cajoled. "It looks to be a fine day and you would enjoy a ride around the Park, admit it!"

"You will not lure me into wasting my time with such diversions. I have a painting I must finish."

Esme refused his offer with little regret. How she wished her family would realize that her art came first. It was not some attempt to thwart their plans, but what she really wanted to do. She really did not enjoy these excursions into London society. Still, Robert would never believe she found such amusements boring. He was such a roisterer himself.

"Well, I suppose I will have to content myself with this evening's jollity," he said in mild annoyance. "But hell you are in danger of putting yourself on the shelf if you continue to secrete yourself in that damned studio." Robert knew Esme would not welcome his real reason for trying to draw her into the Season's excitement. And, in fact, he had mixed emotions about her seclusion. He was afraid if she did consent to all the invitations she received, she might meet some fellow who would win her heart, and Robert found himself hating that idea. She was so much more appealing than his usual round of young women, whose whole purpose was to dance and flirt the hours away in order to capture some poor unsuspecting fool as a husband. The man who finally won Esme, he thought, would be of an uncommon sort. Robert dreaded the day she would meet him. He feared she would never entertain more than cousinly affection from him. He would have to tread carefully not to arouse her suspicions of his real feelings. Perhaps tonight might be the beginning of his serious courtship of his elusive cousin.

Reminding her again of the two promised dances, one a supper dance, he left her reluctantly. She was so unaware of her beauty, he thought. Robert did not want to marry, but if he was forced into bondage within the next few years, he knew that he would never find a bride as satisfying as his cousin. He thought of confiding his wish to his parents, but sensed they would not be receptive. Better to wait until the lady consented, he decided, for once taking a prudent course his father would have approved. Marriage between first cousins, although not unknown, was not completely acceptable, but if he persuaded his father it would be Esme or no one for his wife, he might convince him. Plenty of time, he thought in his light-hearted way, to win Esme's heart.

Joseph Gorton, owner of a small gallery off St. James Street, had little of the aesthete in his appearance. He cultivated a suave, ingratiating air, his portly figure, round face topped by a fringe of brown hair, and ever-present smile giving a false impression of amiability. Beneath his smiles and bows he was a shrewd businessman who had parlayed his small talent, inherited from a street artist father, into the successful ownership of a gallery, which was just now coming into fashion. And among his most valued clients was the Duke of Milbourne, although he was a difficult one who knew his own mind and was not apt to be persuaded to buy a meritricious daub. The duke's patronage was highly prestigious and when His Grace entered the gallery the morning after his dinner with the Prince Regent, Joseph Gorton welcomed him effusively.

"Good morning, Your Grace. A splendid spring day, is it not? Have you come about another Constable? Your man collected that small landscape you favoured yesterday?" Gorton said, ushering the duke into his private sanctum. "I regret I have nothing more from that artist right now, but I expect he will be sending some paintings around to me soon. And, of course, you will have the first opportunity to view them."

Gorton rubbed his hands together obsequiously, which the duke found intensely annoying. He disliked toadies and Gorton's undoubted expertise in his field did not excuse his oily manner. But the duke was accustomed to such treatment, and although it wearied him, he was resigned to it.

"Of course, I am always interested in Constable, Gorton. But I am here on another errand." He hesitated, suddenly doubting that Gorton knew that the purchaser of the Arethusa oil was the Prince Regent. He would be cock of the walk if he did, and his prices and his conceit would rise accordingly. The prince, no doubt, had bought the painting through an intermediary, and the duke must not reveal his secret.

"I came across a rather interesting find the other day, done by an unknown artist, at least unknown to me," he said, choosing his words carefully. "I wonder if you could assist me in discovering a bit more about the artist. The painting had an unusual quality. It depicted a young boy against a seacoast background, and was signed, somewhat enigmatically, with the name Arethusa—no doubt an attempt at anonymity. Do you remember this work?"

Surprisingly, Gorton did not rush into an enthusiastic tribute to the anonymous artist. He lowered his eyes and turned away, as if marshalling his thoughts.

"I did sell a painting to Sir John Leicester, Your Grace, by this Arethusa. I was rather surprised at his interest, for the work had none of the grandeur, the color, which usually appeals. In fact, I thought it was rather derivative. But I must be guided by your superior judgment, and by Sir John's, of course." Gorton gave a spurious smile.

"Nonsense, my good man. The painting was very unusual, and I want to buy some of Arethusa's work before the artist becomes the rage and you raise the price accordingly. Now where can I find the artist?" the duke insisted haughtily, angered by the man's evasion. "Is Arethusa a woman? I have a sense that is the reason for the pseudonym."

"How clever of you, Your Grace. The artist is indeed a woman, and therefore prefers not be known by her real name. But alas, I am not at liberty to reveal her identity. It pains me to disappoint you, but I have promised the lady she shall remain unknown. Of course, I would not be averse to selling you another of her works when it comes on the market. I have the exclusive rights to her efforts," Gorton explained, anxiously trying to mollify his most important customer.

"Do I understand correctly that you refuse to tell me what I want to know?" the duke demanded coldly, his temper rising.

Gorton remained firm. "I am afraid so, for the moment, Your Grace. Of course, I can beg the lady to be less intransigent. But I fear I must, for now, respect her privacy. I will endeavor to tell her of your interest and that it would be to her advantage to reveal herself. I can only say she is a lady of quality who fears that her hobby might attract undue notoriety." Gorton was caught between two stools. The lady had powerful protectors, almost as influential as the duke, and if he betrayed her, he might suffer as much as from the duke's withdrawal of his custom. It was a situation that required all of his considerable tact.

"If you are honor-bound to keep her name secret, I must not coax you, I suppose. Perhaps I can gain my information from another source. But, remember, Gorton, I want to see the next work she produces. It will be on your head if you sell it to Leicester or anyone else before I have the chance to purchase it," the duke warned, casting a black look at the gallery owner. While he respected the man's attempt to shield the artist, he was frustrated at not achieving his goal.

Seeing no reason to prolong the interview, he bid Gorton a curt goodbye and left the gallery.

At his departure, Joseph Gorton wiped beads of perspiration from his forehead. He only hoped he had not alienated the duke permanently, but what could he do? He had his own well-being to consider. And his pocketbook. If the artist should suddenly become popular and refuse to employ him as an agent, he would sacrifice some healthy profits. But if the duke took away his custom he would be equally the poorer. It was unfair that he should be the victim of these aristocratic caprices. Well, all was not lost yet, and he would certainly try to persuade the diffident Arethusa that she could not hide behind him indefinitely.

*Chapter Four*

Invitations to the Russian Embassy were highly prized. The ambassador and his wife, the Prince and Princess Lieven, reigned as the social arbiters of London. The princess, a striking brunette with large brown eyes and a lively manner, could be haughty and exclusive when her position warranted it. In spite of a series of distinguished lovers, which included the Austrian prime mininster, Prince Metternich, she remained impregnable. But she frowned on similar moral deviations from the less favored members of her milieu. She was a strict patroness of Almack's, known irreverently as "The Marriage Mart" to some, and could refuse vouchers to its portals for the slightest infraction of her hypocritical code. Few had the temerity to challenge her, for her displeasure could ruin any debutante's chances to secure a suitable husband. She was a passionate and intelligent intrigante and a friend and confidante of the Prince Regent, Wellington and Castelreagh. She craved power and attained it, allowing her cuckolded husband to go his own way.

Since the princess had waltzed with the Tsar on Alexander's much-fêted visit to London in 1814, the dance had become all the rage, despite the fact that more sober citizens felt it an excuse for "squeezing and hugging."

The Lievens' entertainments were usually lavish, and this evening was no exception. Carriages thronged Harley Street before the embassy, and guests had to wait quite three quarters of an hour before gaining entrance to the mansion. The mirrored great hall, where the Lievens were receiving, reflected the light of hundreds of wax tapers. The over-powering scent of hot-house flowers permeated the room.

Waiting in line with the Cranfords as the elegant crowd inched its way toward their hosts, Esme wondered why she had accepted this invitation. Already her head had begun to ache from the press of people and close, cloying atmosphere. She had yielded to Fannie's pleas and was wearing her most attractive gown, a cream silk with a matching gauze overskirt iridescent with seed pearls. Her honey-colored hair was caught in a Psyche knot. A few strands escaped to heighten the graceful effect of her long neck. As her only jewelry, she'd worn her mother's modest string of pearls, aware that most of the fashionably dressed ladies would put her to shame with a glittering array of diamonds, emeralds, and sapphires.

At last Esme and the Cranfords were welcomed by the Lievens. The princess gave a cool, appraising nod to Esme before greeting the Cranfords with more enthusiasm. At last they were free to join the dancers in the gaily-decked ballroom. Robert eagerly claimed the first dance, which Esme had promised him, aware that her entrance onto the dance floor was the signal for other partners to make their claim. As they slid into the waltz, she remarked on the luxury of the appointments with some derision.

"The cost of this evening's ball would support a score of East End families for more than a year!" she said.

"Don't be such a little Puritan, cousin," he chided her. "Think of the employment the Lievens are providing for the caterers, modistes, and musicians. They have to live, too, you know."

When she had first come to London a few years ago, Esme had been appalled at the poverty of the city. If her guardians had not been so disapproving, she would have made some personal efforts to alleviate the shocking indifference of the *ton* toward the general populace. But the Cranfords had forbidden her to expose herself to disease and squalor, and their objections were so heated she had abandoned her more ambitious plans. She did, however, volunteer her services, over their protests, to a local orphanage.

Robert, a complete hedonist, paid little attention to such serious concerns and did not understand his cousin's distress. He did not want to quarrel with her on this rare festive evening, but Esme would not be easily gainsaid.

"I suppose you have a point, Robert," she admitted as they dipped and swayed to the beguiling strains of the Viennese music, "but I find it unconscionable to put on such an ostentatious display while children are starving a few blocks from here." She looked around with contempt. "Everyone looks so bored, sated with the round of pleasure that consumes them. It's quite disgusting!"

"Oh, Esme, when will you learn that a bit of fun and frivolity does the soul good?" Robert found Esme's social conscience her most annoying quality.

Esme laughed, realizing that now was not the time to convince Robert to take life seriously. She would postpone her strictures to a more opportune occasion, and surrender for now to his blandishments.

Once more in accord, they finished the dance, and as the last chords of the waltz died away, new partners clamoured for Esme's attention. Her popularity surprised her and, not being conceited, she concluded that it sprang from novelty. After all, she did not often make an appearance.

When she had first come to London for the Season some three years ago, she could have made a brillant marriage, for her birth was respectable and her unusual beauty attracted many admirers. But she had soon tired of the vapid young men and older roués who sought her out. She now considered herself a spinster, well beyond marriageable age when so many younger women graced the scene. It was a situation she welcomed.

Aware of Robert scowling by her side, she laughingly accepted the shyest of her partners for the country dance that followed and allowed several other young men to scrawl their names on her card. During her dance with the blushing young man, she suggested he might make a bid for Fannie. Her cousin was looking forlorn and partnerless at the edge of the floor, with the countess beside her smiling grimly, disappointed at her daughter's lack of success.

Dear Fannie, such a warm, loving girl, whose lack of beauty masked other more important qualities. As Esme watched, a tall blond man, with sculptured locks and a distrait air approached her cousin. Could this be the poet, Algernon French? Certainly he looked every inch the dreamer. Fannie welcomed him enthusiastically, but the Countess gave only a curt nod to her daughter's partner. As the dance finished, Fannie dragged the scowling man toward Esme, and introduced him with some pride.

"Esme, this is Algernon French. I know you two will become fast friends. You have so much in common," she said, glowing with excitement.

The young man made a correct bow. "I have heard much about you, Miss Sedgewick. I understand you share my appreciation of the arts, and scorn this surrender to social indulgence," he said. He was obviously impressed by the beauty before him.

Since he was dressed to the nines with a cravat that must have taken hours to arrange, his scorn of society's foibles seemed a little ridiculous to Esme. Repressing a giggle at his serious demeanour, she replied lightly, "But you must admit, Mr. French, that a little respite from the muse is most appealing!" Oh, dear, she thought, he so obviously has a great conceit. How could Fannie find that attractive?

"Perhaps you will honor me with a dance later this evening and we can discuss the arts more fully," he replied, in thrall to this goddess who might understand his passion for poetry.

Much as Esme would have liked to refuse him—she feared

he would bore her to tears with long-winded perorations—she consented for Fannie's sake. She greeted her next partner with some relief. He was a pompous guardsman, but he had little conversation and was an expert dancer. Esme surrendered to the lure of the music.

As the evening wore on, her satin slippers began to pinch and she felt increasingly weary. But supper with Robert and a group of his roistering friends helped relieve some of the tedium. When her next partner, Sir Guy Wentworth, suggested a stroll in the gardens as an escape from the crowded floor, she agreed with alacrity. She barely knew Sir Guy, although she recognized his kind—a jaded libertine whose dissipated life showed in the lines of his pale face and cynical faded blue eyes. It did not occur to her, however, that he entertained any but the most respectful intentions toward her person as he escorted her through the Lievens well-lighted, immaculately tended gardens. She was therefore quite surprised when he stopped her behind some convenient statuary.

"It is rumored that you dislike society, Miss Sedgewick, and consign us poor fools to the devil," he said provocatively. They stood well apart from other meandering couples. It was an unusually mild night for April and the light breeze that had sprung up was a welcome relief to Esme's fevered cheeks.

She replied lightly. "Oh, I don't know, Sir Guy. I admit that on occasion it can be quite amusing to join in the dissipations of the *ton*. I have enjoyed myself this evening."

"You are far too attractive and intriguing to hide yourself away from us all," he continued silkily. "I suspect there is a wanton lurking beneath that prim exterior. Shall we find out?" Before Esme knew what he intended he had taken her in a rough grasp and endeavored to force a kiss upon her lips. Before he could complete his assault, he was rudely shoved aside by a tall dark stranger.

"Up to your old tricks again, Guy?" the stranger asked harshly, looking at Sir Guy with contempt. "You really must resist forcing your attentions on innocents. Bad *ton!*"

Sir Guy recognized his assailant and made no attempt to fight back.

"Are you convinced she is an innocent, Milbourne?" he sneered, but kept a safe distance. He feared that punishing right the duke perfected weekly at Gentleman Jackson's boxing saloon.

"I think you'd best take yourself off before I really lose my temper, Guy," Milbourne threatened, a dangerous light in his dark eyes.

Esme kept silent after one startled look at the intruder. She recognized the elegant peer who had kissed her on the stairs at Harriette Wilson's and was covered with confusion and a smoldering anger. Who was *he* to criticize Sir Guy for trying to kiss her when he had attempted the same outrageous breach of manners and succeeded?

The duke had noticed Esme immediately upon her arrival at the Lievens and had watched her ever since. He'd seen her leave the ballroom with Sir Guy, frowning at her choice of companions. Didn't the little fool realize what kind of man he was? The duke, gave no thought to his own shocking attack on the girl just two days past. He brooked no interference with his own desires, but did not extend that license to the men he despised.

Sir Guy, judging that discretion was the better part of valor in this case, backed down hurriedly.

"The lady seemed willing, but I would not poach on your prior claim, Milbourne. Let us forget it," he fawned, earning a black look from Esme.

There was not a farthing to choose between them, she thought disdainfully, although she felt some gratitude for the duke's rescue. But she did not like his manner, so self-assured, so haughty. She looked at the routed Sir Guy with contempt. He had retreated at the first sign of violence. He was a coward and a poltroon, not worthy even of her scorn.

"I think Miss Sedgewick is awaiting your apology, Sir Guy,"

the duke said softly, grasping the man by the arm in a fierce way.

Giving the duke a look of loathing, Sir Guy bowed curtly to Esme. "I am sorry if I offended your sensibilities, Miss Sedgewick. Pray forgive the liberty."

"Yes, of course, Sir Guy," Esme murmured, uncomfortable with the situation.

Sir Guy, giving her one last insolent look, removed himself before he could encounter any more trouble.

The duke turned to Esme, his eyes kindling with disgust. "Whatever possessed you to allow that man to escort you into the garden? Could you possibly have been eager for his embrace?"

"Don't be ridiculous, sir. And it hardly behooves you to take him to task when you are not above such assaults yourself," Esme replied sharply, annoyed that he was trying to put the burden of the encounter on her shoulders. Really, these libertine refused to take any responsibility for their own actions, and were eager to put the onus on the woman in every case.

"Perhaps I should not have interfered. Doubtless I ruined your enjoyment of his love making," the duke said. "You are rather an enigma, Miss Sedgewick. If I had known who you were I would not have treated you so when we met at Harriette's, but I hardly expected to meet the Cranfords's niece at such an establishment!"

"Do I understand you to mean that you only kiss women of the lower orders?" Esme asked coldly.

The duke smiled, reluctant admiration in his eyes. He put out a careless hand and stroked one wayward curl. Esme experienced a frisson of sensation at his touch.

"You are uncommonly lovely, and talented, too. I find you quite incomparable, my dear. I cannot regret our encounter." He spoke softly, watching the agitated rise and fall of her breast with some amusement.

But Esme had no interest in his flattery. "I am not one of

your bits of muslin, Your Grace. I suppose I should thank you for my escape from Sir Guy. It is my own fault for being so naive as to allow myself to fall into such a disagreeable situation, but I should have known coming to this ball was a mistake. I dislike these shallow social occasions. I dislike even more those who prefer this idle round of pleasure to other more worthwhile pursuits!" He might be an aristocrat with influence and power but he was not going to cajole her with compliments. He was the epitome of all she despised.

"Dear me! Rather puritanical for a young miss who doesn't hesitate to associate with Miss Wilson. I gather your aunt and uncle are in ignorance of your activities. You should be kind to me, or I might blow the gaff," he said, and tilted her chin up to give her a smoldering look she refused to meet.

Ignoring the clasp of his hand on her chin, she flushed and replied with some derision. "Are you blackmailing me, Your Grace?"

"Perhaps. I think it behooves you to show a little appreciation for my forbearance. I could make matters quite difficult for you, you know. Respectable girls do not paint pictures of demimondaines," he insisted, not relinquishing his hard grasp of her chin.

She read his intention in his dark eyes before he lowered his head, but was powerless to stop him. His kiss was surprisingly gentle this time, insinuatingly provocative, causing shudders of some unnameable emotion to course through her body. When he realized she was not rejecting him, he deepened the kiss and his hands roamed suggestively down her body, exploring the curves of her breasts, and evoking a shameful delight.

Gasping, Esme finally tore herself free, and raised her hand. But before she could slap him, he caught her wrist in an iron grip.

"Not again, I think. You really are a termagant, Miss Sedgewick. And a much too enticing one at that," the duke mocked, unmoved by her anger. He made no effort to stop her when she stormed away, eager to put as much distance between them as possible.

She heard his sardonic laugh as she fled back toward the ballroom. What a monster the man was, far worse than poor Sir Guy! She paused on the terrace to bring her emotions into some order. She would not let the duke threaten her composure with allusions to what he knew about her secret life. Accustomed to satisfying his every fancy, the man had no decent instincts. Well, she would not be one of them! She would not allow herself to be handled so at their every encounter.

Taking a deep breath, Esme pinned back her falling hair, and straightened her gown. She only hoped he had a few gentlemanly instincts and would not divulge his knowledge. She knew only too well how her reputation would suffer from such revelations. And it would be a terrible blow to her aunt and uncle, as well as her two cousins. But she would not plead with him to keep silent. She would not pander to his conceit by throwing herself on his mercy.

She recalled with embarrassment that she had not exactly remained unresponsive to his kiss. Why had she behaved in so shameless a fashion? There was nothing about the man to attract her. He was arrogant and rude, a libertine and a despoiler of women. What had possessed her to abandon all restraint and allow him such shocking liberties? She was nearly as depraved as he was!

She could not even excuse herself by pleading innocence. She knew more than she cared to about the Duke of Milbourne from Fannie's titillating gossip. Perhaps she would quiz Fannie in order to learn how to deal with the duke if he threatened her again. It would be too much to hope that she would not see him again. Somehow she knew another encounter was fated.

For now she must return to the ballroom and pretend that she had not just been involved in an outrageous embroglio. She examined her dance card distractedly. She must not avoid her dance with Algernon French. Fannie was depending on her, and her own problems must wait until a more suitable time.

37

# Chapter Five

If Esme wondered about her reaction to the duke, he had no such trouble in divining her response to his ruthless kiss. Accustomed to seducing the fairer sex, he had not been surprised at her untutored response. But he made no further attempt to approach her at the Lievens ball, content to watch her for the few remaining dances. He was amused at her partnering Algernon French, the young popinjay who fancied himself a poet. But he frowned at her obvious rapport with Lord Robert Weirs.

He would make it his business to learn all he could about the maddening Miss Sedgewick for he had plans for her. She was a fetching piece and no doubt would be a provocative mistress. Undaunted by her birth or her obvious innocence, and entertained by her animosity, he anticipated a lively chase—just the distraction he needed to dissipate his ennui. He was bored to death with the greedy, stupid Cyprians, and better-bred ladies made unreasonable demands. Miss Sedgewick would have to consent to his desires or face having her secret life revealed to the Cranfords, who would no doubt eject her from their household.

He would be generous with her—once she submitted to his demands. He had no objections whatsoever to her painting, that was, when she was not more pleasurably occupied.

Not for a moment did the duke feel any remorse for the role he had chosen for Esme to fulfill. His was not an over-active conscience, and he was accustomed to achieving what he wanted. Since he had met her on Harriette's stairs, she had rarely been out of his mind, and he was convinced the only way to rid himself of his obsession with her was to possess her. Her feelings were of little moment.

Spoiled, disillusioned and world-weary, Carstairs took a jaundiced view of the fairer sex. His experience had led him to think they could be cajoled, flattered or bought, and he had evidence that his skilled love making satisfied the most exigent female. His cynicism lay deep in his character, dating from his youth when he had been coerced into a marriage with a neighbor's titled daughter by his domineering father. Although there was much about the lovely Maria Rhodes, with her golden hair and blue eyes, to recommend her to any romantic young man, she had little conversation and less wit, and she retreated soon after their marriage into fancied invalidism as an escape from Hugo's passionate demands. Within a few years she had become a drunkard, and Hugo, disillusioned and disgusted, sought more attractive and willing females. By the time the duchess had drunk herself to death, a horrifying and piteable end to a lovely girl, Hugo had long since found relief in the dissipations that marked him now, in his thirty-first year, as a scandalous rake.

Few decent women would associate with him, and most of London's drawing rooms were closed to him, despite his title and wealth. The Princess Lieven was one of the few who regarded his conduct with amusement rather than shock. He was indifferent to society's judgments and generally found his amusement with folk of a far less reputable type. Of late, however, his usual round of drinking, gambling and wenching had left him restless and dissatisfied. Only his interest in art seemed rewarding.

Perhaps some of Miss Sedgewick's appeal was that he knew her to be a painter. No doubt she was the merest amateur who daubed in a ladylike way at her hobby, though he doubted the critical Harriette would have engaged her to paint her portrait if Miss Sedgewick had not shown some germ of talent. Yes, she would do very well as his newest inamorata, he decided arrogantly.

Suddenly he remembered the Prince Regent's picture. He had promised to track down "Arethusa." Between that pursuit and the pursuit of Miss Sedgewick, life was looking far more stimulating. How fortunate that he had accepted the Lievens's invitation.

Esme, unaware of what the notorious duke had in mind for her, nevertheless sensed that it would behoove her to discover something about him that would protect her if their paths crossed again. Certainly, if she painted Miss Wilson, she might not be able to avoid him.

The morning after the ball, Esme and Robert rode, as usual, in the park. Normally Fannie accompanied them, but last evening's revelry had left the girl languid and restless. She preferred to sleep and dream of Algernon, Esme suspected, although that vacuous conceited young man had few charms that Esme could appreciate. She would have to tread carefully when Fannie asked her opinion. The morning's crisp air and the exhilaration of an early gallop through the park lightened her spirits considerably, and she was loathe to dispel her mood of contentment by introducing the duke's name but wisdom demanded it.

"Tell me, Robert," Esme said carelessly, "What do you know about the Duke of Milbourne. I have heard the most shocking tales!"

"Where did you meet the fellow, Esme?" Robert replied as they slowed their horses to a walk and conversation became possible. "He's not received in most decent households, you know, and with good cause. He's a true libertine, not to be trusted around any female." He frowned, displeased that Esme would inquire about a man of Milbourne's stamp.

"Oh, surely, he can't be completely beyond the pale! I

understand he has a splendid art collection." Esme had learned that much from casual conversation the evening before.

"Your damned daubing will lead you into trouble, yet, my girl," Robert said jealously. "Just because the man has some knowledge of art, and I believe even the Prince Regent acknowledges his expertise, does not mean he is a fit person for you to be associating with, or even talking about!"

"Well, he can't be so dreadful if he appreciates painting," Esme teased. "Is he married?" she asked, then immediately wondered why she had chosen to pursue that particular line of inquiry.

"He was, but his wife died of drink several years ago. Nasty affair, and quite a scandal, but he shows no signs of mourning her. No doubt, he drove her to it," Robert growled. He wanted Esme's attention to be directed to him, not to a dissolute rake who was the talk of the town. "He never associates with decent women," Robert concluded as if that ended the matter.

"Well, he was at the Lievens's ball last night, so he cannot be thoroughly abandoned by society," Esme persisted.

"There were quite a few disreputable people at the Lievens's. I saw you dancing with Sir Guy Wentworth. You go out into society so seldom, Esme, you have no idea of the pitfalls awaiting a respectable girl. Wentworth and Milbourne! There's not a more dishonorable pair in London. You can't know how your reputation would suffer if you took up with their sort!"

"And that is precisely why I am asking for information," Esme replied, rather touched by his protective air. "I do not intend to take up with them, but it's well to know the danger."

"If you want to enjoy the jollities at last, *I* will escort you. *And* see to it that such men don't bother you," Robert said caressingly, looking at her wind-tossed hair and elegant figure with a wistful sigh. Much as he wanted her to lead the normal life of a young well-born woman, he did not want her to become interested in other men.

"Don't worry, Robert. Neither of those so-called gentlemen are to my taste. But I was curious. I am not above a little scandal, you know. No doubt it is shameful, but we females love gossip," Esme joked lightly.

Robert frowned and looked at her with a searching gaze, but Esme decided it was time to change the subject.

Later that week, when she had heard no more from the troublesome Duke of Milbourne, Esme decided that his threats had been mere diversions. No doubt his amusement in baiting her had lost its attraction. She refused any further invitations to parties where she might encounter him, vowing never again to place herself in such an invidious position.

If she had followed her instincts, she would not have attended the Lievens's ball and saved herself much embarrassment. Sir Guy Wentworth was easily balked in his attempts to see her. She was not at home to him when he called, and soon he, too, gave up his pursuit. Algernon French, Fannie's poet, continued to appear at frequent intervals, but Esme decided that any protest she made to Fannie about his unsuitability would only whet her interest, so she was carefully noncommittal when her cousin quizzed her about the young man.

Gratefully, she settled down to an arduous program of painting, working diligently at her portrait of Harriette Wilson. Esme decided that the demimondaine was much maligned by the gossips. Miss Wilson treated Esme with polite charm. Indeed, her manners could not be faulted, and Esme believed her subject was far more of a lady than those who criticized her style and profession. At first she had feared she might meet the duke at Harriette's but her fears proved groundless and she continued the sittings with an increasing sense of relief. If she had known the duke better, she would not have been so sanguine.

Hugo, having made no progress in ferreting out the identity of Arethusa, was becoming increasingly frustrated, but was still determined. The gallery owner, Joseph Gorton, had no further news for him about the mysterious artist, although he kept assuring the duke he would notify him if another painting by the artist appeared in his galleries. The duke gave some thought to employing a Bow Street runner to track down the painter, but preferred to trust his own sources of investigation, having little faith in those guardians of the law.

And, contrary to Esme's hopes, he had not abandoned his interest in her, but was too skilled a hunter to show his hand. He would allay her suspicions and then pounce, he decided. Why the enigmatic Miss Sedgewick should prove such a challenge he could not decide. She had a certain piquant charm, but he had engaged far more beautiful mistresses. Neither her innocence nor her breeding deterred him. He wanted her and he would have her.

If she should prove to be chaste, he had no qualms about taking her virginity, for he was convinced all women were promiscuous at heart. His early and disastrous marriage had disillusioned him thoroughly. And he did not fear more respectable rivals. Who could compete with the Duke of Milbourne? Few men could offer what he could. That Esme would not be tempted was inconceivable.

He let a week elapse before confronting her where she was most vulnerable.

Harriette liked Esme, and was pleased with the progress of her portrait, but she was too pragmatic to protect Esme from the duke's obvious intent. She found the situation amusing. She doubted that he would find the girl as pliable as his usual conquests. Pressured, she surrendered to his demands and told him when Esme was next expected for a sitting.

Hugo's approach was completely unexpected. Esme had nearly completed the portrait and promised Harriette that one more hour would see the end of her work. Bidding the demimondaine a cheerful farewell, she donned her shawl and proceeded down the stairway from the morning room where she had set up her easel. As she crossed the hall, the duke appeared suddenly, startling her.

"Ah, we meet again, Miss Sedgewick, as I promised we would," he said suavely, raking her with a suggestive glance.

Confused and wary, Esme nodded briefly. She would make

no effort to mollify the man. He was dressed informally in riding clothes, but looked every inch the aristocrat, his arrogant stance and smooth address overwhelming.

"We must have a talk, my dear. Come into this small salon. We will not be disturbed," he invited smoothly, as if there was no possibility that she would demur.

"I am afraid I cannot spare the time, sir. I am late for an appointment," Esme answered curtly. She would not let the rake see that his sudden presence had thrown her into confusion. But beneath her calm demeanour she quailed. He had it in his power to cause her great distress and she doubted that any appeal to his gentlemanly code would prove effective.

"I think it would be to your advantage to postpone your departure," he said softly, raising his eyebrows at her refusal. "I am in a position to insist, my dear, as I think you will agree."

Feeling very much like a mouse stalked by a great cat, she surrendered and preceded him rigid-backed into the salon.

"Please be seated. We have a little matter of business to discuss."

Esme sank into the chair indicated by the duke, hoping her trembling legs and her inner disquiet was not evident to his piercing gaze. As he loomed over her, she took a firm grasp of her courage. She would not let this man gain any ascendancy over her.

"You look quite charming this afternoon. The gown hardly does you justice, but then your attributes transcend any costume," he mocked, his bold hard eyes insulting as they undressed her.

Esme refused to be baited. She folded her hands primly in her lap, as much to stop their shaking as to give him the impression that she was not frightened.

"Can you guess what I require of you?" he asked in his most arrogant tone, not willing to make any effort at cajolery. He stood over her, his feet apart, looking more intimidating than lover-like.

"I have no idea, Your Grace," she replied guilelessly, refusing to meet his dark stare.

"My name is Hugo," he said repressively. Her obvious indifference to him as a man sharpened his desire to possess her. No doubt once he had taken her to bed a few times his unnatural preoccupation with her would fade. She was certainly attractive with her honey-gold hair, her deep gray eyes, which promised hidden mysteries, and her challenging coolness. She was a trifle too thin, not in the voluptuous style that most of his partners displayed, but she had a rare and provocative elegance of manner. Hugo prided himself on his discrimination, his ability to search out the unusual, and Miss Sedgewick was certainly that. Then there were her artistic talents which heightened his interest. She was not in a position to refuse him, and once she had submitted, she would probably enjoy their passionate duels, for he was convinced that strong emotion lay behind that prim facade she had erected. All in all she would be a fascinating antidote to his boredom.

He leaned over her and raised her chin so that she was forced to look into his hot, dark eyes. "Perhaps I should remind you that you have placed yourself in an invidious position. You are consorting with a notorious demimondaine, whose influence could ruin your reputation and bring your uncle and aunt into disrepute."

Esme gave him one scornful glance and then averted her eyes, making no attempt to struggle against his hand.

"You are at it again, blackmailing me into submitting to your infamous suggestions," she replied with contempt.

"I haven't made any infamous suggestions yet, but you are quite right. I intend to take you to bed one way or another, and you could save yourself a great deal of trouble by assenting now to the inevitable."

"I do not see it as inevitable, and I cannot understand why you would wish to force an unwilling woman. Surely there are enough females, who if not attracted by your looks, which I admit are compelling, would certainly enjoy your wealth." Esme argued reasonably.

The duke did not like her pragmatic assessment of what he could offer, although he observed she did not find him

45

repulsive. She certainly was a cool one. Completely in his power, but still trying rationally to find a way out of her dilemma.

"Is the idea of pleasure in my arms so hateful to you?" he asked, in false surprise.

"Yes, Your Grace, it is. My work would be interrupted, my family disgusted and my whole life disarranged for an alliance which would bring you only passing satisfaction, if that. My understanding is that men of your stamp find virgins boring." She said it matter-of-factly, as if they were discussing the purchase of some trifling account. She would not show him how his frank sensuality shocked her. She surmised that was exactly the reaction he wanted.

"Once you have a taste of it," he interposed smoothly, "I am persuaded you would find the pleasures of the bed to your liking." The duke continued to look at her with what she considered an insultingly intimate gaze.

"If that were the case, I am sure I could find a satisfactory legal recourse to my needs. A suitable husband is not out of court, you know," she countered.

"But a proper husband might make unacceptable demands on your time and talent. I would never do that. I am quite prepared to set you up in a studio and allow you to paint away at whatever takes your fancy," he promised casually, as if her painting was a mere diversion. "I have quite an interest in art, myself. And I might engage Turner or Lawrence to give you some lessons as an added inducement."

Astonished at the man's arrogance and careless bribery, Esme was within an ace of losing her temper and storming at him. He was a callous monster with no manners and less sensitivity. She refrained with difficulty and rose to her feet, meeting his eyes with a calm she was far from feeling.

"I can see there is no use appealing to your chivalry, because I doubt you have any notion of such a thing," she said hotly. "You must look elsewhere for your newest light of love. I doubt that you will have difficulty. And now you must excuse me. I am already late for my appointment."

"Quite right. I put little stock in chivalry. I can see I shall have to use more stringent measures to bring you around, Miss Sedgewick. But make no mistake. In the end I will have you, one way or another," he said firmly. A hot tide of passion rose in him as he looked over her alluring figure.

"You disgust me," Esme said severely, wondering at her temerity in baiting the man. "You may do your worse, Duke. But I warn you, I am not an easy prey. I have my own methods of dealing with lecherous immoral rakes!"

"Since you hold me in such contempt already, I will lose nothing in tasting some of the delights to come," he said silkily.

Quickly he took her in iron-hard arms, restraining her attempts to shake him off. His kiss was hot and possessive, causing strange sensations to rise through her body and arousing her emotions to a fever pitch. His tongue pressed its way into her mouth, touching her intimately in a way she had never before experienced. His hands roamed down her smooth form. She hardly knew what she was doing as her hands crept up around his shoulders and wandered through his thick hair. She felt his arousal, shocked by the languor he induced and her inability to resist his increasing demands.

"I could take you now, on the floor in this salon," he told her, "but your initiation should be in more comfortable surroundings. I will reluctantly postpone what will be a memorable experience to a more suitable time." He removed her hand from around his neck and stepped away, noting her flushed cheeks and quick breathing with amusement. "Until we meet again, Miss Sedgewick," he promised with a grin.

Esme was astounded by his effrontery. With a scathing look, her chin jutting out defiantly, she left the room without a word shutting her ears to his laughter.

# Chapter Six

Esme sank back against the squabs of the hackney she had hailed upon leaving Miss Wilson's and tried to gather her emotions together. Ashamed of her response to the duke, she was still flushed, and her heart pounded as she remembered how wantonly she had behaved. How could she have submitted so tamely to his bold advances? She despised everything about the man, his ruthless conceit, his cynical view of her sex, his assumption that he need only reach out his hand and any silly female would drop into it like a ripe plum. Esme had never been in love, had never understood that emotion. All of her considerable passion went into her work, and now she sought the only refuge which could comfort her.

She directed the coachman to Somerset House on The Strand. An hour contemplating the masters would restore her shattered senses, she hoped.

Today, however, the great collection, which had been opened in the last century, did not have the usual soothing effect. Usually she could lose herself in the incredible brushwork of Gainsborough, a painter whose portraits she particularly admired, but today his skill did not distract her from her worries.

Finally she sank into a convenient, if uncomfortable seat and let her thoughts roam over her various problems. She desperately wanted to complete the commission Harriette Wilson had requested, and another hour or two's work would see the end of it, one of the best portraits she had ever done. Did she dare continue, knowing that she might suffer another encounter with the duke? And what about his threats to tell the Cranfords about her secret life? If she felt no deep affection for Aunt Mildred and Uncle Egbert, she did feel gratitude for their guardianship of her. She could not expose them to scandal, for their notions of propriety were strong and deep-rooted. They would be dreadfully appalled to learn of her association with Harriette Wilson and with the reprobate duke. They must be protected.

There was always Robert. Esme realized that his attentions could also cause pain to the Cranfords who hoped for a different alliance for their only son and heir. Not that she had any inclination to accept him. But he could provide some protection from libertines like the duke.

As for Hugo Carstairs, how she would like to see his downfall! He wanted her for the moment, but if she could keep out of his way, no doubt he would soon lose interest when a more exciting female crossed his path. If only she could escape to the country, be left in peace to get on with her work.

Perhaps she could suggest to Aunt Mildred that it might be advantageous for her to leave London and return to the ancestral home in Dorset. Surely the duke would not seek her out there. Even if Fannie and the countess would not return to Dorset, they might look kindly on her request to do so. Old Aunt Caroline lived on the estate and would be chaperone enough. And Esme shrewdly suspected that Aunt Mildred thought Fannie's chances of securing a husband would improve if her cousin were absent from London. With a sigh, Esme rose to her feet, eager to put her plan into action.

Hugo Carstairs had plans, too, and Esme's rebuff had caused them no alteration. Her apparent dislike did not deter him, nor did her position in society. His own desires were the decisive factor, and he was surprised at how compelling was his passion for the girl.

From his first encounter with Esme Sedgewick, the duke had been intrigued. But he would probably have relegated her to oblivion if he had not caught a glimpse of her at the Lievens' ball. He had not recognized her at first, never expecting to see a light skirt in such company, but then a distinctive turn of her head with that lovely fall of honey-gold hair, and a look from those haunting gray eyes had startled him into realization that this was indeed Harriette's unusual visitor. Cleverly he sought out acquaintances at the ball who could reveal some facts about the puzzling girl. It had not taken long for him to learn her name and her circumstances. He found it vastly amusing that a well-bred female, a member of one of the starchiest families, should have been consorting with such as Harriette. But he did not deride her for her choice of companions, rather the reverse. He found it stimulating, and watching her go through the motions of the waltz with her cousin, wondered idly how he could turn this discovery to his advantage.

Probably if he offered marriage she would fall into his arms gratefully, he thought, but he had no intention of upsetting his life with such a drastic solution. His sister, Lady Hansford, was forever after him to wed and beget an heir, but of course Emily was dynasty-minded since she had not been able to provide her husband with a son. The Hansfords had three gawky daughters and Emily was beyond producing another baby by now. She took an inordinate interest in her brother's affairs and he found her reproaches tedious. No doubt, if she knew of his pursuit of Esme Sedgewick, she would encourage him to make her an honorable offer. But the idea of tying the parson's knot, to exposing himself to a lifetime of the vagaries of one woman alone was unthinkable to Hugo. Esme Sedgewick was just the type to expect fidelity and a husband who would dance attendance upon her. He looked forward, however, to having her outside the bounds of holy wedlock. If she would not come willingly he had the means to force her, and had no compunction about the scheme he put on hand. Once she had submitted to him, he would make sure she enjoyed the situation as much as he.

"There! It is finished. You may relax, Miss Wilson. And you may view the work, now. I have done all I can," Esme said, pushing a loose lock from her face with a paint-smeared hand. She stood back a few paces from the portrait, and Harriette joined her.

"You have done a masterful piece of work, Miss Sedgewick! And flattered me in the bargain!" Harriette looked at the canvas with an appraising eye. Esme had indeed caught Harriette's rare character, the flashing eyes and pointed chin, the dark hair arranged in classic fashion. She was not a beauty and knew it. Her attributes were more subtle and Esme had captured the unusual quality that had made Harriette Wilson the chère amie of so many distinguished aristocrats and statesmen. Hers was not a sensual beauty but a combination of intelligence and vivacious appeal. In her simple white dress she looked vibrantly alive. Esme believed it was her best work to date.

Harriette stepped closer and peered at the lower corners of the portrait. "You have not signed it, Miss Sedgewick," she protested.

"No, I think it best that the work remain anonymous," Esme explained. "I fear disclosure, and my family would be horrified. I hope you understand, Miss Wilson." This painting would be displayed to a score of knowledgeable critics, Harriette's clients were all members of the *ton*. Even her sobriquet "Arethusa" might lead to discovery. Esme thought of the duke. He knew her as an artist but not as "Arethusa." She wanted to keep that secret—especially from him.

"Of course, I would not want to cause you embarrassment, Miss Sedgewick. It will be as you wish. But I feel you might gain several prominent commissions once this portrait is seen and admired." Harriette was rather amused at Esme's

51

insistence on remaining anonymous. Shrewdly she guessed that Esme had already encountered some difficulty from the duke and wondered what he had in mind for this gently bred girl who appeared completely devoted to her art. Harriette knew that Hugo Carstairs would not be thwarted. Poor Esme. She would find him a difficult paramour. Harriette, for all her sophistication, retained enough romance in her temperament to sympathize with Esme.

"The Duke of Milbourne has discovered who you are, hasn't he, Miss Sedgewick?" Harriette said softly, turning from the portrait. "He is not above using that knowledge, you know. Hugo is not much of a gentleman when it comes to the ladies."

"He has already tried to blackmail me, but I refuse to be intimidated by that rake," Esme said scornfully, hiding her disquiet that Harriette had gauged the situation with all its perils.

"You know your own business best, and I would not presume to advise you. But he is a clever and cruel devil who will not be balked of what he wants," Harriette persisted. "Let us hope that he does not want you, Miss Sedgewick. After a few weeks he would grow weary and turn away without a passing thought to your feelings. He is not a proper object for your affections."

Esme smiled at her patroness. "Of that I am sure," she said. "Don't worry, Miss Wilson, I'll stay well clear of the duke." If I can help it, she thought.

The two parted, after Harriette had given a generous fee to the reluctant Esme. They would probably never meet again, and Esme regretted this. She had come to admire the demimondaine for her ability to cope with a life many considered discreditable and unfortunate. At least the woman had gained some measure of independence, Esme thought wistfully. And she had the wit to conserve her fortune for years when her physical appeal would have faded. Harriette had made a choice which she obviously did not regret, and she had accepted whatever indignities her chosen career had imposed.

Esme, untutored and innocent, could not help but wonder how the disciplined Miss Wilson regarded the physical aspect of her affairs, but she seemed amazingly untouched by that more sordid side of her career. Esme chided herself for such musings. She spent entirely too much time wondering about the relationships between men and women in and out of the marriage bed. She would not admit that such concerns had rarely troubled her until the duke had burst upon her awareness.

She scurried from the house, relieved to have avoided him. Now she must persuade the Cranfords to let her leave London. The sooner she removed herself from any chance meeting with Hugo Carstairs the better.

Esme would find that Fannie was her accomplice in this task. The plain girl had been deeply hurt by Algernon French's defection. He had haunted the Cranford's Mount Street house since his meeting with Esme at the Lieven's ball, and Fannie soon realized that she had been supplanted in the poet's mercurial affections. He insisted on reading long screeds to Esme's eyes, hair and general appearance, much to that lady's annoyance, and his abandonment of his previous interest in Fannie had made relations between the cousins difficult. Arriving home from Harriette Wilson's, Esme was annoyed to find the poet in attendance, obviously waiting for his new inamorata. Fannie was entertaining him in the drawing room, under the disapproving eyes of her mother, who noted Esme's arrival with relief. She had no objections to her niece encouraging Algernon, but he would never do as a husband for her daughter.

"Ah, there you are, Esme, back from your errand at last," Lady Cranford greeted Esme as she entered the room, noticing that her niece did not seem delighted at the presence of their visitor. "Mr. French has been waiting to take you riding in the park," Lady Cranford said with a tight smile. She was a woman of rather stern, handsome looks, with dark hair always confined in a severe style, and strong features. Fannie in no

53

way resembled her august parent, except for a certain stubbornness in her chin. Esme had often thought that the Cranfords were disappointed in their only daughter. They certainly did not appreciate Fannie's finer qualities of heart, and criticized her often for her warm feelings and inability to catch a husband. Algernon French's obvious preference for Esme only heightened that discontent even if they considered him an ineligible parti.

"I regret, Algernon, I cannot find the time today," Esme demurred. "Why don't you take Fannie? I am sure she would enjoy an outing. It is a splendid day." Esme noticed that Fannie looked mutinous, and sighed with frustration. She wanted her cousin out of the way so she could put her suggestion of leaving for the country to Aunt Mildred.

Algernon assumed an expression of martyrdom, but seeing the determination on his goddess's face, could only consent politely. "I would be delighted to escort Lady Fannie, but could we not prevail upon you to join us? I have a new poem I want you to hear."

Esme looked at the young man with barely concealed irritation. What could Fannie find so attractive in this vapid poseur? He was handsome enough, in an effete way, with a carefully coiffed shock of blond hair and soulful blue eyes. But his figure was reedy and not improved by his dandified dress with shirt points almost too ludicrous to be believed. A profusion of gold rings, and a gaily bedecked waistcoat accentuating his ridiculous attempt at fashion. Obviously he did not heed Beau Brummel's strictures on plain, unadorned dress. Before she could continue her objections to his invitations, Lady Cranford intervened.

"I need Fannie to accompany me on a call to Mrs. Burrell this morning, Esme. I believe you must take pity on poor Mr. French. He has been so patient," she insisted smoothly, giving Esme a minatory look.

Esme decided that her best course was to agree. She would tell the young man when they were alone that she could no longer countenance his attentions, and if she was firm, he must desist. He was just one more annoyance in a long list of aggravations, but one that could be dealt with in no uncertain manner.

"Oh, all right, Mr. French. I will ride with you, but you must wait until I change into something more comfortable." Leaving Lady Cranford to entertain Algernon, Esme prevailed upon her Fannie to accompany her to her bedroom.

Once they had gained the privacy of her chamber, Esme wasted no time in explaining to her cousin that she had no interest in the ubiquitous Mr. French.

"Really, Fannie," Esme said as she threw off her morning dress in a fit of exasperation. "I cannot believe you find Algernon entertaining! He proses on about his bad verse at interminable length and has a great conceit. You would not be happy with such a man."

"Shall I ring for your maid?" Fannie said, ignoring Esme's explanations and very evidently sulking.

"No. I will cope." Esme plucked a green silk riding dress from her wardrobe and hurried into it, giving little attention to her appearance. "Button me up, please, Fannie," she pleaded, sympathizing with her cousin, but determined to make her see the folly of her infatuation.

Fannie pouted, but she was too kind a girl to refuse Esme. Her usual good humour and sense of fairness would not allow her to stay in the sullens for long.

As she bent to her task, Fannie muttered, "I suppose you are not to blame for Algernon's interest, Esme. Naturally he would find you more appealing. Anyway, Mother doesn't like him and would never entertain an offer for me even if he were so inclined. I am a ninny to be jealous." Fannie finished the last button.

Esme turned to face her. "Yes, you are, Fannie. I find Mr. French vapid and conceited, with very little talent to boot. I am happy to see your normal good sense is rising to the surface. You are much too nice to be cozened by that foolish young man. Believe me, I am doing you a favour by distracting his attention from you. He would make a very tedious husband, and you need a man who will appreciate your fine qualities, Fannie dear. Let us not wrangle over such an unworthy cause. I intend to let him know his constant calls are not welcome. I will get rid of him in short order and then we can return to our normal comfortable state," she promised, giving her hair a cursory pat and eyeing her cousin in the mirror.

Fannie sighed. "I suppose you are right as always, Esme. I know you are not a spiteful girl who would deprive me of a man who really cared for me."

"Well, I am glad to see that we are not at daggers drawn any longer. I want your help, Fannie, in a plan I have to broach to your parents." Esme seated herself on a nearby sofa and patted the cushion next to her. Her cousin sat down, and gave Esme a contrite hug.

"You know I will do all I can to aid you, Esme," she declared.

"I want to return to Dorset and get on with my painting. I find all the trials of London life very upsetting, and in the country I can be left in peace to get on with my work," Esme said.

"Oh, but Esme, you know mother will not let me leave in the middle of the Season, and I doubt if she would let you go alone," Fannie stifled relief at the thought that her attractive cousin could contemplate such a flight. It would make her own path much easier, she thought secretly, and was ashamed of her feelings.

"Aunt Caroline is there to chaperone me. You would not need to absent yourself from all the pleasures of London. And I suspect Aunt Mildred would be relieved to see the back of me."

"Well, of course I will support you, if that is what you want," Fannie agreed. "But I thought you were painting happily away in your studio here."

"Yes, and I have completed some good work, but I long for the fresh air and inspiring sights of Dorset! London does not offer quite so much creative inducement. I will miss you, Fannie, but you will be coming to the country before too long, and perhaps with some exciting news."

"If you mean a promised husband, I doubt it. But I will put your case to the parents. Robert will be angry," she pointed out shrewdly, having an idea of her brother's interest.

"He will survive. There is plenty of distraction. Thank you, Fannie," Esme hugged her cousin. "You are a darling. And now I am off to do battle with the annoying Mr. French. Wish me luck."

Fannie smiled despite herself. Really, Esme was a wonderful cousin and friend.

# Chapter Seven

The Park was quite deserted as Algernon French and Esme drove sedately through its greenery at this unfasionable hour. Most of the *ton* preferred to take the air in the late afternoon and there were few equipages joining them on the raked paths. That was just as well, Esme decided, for Algernon was not a skilled driver, and his horses appeared a trifle skittish. She recalled him to his duties rather sharply as the off leader tried to escape on his own pursuits.

"Your horses appear very fresh, Mr. French. Do have a care!"

"I can handle them, never fear," the poet insisted, sawing ineffectually on the reins. "They are overfed. My damn groom has no idea of horseflesh."

The horses now broke into a swift canter. Algernon tried again to bring them under control, not liking to be distracted from his intent, which was to regale Esme with his devotion through measured verse. He had hoped that by getting her alone, he would find her more receptive to his odes to her beauty.

Esme wondered if he realized how ridiculous it was to suppose this was the proper setting for empassioned poetry. Really, the man was a fool, and Aunt Mildred had no business sending her out on this expedition with him just to thwart

Fannie. She braced herself as the phaeton careened between the trees, holding onto her straw bonnet, which was endangered by their pell mell flight.

"Can you not slow them down?" she gasped, thoroughly annoyed.

Algernon, who fancied himself an expert driver, swallowed a curse. The horses now had the bit between their teeth and only an iron hand on the reins would prevent disaster. Esme looked around wildly for a rescuer but saw no help. The maddened horses bolted off the gravel path and headed straight for an ornamental pond that bordered the road. Before she could take any measures to avoid the accident, the phaeton lurched under a low-lying set of trees and spilled its occupants into the water.

Sputtering with indignation and shock, Esme staggered to her feet, the water cascading from her shoulders. She was in no imminent danger, for the pond was only waist deep. Algernon had avoided a complete ducking, but he was a dismal sight. With a lily frond lying dripping on his waistcoat and his boots covered with muck as he struggled to extricate himself, he seemed to have no thought for Esme's plight. She cast him a glance of loathing, then floundered from the water, her wet skirts impeding her progress and revealing rather more than was seemly of the outline of her legs.

"Rather early in the year for a swim, don't you think?" came a cool voice from the path. Esme looked up to see the Duke of Milbourne, astride a huge black stallion, grinning evilly at the picture of the drenched couple. Disdaining to answer him, she turned away and busily wrung the water from her skirts, and tossed back her hair, which had become loose from its neat chignon and was hanging down her back in disarray. She had lost her bonnet and parasol and knew she looked a veritable wretch. But that did not concern her as much as the annoying spectacle of the duke, who was grinning with enjoyment.

Determined to ignore her tormentor, Esme turned to Algernon in exasperation. "Will you not make some push to secure your horses, Mr. French and escort me back to Mount

59

Street," she ordered shortly.

Algernon, embarrassed at being discovered in such a mess by a leading light of the *ton*, looked confused and apologetic as well as pitiable. He seemed unable to take any decisive action. The horses, having shot their spleen, grazed nearby, peacefully awaiting events. The duke, seeing that Algernon was completely overset, dismounted and approached Esme.

"Really, my dear, you are in a state, but charmingly disheveled for all that," he said, laughing at the look of disgust she gave him, and paying no attention to the rigid back she turned upon him. "Come, we must get you out of those damp garments before you catch your death," he advised.

"We do not need your assistance, Duke. But instead of standing there enjoying this debacle, which you appear to think was arranged especially for your amusement, you might try to help Mr. French extricate his horses so that I may return home with all possible speed," Esme said in icy tones. Of all the gentlemen in London to come upon them in this ridiculous situation, why did it have to be this sarcastic devil?

"Let French be damned. His own stupidity caused this accident. Let him retrieve his affairs as best he can. I have no interest in him," the duke said. "For God's sake, man, you have no business taking a lady riding if you can't control your cattle," he said, directing his tirade at the poor poet. Algernon avoided the accusing glances of both the duke and Esme, busily trying to restore some order to his clothes. At last he stalked over to his horses and gathered up the reins of the now docile beasts. "If you are ready, Miss Sedgewick, I believe I can now drive you home without further mishap."

"Don't be a fool, French. No sensible female would allow you to take her anywhere after this disgraceful performance. Look to your horses, man. I will take care of Miss Sedgewick," ordered the duke in peremptory tones. And before Esme could demur, he picked her up, heedless of her dripping, sodden state, and carried her to his horse.

"What are you doing, sir? Put me down at once," she

protested, appalled at this impertinent treatment. But the affect of her brave words was spoiled by a deafening sneeze which the duke heard with a nod of satisfaction. "See, my girl, you are in definite danger of pneumonia."

He threw her onto the stallion and mounted quickly behind her, settling her into the crook of his arm in a masterful fashion. "Come, Miss Sedgewick, your faint-hearted escort must be left to his just deserts. I only hope this will prove a lesson to him."

Mortified and at a complete loss, Algernon had no recourse but to allow the duke to have his way. He wanted only to escape from this deplorable situation before the notable Corinthian could humiliate him further.

Seeing that there would be no help from Algernon, Esme submitted with as much dignity as she could command, aware that she cut a sorry figure, damp and shivering from her ducking. Still, she was not about to let Algernon depart without speaking her mind. "Let this be a lesson to you, Mr. French. It would behoove you to take some time from your scribbling to take a lesson in horsemanship before you invite some other poor female to accompany you on a tour of the park," she said sharply.

Algernon could only mutter a weak apology, and watched helplessly, holding his horses' reins in a limp hand, as Esme was spirited away by the redoubtable duke. He would not soon forget his lamentable ineptitude before one whom he had wished to impress, but for the moment he wished never to see either the duke or Esme again.

Very conscious of the duke's lean strength at her back, Esme tried to rally her shattered dignity and control her shivering. She was only too aware of her disreputable condition, her hair tangled and wildly curling, her gown clinging damply to her figure and outlining every curve in a most revealing fashion. The duke held her securely, apparently unperturbed by their closeness. She, however, had difficulty in ignoring the warm scent of his body, the force of his masculinity that set loose a welter of sensations in her trembling form. Esme had never before been held in such intimacy. She tried desperately to hold herself rigid, to ignore the implacable presence that caused her such a distressing reaction, keeping her eyes fixed on the lean, tanned hands that held the reins so expertly.

She prayed no curious eyes would see their progress from the park, for her position was most compromising, perched on the duke's horse like a piece of careless booty. As they crossed the road, she was distracted by the direction they took.

"This is not the way to Mount Street," she protested.

"No, I am taking you to Grosvenor Street, to my house, which is closer. You cannot arrive at Mount Street in this deplorable condition. Your appearance could easily give rise to rumors you would find most distasteful. We will slip in through the stables before any gape-seed can wonder at your dilemma." As he spoke, the duke tightened his grip, as if she might consider leaping from his arms.

"Sir, you are taking unwarranted liberties," Esme protested.

"And what in the world were you doing gallivanting in the park with that nodcock? You could have been seriously injured! You have most probably caught a severe cold, which will serve you right. You should be thanking me for coming to your aid."

"No doubt it would give you the greatest satisfaction if I my health went into a decline," Esme retorted. "Well, let me inform you I am never ill, so this concern is not necessary." She hated the cowardly lassitude that prevented her from giving the duke the raking down he deserved.

Although she agreed heartily with his assessment of Algernon French, she would not give him the satisfaction of accepting his judgment. "Mr. French is artistic, a poet, not a member of the Four-in-Hand Club. There was no need for you to whisk me onto your horse in such a high-handed fashion. I am sure he could have delivered me safely to my home without further mishap. My aunt and uncle will be wondering what happened to me, and I doubt they would approve of your interference. You are hardly cut out for the role of saviour. And now you are kidnapping me! I demand to be taken to Mount Street."

His answer did nothing to calm her. "You go riding with that rubbishy fellow, in whom you have not the slightest interest, but object to my company. At least I would not have dumped you into a pond and endangered your health. Look at you, shivering and sneezing, incoherent, a poor thing, indeed. Would you have your relations see you in such a condition? I wonder why I bother with such an ungrateful chit," he replied in a bored tone.

Stung by his reproof, and honest enough to admit there was a small amount of truth in what he said, she murmured, "I suppose I should thank you. But although you may wish to protect my health, there are other perils in your company."

"Stop wriggling and behave yourself or you'll end up in the mud," he answered impatiently as they entered the courtyard of an imposing mansion. The cobbled square was quiet, but on their arrival several grooms hastened from the stables to assist them. A hostler held the duke's horse while he dismounted with his booty.

Esme struggled to escape his arms, but he merely tightened his grip and strode forward, giving a curt order to his servants. They did not appear surprised by his arrival with a strange female in a distressing state, and she doubted they would heed any pleas from her. It was beneath her dignity to scream that she was the victim of an abduction. She set her lips tightly and gave the duke a look of intense loathing. He ignored it, carrying her through a door into what seemed to be a vast kitchen.

"Rather an unorthodox approach, but necessary, I believe," he said suavely, depositing her on the floor, but keeping a grip on her arm in case she had ideas of fleeing.

Esme felt disoriented and desperate as she looked around the room. Several minions were basteing a roast over a huge spit, and a chef in a white hat was stirring something savory over a stove.

The staff looked up, startled by this invasion of their premises, but seeing the duke's ferocious frown, turned back to their work. They were accustomed to his rages and untoward actions and valued their posts too much to question this unusual arrival of their master. Dragging her across the stone floor, he pushed her through a green baize door into a long hallway, and met his major domo, who was hurrying to receive them.

Realizing she could not make a scene before such a person, Esme allowed herself to be chivied along, wondering if perhaps she was making a great deal out of nothing. Perhaps the duke was really trying to see to her well-being and it behooved her to act more graciously.

"There you are, Roberts. Miss Sedgewick has suffered an accident and will need some warm clothes and a hot bath. Escort her to the Lilac Chamber and see that she has what she needs," the duke ordered. "I will need to change also."

Somewhat reassured by these unexceptional orders, Esme was tempted to express her gratitude to the duke, but his expression did not welcome any overtures from her and she remained silent. She was beginning to feel most tired and uncomfortable, unhappy about the poor figure she was exposing to the butler's bland gaze.

The duke, sensing her indecision, soothed her. "I promise to return you to Mount Street after you have been cleaned up and had some refreshment. Not that you do not look most enticing in this rumpled state . . . But come, I am mean to tease you. Go along with Roberts. He will see to you," the duke reassured her gently, then turned away as if suddenly weary of the whole affair.

Realizing she would be foolish to make any more protests, Esme trudged after the butler up the great staircase, wondering why she was so reluctant to accept the duke's hospitality. Obviously he really wanted to see to her comfort and she was behaving in a silly fashion. She did owe him some gratitude for his rescue. Thanking Roberts, who ushered her into a magnificently furnished chamber, she acknowledged she would appreciate some hot tea and an opportunity to restore her appearance.

"I will send a maid to you shortly, madam," Roberts said, pulling back the curtains to reveal a tasteful bedroom, decorated in the latest style, with accents of rich lilac silk covering the tester and the chairs and sofas. His stoic manner did not soften as he bowed himself from the room, leaving Esme to make what she would of her situation.

At least she had some time to gather her defences and consider how to deal with her dilemma. She crossed to the cheval mirror, where her first sight of the picture she presented gave her quite a shock.

The green silk riding dress was completely ruined, sopping and mud-spattered, with a nasty rent down the bodice, too. And her hair, a complete tangle, gave her the look of a veritable hoyden. She picked up a comb from the nearby dressing table and attempted to restore some order, but threw down the comb in disgust as the maid entered the room with a tray.

"I understand you have suffered an accident, madam. If you will allow me, I will take your garments and do what I can to put them in order. A hot bath will be up shortly. Here is a nice hot cup of tea to warm you," the woman said matter-of-factly. It was as if such visitations from disheveled females were all in a day's work.

Esme drank the tea gratefully, feeling some strength and comfort returning to her. The maid, too well-trained to ask questions or show any curiosity, bustled about stirring up a fire and readying the room for the bath. But Esme could not dispell a certain uneasiness. What must the woman think of her tempestuous arrival in such a state? A flush rose to Esme's cheeks, but she bit back any explanation. The maid awaited her pleasure, having skillfully helped Esme to step from her crumpled gown and taken a peignoir from the wardrobe.

The dressing gown of rose chiffon and lavishly trimmed in

lace was not a chaste covering, and Esme's blush deepened as she realized it was probably kept for one of the duke's numerous chères amies. She hated wearing the wretched garment, but she had little choice until her own clothes were made respectable. The peignoir was cut very low in the bosom, and barely concealed Esme's body in its chiffon folds. She was about to ask for a less indelicate covering when they were interrupted by two burly footmen carrying a hip bath filled with steaming water.

They placed it before the fire. Their bland faces showed no emotion, but Esme could only feel embarrassed at any man seeing her in such a gown. In a surge of indignation at her position—the fault of the odious duke, she decided rather unfairly—Esme dismissed the servants imperiously, indicating she could manage on her own. The maid, prepared to assist Esme with her bath, received her banishment with no comment but a toss of her head. She bundled Esme's clothes together and left the room.

Finally alone, Esme crossed to the door, determined to lock it. She did not doubt for a moment that the duke would have the effrontery to enter without any warning. To her dismay, she discovered the key was missing, which intensified her suspicions. Well, she thought, she could not stand here shivering and sneezing. If she did not avail herself of the tempting bath, she would be even more miserable than she was already. Esme quickly removed the gown and lowered herself into the tub.

She was grateful for the scented warmth of the water and the soothing comfort it brought her aching limbs, but she dared not luxuriate in the reviving bath, fearing an intrusion. Although she would have liked a good long soak, she hurried with her washing and rose to wrap herself in the towels laid out for her use. The maid had taken not only her dress but her chemise and other undergarments. She had no alternative but to cover her nakedness again with the provocative rose peignoir. She was brushing her hair, steeling herself for the inevitable encounter when the duke entered the room quietly.

Esme whirled to face him. He locked the door with the errant key, which he pocketed casually, an action that did little to calm her apprehension. He too had changed from his riding clothes, and was dressed in black trousers and a white shirt, unbuttoned to reveal a great deal of his chest. His dress implied an intimacy Esme did not welcome.

"What do you think you are doing?" she challenged, determined to keep the upper hand in this interview. He no doubt found the situation amusing, accustomed as he was to intimate rendezvous of the most sordid kind. Well, Esme would soon set him straight, she decided, although she feared this might prove more difficult than she imagined.

"I am seeing to it that we are not disturbed," he answered calmly, his gaze passing over her in a possessive fashion which quite unnerved her. "I must say, my dear, you look most enticing."

He smiled, ignoring her outrage. Indeed she did look appealing, her cheeks rosy from the bath, her gold-streaked hair tumbling down her shoulders. Her figure was enticingly evident beneath the chiffon folds of the peignoir. Only her stormy gray eyes belied the picture of a mistress awaiting the pleasure of her master.

She stood, trying to subdue the trembling his passionate gaze evoked. She wanted to escape that assessing, hungry look, but where could she go? Her only recourse was to turn her back, ignoring the intimacy of the scene. Her limbs felt leaden, unwilling to obey her mind. She did not hear his footfall over the beating of her heart, and before she could react, she felt his kiss on the back of her neck.

His lips seared across her tender skin, evoking a storm of feelings that held her immobile. Before she could wrench herself away, he had turned her directly into his arms. Placing a hand under her chin, he raised her head to look searchingly into her eyes, his own hot with desire.

"Are you sure you still want to return to Mount Street? We

could deal very well together, you know," he promised.

She jerked away, alarmed as much by what he inferred as her own lack of resistance. The devil was luring her into compliance with his suave, compelling manner, behaving as if this assault on her senses was welcome.

"Of course, I do. I resent being held here against my will, sir." Esme spoke bravely, but his arms only tightened around her, and her desires made her a liar.

"I think not. You have been asking for this, you know, tempting me beyond reason with your jibes and insults, daring me to make love to you." Sensuality was heavy in his voice.

But she would not submit, although every nerve in her body rose to his seductive assault. She would not join that legion of women who found him irresistible, surrendering to his momentary desire, satisfying his transient urge to bed her, and then abandoning her without a thought to her feelings.

"Love—hah," she cried. "You don't know the meaning of the word. What you are talking about is lust, and I don't intend to satisfy that." But Esme's resistance weakened under the onslaught of his demanding hand. It roamed down her body and rose to seek the flesh beneath the shameless dressing gown. Expecting further attack she steeled herself to rebuff him. But he surprised her, dropping his arms and raising a sardonic eyebrow as if her rejection was acceptable.

"You wound me, Esme. I am quite famed for my expertise in the boudoir. If you would abandon this missish pose, you might find the experience quite enjoyable." He seemed unimpressed by her gasp of outrage.

Hugo admired her display of pride, but he had no doubt about the outcome of their duel. Beneath that facade of propriety lay a passionate creature destined for lovemaking, and he would be the man to initiate her into its delights. He did not want a tame surrender, the cloying scented embraces he found so wearisome, but neither would he force her against her will. From their first meeting he had known he must have her.

Her innocence, her disdain, her disapproval of him only whetted his desire. Why he found her so arousing he could not fathom, but as he looked at her now, trembling but determined, a tide of hunger overcame whatever lingering hesitation he might have had about her seduction.

She was a constant ache, disturbing his peace and self-control, but once he possessed her, he would be satisfied, able to forget her and to turn once again to more complaisant women for enjoyment. With a muttered oath he pulled her closely into his arms, his mouth silencing any outcry she might make, forcing a hard demanding kiss on her soft mouth.

Astounded by the sensations he was evoking with his plundering mouth, and even more by her own instinctive response, Esme tried to remain unmoving. Resistance would only excite him to further shocking assaults on her senses, she felt instinctively. He wanted her to struggle, but she would deny him that satisfaction. His kiss deepened and turned warmer, his tongue forcing itself into her mouth in the most intimate of gestures, and his hand wandering down to the opening of her dressing gown, seeking the pliant flesh beneath. She bit back a cry at this unexpected violation, but he seemed impervious to her resistance, a hot fire gleaming in the eyes that roamed her possessively. She must not let him do this, must not submit like some tame acquiescent fool, she thought desperately. But it was increasingly hard to deny her own response. Her skin felt hot and tingling, the pounding of her heart deafening, and she could no longer resist the clamoring of her senses that his caresses induced, the strange frustration that threatened to overcome her.

Before she could tear herself away from his arms, he lifted her, still kissing her deeply, and walked to the huge bed that loomed so menacingly behind them. Lowering her to the counterpane, he subdued her attempt to roll away and pinned her arms above her head with one ruthless hand, while the other roamed expertly over her body in display of mastery. She could not counteract the emotions he induced so easily and shame mingled with some other strange emotion flooded her from head to toes. His lips and hands were causing an acquiescence that prevented her from fighting him, but as he began to undress her, her fear returned and she writhed beneath him, attempting to evade the determined hands which promised undreamed of pleasures. Even more frightening was his silence. No words of reassurance or affection passed his lips as he continued to bring her to an awareness of his body. Just when she had abandoned all hope of retaining any control, they were interrupted by a loud pounding on the door.

"My lord. You must open the door. There is a gentleman demanding the lady's presence below and he will not be denied," came the harried voice of Roberts.

At first Esme thought the duke was so far gone in passion that he did not hear the intruder, but then he cursed and rose slightly, turning his head toward the sound of the untimely interruption.

"Damn it, Roberts, throw the fellow out. I cannot be disturbed," he growled, watching sardonically as Esme colored and tried to restore her garments to decency.

"I know you are in there with Esme. Open this door immediately," came Robert Weirs's furious voice.

"Oh, my God. It's my cousin! Let me up this instant, sir," Esme implored. Shame and outrage had banished all of her arousal. What could she have been thinking of—to allow such liberties, to surrender so easily to this lecherous womanizer. She could not let Robert find her like this. She scurried from the bed, tying the dressing gown firmly around her, as the duke rose impatiently, giving her a mocking look of amusement.

"How timely. Your gallant cousin to the rescue," he gibed, walking casually to the door and throwing it open. He faced an apologetic butler and a raging young man who shouldered his way into the room. Robert's eyes looked around expectantly for Esme, and found her standing quietly by the window.

"Are you all right, Esme? Has this bounder laid a finger on you?" he asked, ignoring the duke, who stood negligently aside, his shoulders propped against the fireplace while he watched the scene with boredom.

"Unable to answer, Esme stared at her cousin, knowing what he was thinking and unwilling to admit he had saved her from unmentionable indignities.

"I am fine, Robert, as you see. How did you find me?" she asked in a soothing tone, for she did not like the ugly look in her cousin's eye.

"That fool French came sputtering into the house, telling us some tale about a runaway horse and your rescue by this rake-hell here. I feared for your reputation and worse, alone here with him," Robert explained, breathing heavily. But he calmed slightly in response to Esme's equanimity. He did not recognize the fragility of the facade she had erected, did not suspect she was hanging on to her composure with the utmost difficulty.

Taking a deep breath, she turned to the tall man watching them ironically. "I am sure my dress has been freshened by now. If you will summon the maid, I will don it and Robert can escort me home, Duke," she said evenly, her eyes giving him a warning. She would entertain no confrontation, and she defied the duke to tell Robert just what he had interrupted.

He surprised her by giving a negligent wave of his hand and assenting. "Of course, dear lady. It shall be attended to, and then you and your cavalier may leave this sinful house without more ado," the duke sneered, as if they had not, a few minutes past, been locked in the most passionate of embraces. The devil did not appear one bit annoyed by Robert's timely interference.

Hugo did not intend to challenge the young man's suspicions, leaving him to think what he might about any loss of Esme's innocence.

How typical, Esme thought. But, of course, he thought

71

nothing untoward in having his afternoon's seduction interrupted. After all, he could satisfy his craving with a variety of other, more willing women. Esme wondered why that thought should cause her such anger. No doubt he was accustomed to being discovered by jealous husbands and lovers, hence the bored, polite scorn. She supposed no woman was worth the trouble to him.

Robert, tight-lipped, faced the duke. "I shall call you out, sir, for your reprehensible behaviour. If it weren't for the scandal which would fall on Esme's head, I would not hesitate to do exactly that."

"That would be foolish. The lady will tell you she is still a model of chastity, unharmed in any way. All I did was remove her from the company of that nodcock French and bring her here for some restorative measures," Carstairs drawled, his eyes roaming over Esme suggestively. He then pulled the bell to summon the maid.

"Perhaps we might leave Miss Sedgewick to dress, and you can join me in a glass of wine below, Lord Weirs," he invited blandly.

"I'm damned if I'll accept your hospitality, sir," Robert answered heatedly.

"As you will, Weirs. But we must continue our quarrel elsewhere. Miss Sedgewick needs some privacy, I believe." He ushered Robert to the door.

Robert hesitated, then in response to the beseeching plea in Esme's eyes, he said stiffly, "I will await you below, Esme, but don't be long. The parents are quite worried about you."

Esme nodded and dropped her eyes, unwilling to see the amusement in the man who would so easily have seduced her if not for the interruption.

On the maid's appearance with her sponged and cleaned dress, Esme threw off the offending garment that had imperfectly clothed her during the recent encounter, looking at it with loathing. She hurried into her dress, smoothed her hair quickly. Looking at herself in the mirror, Esme wondered

72

how she could appear so unchanged, so calm, as if nothing had happened in the last tumultuous hour. Just as well she could deceive the casual eye, for she suspected that Robert would prove most exigent in the next few minutes. The Cranfords, too, would have a great deal to say. And none of it her doing. She was an innocent victim of the duke's lust, but now she alone would have to pay the price.

# Chapter Eight

"Really, Esme, how could you have accompanied that lecher to his house? You know his reputation, and no doubt all the town gossips saw you riding disreputably on his horse through the streets. I cannot conceive what you were about, allowing such outrageous behavior," Robert railed as he drove Esme from Grosvernor Street to the Cranford's house.

"I did not have much choice, Robert, Esme explained wearily. "He abducted me, and I was in no case to make any protest." Recollecting that Robert had rescued her from an embarrassing position, if not worse, she softened her tone. "You were kind to come to my aid. I have not thanked you properly." She looked at him with affection, noticing his scowl and his barely repressed fury. Just what had that ridiculous Algernon implied? she wondered. Whatever he had said, it was no less than the truth. At all costs she must keep the real facts from Robert. He would attempt some foolish revenge and suffer in the doing. Her best refuge could only be the role of the injured innocent. This was not in her customary style, but she had to protect Robert. She felt that in any confrontation with the duke, Robert would not emerge unscathed.

"I do hope you have not challenged the duke to a duel or some such folly," Esme said broaching the subject gingerly. She must know what had gone on between the two men while

74

she was dressing. They had appeared cooly indifferent to each other, not at daggers drawn when she had joined them in the drawing room.

"Damn the fellow. He behaved with every politeness, completely disarmed me. He admitted that perhaps he had been a bit impetuous, wresting you from French in such a hurly-burley fashion. And he agreed to meet me at Gentleman Jackson's Saloon later today in order to allow me to take what recompense I wanted in a sparring match. He made me feel that I had overstated the situation, but was perfectly acceptable to any punishment I wanted to inflict."

Robert reddened at the remembrance. He had not conducted that meeting with quite the aplomb he had wished. Somehow the duke had put him in the wrong, treated him like a callow youth raising the dust over a mere peccadillo. But Esme's danger had been real. He should have been more devisive, brought home to the duke his transgression. Robert did not want to admit to Esme that the duke's suave sophistication, his casual acceptance of responsibility, his flattering *we are men together* attitude had disarmed much of his righteous wrath. And he had a sneaking suspicion that in any encounter with pistols across a greensward, he would come out the loser, an admission he was loathe to make. Not that he was a coward, just that he lacked the experience that made the duke such a formidable opponent. Ashamed, he put the blame on Esme.

"Really, Esme," he complained, "it is not as if you did not realize the duke's reputation. His least attention to a well-bred female can put her respectability in jeopardy. You should not have accompanied him, riding hobble-de-hoy on his horse, with your skirts rucked up for all the world to see."

Esme's relief at being rescued from the duke now became anger at men in general. She gave Robert a look of pure disgust. "And just how was I to achieve that, I wonder? I would remind you, Robert, that I did not want to accompany Mr. French on that ride in the first place. Your mother insisted, and I could not know he was such a ham-fisted driver that his horses would run away with the phaeton. I might have been seriously injured if the duke had not fortuitously halted the run aways. But I suppose that would have been far better for my standing, to have been brought home bleeding and unconscious, rather than have my association with the duke questioned. The strictures of the *ton* are beyond me, and the sooner I am out of London, away from all this ridiculous hypocrisy, the better!''

The duke and Robert may have settled their own differences, but neither of them had apologized to *her*. And Robert could not seem to realize that her participation in this mess had been entirely innocent. She hesitated a moment. *Had* she been entirely guiltless, as valiant against the duke's assault on her senses as she should have been? Esme did not deceive herself. She had been within an ace of surrendering to the devil. Well, he would not have a second opportunity to compromise her. Suddenly Esme's spirits lifted. She knew just how to turn this embroglio to her advantage. Now the Cranfords would have to let her return to the country! She smiled, believing she had found the solution to her troubles. But Robert, glancing at her, was suddenly suspicious.

"What are you planning, Esme? I know that expression of yours. You have decided on some ploy. Well, let me tell you, my girl, you had better watch your step. You are not out of the woods yet, and there will be retribution for this day's work," he promised, hoping to shake her self-possession. He wanted her to turn to him for protection, and far more, to give him the opportunity to confess his love.

"If there is retribution, you will bring it on your own head, Robert." Esme said in a quelling voice. "I think it best if we forget the whole affair. I will make my explanations to your parents, and if they wish not to believe me, I am afraid I cannot alter their opinions. I have done nothing wrong, but this episode has convinced me I am not cut out for London life. I have wanted to return to Dorset for some time, and this should persuade Aunt Mildred that it is the proper place for me. Then she can concentrate on Fannie's prospects without any distraction."

Suddenly Esme felt exhausted. She could feel the beginnings of a headache stirring, and she longed to escape Robert's quizzing and smug criticism of her behavior. Next he would be declaring love, and she really could not bear that after all she had endured. Fortunately, before she could express herself more indignantly, they arrived in Mount Street, and she girded herself for the interview with her aunt and uncle.

Robert, who had been within an ace of doing just what she feared, sighed. He was a kindly young man, and as he helped Esme down from the carriage, he cursed himself for being so inconsiderate. She had been through quite enough today without his badgering her with his devotion. He would not be such a cad as to plead his suit while she was in a vulnerable state. Perhaps it would be best to encourage her plan to return to Dorset. She would be out of the duke's way and far from any other bucks who might entertain ideas of pursuing her. Then, he could put his case to her, having given her time to recover and reflect. She needed a protector, a man to stand between her and the world, and he would be her choice. Somewhat reassured by his decision, he took her arm and squeezed it affectionately.

"Don't worry about the parents, Esme. I will defend you, and persuade them your desire to leave for the country is most reasonable," he promised cheerfully.

Esme thanked him. Really, Robert was a dear boy, and a good friend, if only he would abandon his romantic ideas about her. She was sure that in her absence he would find a more suitable object for his affections, one more to his mother's taste, and that would relieve feelings all around. She smiled wistfully as she prepared to meet the Cranfords. She was a sore trial to them, and she could sympathize with their perplexity and irritation at having such a cuckoo in their nest. She must be more forebearing. Straightening her shoulders, she shook off her malaise, determined to conduct the coming interview with patience and charity.

And she needed all she could summon of both those qualities, for Lady Cranford was most scathing in her remarks, blaming Esme entirely for the affair, and questioning Robert with such avidity that he finally abandoned his usual role of good-humored tolerance toward his mother. "That's quite enough, Mother!" he said forcefully. "You have heard what happened, and I might add, that *you* bear some responsibility. Esme did not want to accompany Mr. French, or at least would have preferred to take Fannie with her, but you made the arrangements. You might have known that starry-eyed poet could not handle his cattle. Give over rating Esme and let the poor girl get some rest after her shocking experience."

Taken aback by her son's unusual asperity, Lady Cranford suspected Robert's championship of his cousin might have a more worrisome implication. She was completely receptive to Esme's suggestion that it would be best for everyone if she retired to the country. Lord Cranford, who had been as appalled as his wife by the affair, and who knew a great deal more about the duke than the women of his family, gave a sigh of relief that Esme had brushed through the escapade so successfully. He thoroughly agreed she would be best sequestered for a time.

So arrangements were made for Esme to retreat to Dorset by the end of the week. It was with relief that she at last gained the sanctuary of her room and lay down on her bed, determined to erase her late encounter with the wretched Duke of Milbourne from her mind and heart.

Esme would not have been so sanguine if she had known of Hugo Carstairs' determination and frustration. Standing at the large bowed window that overlooked Grosvenor Street, watching Robert tenderly bundle his cousin into his phaeton, he had cursed roundly. She needn't think that Lord Weirs's providential interruption of that recent interlude meant the end of everything between them. She might profess to detest him, but—he smiled cruelly as he remembered—she had responded with a depth of passion that had surprised him. He had suspected that beneath that cool facade lay a woman ripe for lovemaking, but he had not anticipated the force of his own reaction. He had been within an ace of losing control, a situation no woman had brought him to since his salad days.

Then she had retreated so quickly, cloaked herself in that maddening reserve, acting as if what had happened had been a mere aberration. He knew he was a skilled lover, able to give women the enjoyment that kept them eager for more. Usually, he became bored before his partners tired of him, and had to extricate himself from their panting clutches, but in this case he had not had the opportunity. The maddening Miss Sedgewick had removed herself from temptation, and in a manner that indicated she would not easily be brought to such a pitch again.

Carstairs turned away from the window, his mind busy with a plan. She could not hide from him forever. For a passing moment he wondered if she cared for her callow cousin. The young Lord Weirs had proved to be a very ardent champion of his cousin's chastity, but Hugo did not entertain him for a moment as a rival. That Esme might truly care for her cousin was a factor which only added spice to his inevitable conquest. What could Weirs offer her but a tame devotion? That she might prefer marriage to Robert to a loveless liaison with him was not worthy of consideration. For so long Hugo had not accepted any restraints on his own desires that it never occurred to him that this case might be different. Having come to a decision, he was impatient to put his campaign into action. He crossed the room and rang the bell to summon his secretary. Charles would be shocked, but he would obey orders.

Esme, believing that she had escaped an horrendous fate, tried to put her unfortunate encounter with the duke behind

79

her, and stubbornly emptied her mind of those last passionate moments on his bed. She finished some paintings that she had postponed for Harriette's portrait and packed up her easel and painting gear, ready for transport to the country. She avoided any invitations that might lead to a meeting with the duke, although he rarely appeared at the proper functions her aunt and uncle honored with their presence.

She also eluded Robert and his attempts to get her alone for an avowal. She would have to deal with her cousin's infatuation before too long, but she hoped her sojourn in the country would dampen his ardor and he would turn to the distractions London offered an attractive young man who was plump in the pockets. She knew the Cranfords expected him to make a brilliant match, even if they despaired of Fannie's doing so. He did not need a fortune, but they would insist on a well-dowered, titled young woman for their heir.

Esme wondered what their reaction would have been if she and Robert had been sincerely in love. That emotion had no place in their reckoning. She suspected that Aunt Mildred found such feelings ill-bred and bourgeois. Poor Robert. Well, he was a darling and some woman would find in him the fulfillment of all her dreams—Esme hoped. Then he would laugh at this youthful passion for his cousin, a desire compounded of propinquity and her uncommon type. She wished him well.

At last the day came for her journey to Dorset. Fannie was loathe to see her leave, but promised to join her before too long, once she had persuaded her parents that her Season was a failure. Esme bade her an affectionate farewell and stepped into the luxurious traveling coach for the long ride. The Cranfords, whatever their feelings about Esme's shocking behaviour, would never allow her to travel shabbily, so she was accompanied by a coachman, a footman, and her maid, an impressive entourage.

As the coach pulled out of the city, she relaxed against the squabs, relieved to have eluded both Robert and the duke for

80

the moment. Men were such a trial, so determined to dominate and so sure that no woman could resist them for long. She was well rid of them. And now that she was leaving London, both Robert and the duke could pursue more complaisant females, leaving her free to continue her painting.

She had no illusions about the duke's pursuit of her. He wanted her because she had rejected him, and his pride would not allow such a rebuff. He was intrigued and baffled by her refusal to be impressed by his consequence, his wealth and his undoubted physical attractions. Esme was honest enough to admit that she would not easily abandon those memories of the duke's thwarted seduction. But he had none of the qualities she was seeking in a man, and she knew if she should be tempted to encourage him, she would be the loser. There was no denying the attraction between them, but it was based on nothing more than a carnal appeal, and that could never satisfy her. She despised men of his sort. At least Robert's intentions were honorable, but the duke cared nothing for her, saw her as a means of appeasing his lust, a despicable reason to seduce a chaste female. She disliked everything about the man. She rested her head, in its fetching straw bonnet against the squabs of the carriage and turned her mind to the landscapes she would paint when she arrived in Hampshire.

The journey through London's crowded streets had been slow and tedious, but once the carriage reached Richmond the prospect brightened, although low threatening clouds promised rain later in the day. The Surrey countryside was green and burgeoning with life, but the air hung heavy. Esme insisted on lowering a window to escape the stuffiness of the coach. They had been perhaps three hours on the road when suddenly the equipage drew to a stop. Peering out the window to discover the reason for the halt, she was startled to see several masked men surrounding the equipage. She could not believe it. Here, such a short distance from London, in daylight, they were being held up by highwaymen! Before she could summon her senses, the door of the coach was thrust open and

81

a tall, dark masked man appeared.

"Do not be frightened," he said, as Esme's maid squealed and cowered before the threatening apparition. Esme looked scornful, although her heart was beating hard. She would not tremble and show her fear before this villain.

"What do you want, sirrah? We have few valuables." She set her chin grimly. Her maid started to whine. "Oh, do be quiet, Watson, the men won't harm you. They only want to rob us," she insisted with disdain.

"On the contrary, dear lady. We have no intention of taking your possessions. Please step out of the coach and no harm will come to you." The man spoke silkily, his accent well-bred—and somehow familiar.

"I will do no such thing," Esme replied sternly, a frisson of suspicion darkening her forehead. The man who stood facing them, pistol in his hand, had a curious manner. Could he be one of those gentlemen of the road who had fallen on grim times and made his way by accosting passengers? She remained stubbornly in her seat.

"You would not want us to harm your servants, I am sure, my dear. Now don't be alarmed. We plan no outrage. Just come quietly," the man urged, his tone hard and menacing. Esme hesitated. Could these devils be kidnapping her for ransom? That was unusual. But she refused to show her fear.

"If you insist, sir. But I must complain at such cavalier treatment," she said haughtily, and stepped gingerly down, ignoring the hand he extended to help her.

In the road, she noticed immediately three other varlets surrounding her coach, their pistols cocked. John, the coachman, looked furious but helpless under their weapons. Blocking the highway was another carriage, and her captor indicated she must accompany him toward it. He waved his gun in a negligent manner.

Straightening her shoulders with resolution she walked slowly toward the equipage, giving John a reassuring smile as she walked by him. Within moments she was ushered into the closed carriage, and her captor followed her inside, giving a brief order to the driver. Before she knew what was happening, the horses were whipped up and they had begun their journey.

Her escort, watching her carefully, smiled with a certain nasty appreciation of her stoicism, and commended her docility.

"So wise of you, Miss Sedgewick. Now, I can remove this tiresome mask." Suiting his action to his words, he threw off the offending disguise.

Esme gasped, recognizing the Duke of Milbourne. "You blackguard. I might have known! What do you mean by this outrageous action, sir?" But she knew all too well what his purpose was. She glared at him, powerless to restrain her anger as he lounged carelessly against the squabs opposite her.

"Yes, you must have realized I could not contemplate any further interruptions to our delightful dalliance. I regret taking such drastic measures to secure your undivided attention, my dear Esme, but this time you will not escape me," he promised implacably, eyeing her with unmistakable desire.

Although by now thoroughly frightened, Esme would not show her fears before her tormentor. She tossed her head and looked at him with disdain. "You will regret this action, sir."

"Probably. I am easily bored, and I find the chase much more exciting than the possession. But for the moment, I am anticipating our relationship with great pleasure." He grinned at her, well aware of the picture his suggestive words promised. Then, as if suddenly tiring of the game, he stretched languidly. "Do stop glaring at me and compose yourself, madam, for the inevitable. We have some time yet before we reach our destination, and I can deal with you suitably. I hope you will not spend the hours tediously lamenting your fate. I expect better of you," he mocked, turning away from her furious eyes with a shrug of indifference.

With difficulty, Esme subdued the torrent of angry words that rose to her lips. She would not demean herself and plead for mercy. Obviously he cared little for the sensibilities of his victim, but he would rue the day he took this heinous action. There must be some way of evading what he intended, she decided, her mind busy behind her scornful silence.

The coach rumbled on at a fast pace toward its unknown objective while its two occupants brooded with varying emotions about what lay ahead.

*Chapter Nine*

It was mid-afternoon before the duke's carriage rolled to a stop in the depths of Surrey. They had partaken of a lavishly prepared luncheon en route, but Esme had eaten little and refused the wine the duke proffered politely. She had tried to discover in what direction they were moving and decided they must be bound for some isolated lodge the duke either owned or had commandeered for his wicked purpose. She recognized no landmarks.

The carriage drew up before a small manor house, heavily shrouded by oak trees that allowed little light to brighten the dwelling. In any case, as they emerged from the long ride, a depressing drizzle dampened the atmosphere.

The duke escorted her up the stone steps with a ruthless arm, and advised her that any objections she made would be ignored by the stalwart middle-aged butler who admitted them to the hall. He gave the man a curt nod and asked if a room had been prepared for his guest, not doubting that all his arrangements had been carried out with dispatch.

Esme wished that just once she could see the duke at point non plus—his wishes balked and his cavalier decisions thwarted. But in this instance, she was to be denied the pleasure. The man bowed with servility and agreed that all was in readiness.

"Baines here will escort you to a chamber where you may refresh yourself in preparation for the evening, my dear. I am sure a bath and a change of clothes will improve your humor," the duke suggested suavely, but beneath the smooth tone his determination was evident. She had no recourse but to obey, but she would not allow him to see her apprehension of what faced her.

"You are all kindness, sir," she assented sarcastically, allowing the man to lead her toward the stairs and the upper storey. The dwelling appeared to be a hunting lodge of great age. It was furnished appropriately with oaken chests and the antlers of slain animals adorning the walls.

As she followed Baines across the slate floor and up the stairs, she could not resist looking back. The duke was watching her with an implacable expression. Her back straight despite her fatigue, she hoped her disdain and dislike were evident, but she doubted he found her defiance impressive. She would not submit easily. Nor would she confess her fears to the silent servant who would offer little sympathy.

Baines ushered her into a large room that was tastefully decorated, if a bit stifling with its large old-fashioned, heavy oak furnishings. She ignored the man and walked to the windows, pushing aside the velvet draperies to look out upon a wooded scene that gave no indication of its location.

"A maid will be up shortly with your bath, madam, and there is a change of garments here in the wardrobe," Baines said, his face impassive. Esme gave no indication that she had heard his explanations, and after a moment the man left her to her troubled thoughts.

Obviously the duke had made intricate preparations for this seduction scene, she thought with a moue of distaste. Both Fannie and Robert had told her that the duke's reputation with women was legendary, and he was rarely refused when he tendered a lure. Well, this time he was in for a surprise. Esme suspected that she would be subjected to his famous address, but that in no way compensated for the treatment she had already endured. She had been kidnapped, wrested from her home against her wishes, and had her own plans disrupted, all to satisfy the duke's monumental conceit. Whatever the outcome of this day's disastrous development, the duke would not emerge unscathed, that Esme vowed.

Her ruminations were interrupted by a maid and man-servant, carrying a steaming bath, towels, and a tray of refreshments. She sighed and greeted them politely, although she wanted to scream defiance at their calm acceptance of this hateful situation. She longed for a bath, but would not be smirked at by the duke's servants. With some asperity she ordered them from the room. She was not surprised to find on their departure that the door had no key. She only prayed she would be left alone to have her bath in privacy. She hurriedly undressed and settled into the bath, delighted to wash away her travel dirt. She smiled a bit grimly. Here she was, in expectation of losing her respectability and worse, calmly bathing as if at home in Hampshire or London. She had been in this position before and narrowly averted disaster. This time there would be no escape. Well, what good would it do to spurn the creature comforts which were offered. She was not such a ninny as that.

She did not linger overly long in the water, and on emerging was further enraged to see that her travelling dress had been removed. She had no recourse but to don the rose silk dressing gown, which she found draped across the bed. Furiously struggling with her unbound hair and trying to bring it to a manageable state, she comforted herself with the vengeance she would exact for this day's plot.

She wondered briefly if John, her uncle's coachman, would return to the Mount Street house and instigate a rescue. What would the Cranfords think? Well, they would be in no doubt that she had been forced into this regrettable situation. Certainly she was not here of her own free will. But she realized that their efforts to discover her whereabouts would likely be unsuccessful, and certainly too late to prevent what the duke had in mind.

As she paced back and forth across the room, she was prey to a jumble of disorganized plans for repelling the duke and eluding the fate he had in store for her. What kind of a monster was he that he could so cooly contemplate seducing an innocent girl? Raised in the country, Esme had few fears of the physical act of coupling, but she had no desire to feature as the object of some libertine's lust. Well, perhaps she might now be able to put her own scheme for the future into effect, find a cottage in the country where she would pursue her painting without all this fashionable nonsense her uncle and aunt insisted upon. But that thought in no way mitigated the infamy of her present position, and the duke would discover he had a very unwilling partner in his bed, she promised herself.

Before she could fulminate any further, the duke himself entered the room without warning.

"Ah, my dear. How charming you look! I hope you are feeling better after the strenuous events of the day." He stood with his back to the door and eyed her with what she considered a satyr's look. Evidently he, too, had repaired the ravages of the journey. He had donned a heavily brocaded crimson dressing gown, the intimacy of his attire accentuating the threat that faced her. Obstinately she refused to answer his questioning look, and resolutely turned her back to him.

"How wise of you not to scream and protest your recent treatment. It would do you little good, and I find such recriminations so boring." He smiled sardonically. The chit was stubborn, but she would come around. They all did in time, after they felt it necessary to plead outrage. As his eyes roamed over her figure possessively, his admiration deepened into a hot tide of desire. She was such a lovely creature, with her blond hair streaming over the rose gown, her form outlined against the window. Suddenly impatient, the duke crossed to her, pulled her rigid body into his arms and looked down into the stormy gray eyes that met his fearlessly.

"I did not take our interruption by your cousin the other

88

day in good part, Esme, and it behooved me to see to it that our next encounter resulted in a more felicitious finale. No impetuous gallant will disturb our pleasures here," he promised, his grasp tightening.

His cynical assumption that she would welcome his advances stirred Esme to an angry rejoinder. "Our pleasures!" she sneered. "Don't you mean your own, duke? I was not aware I was consulted in this attempt. I find your suggestions disgusting." It seemed to her that the pounding of her heart almost drowned out the sound of her words. She hoped he would not realize how frightened she was. Looking at the dark face looming above her, she knew she would find no mercy there.

"From the beginning you were destined to grace my bed," he said, "and your pathetic efforts to delay the inevitable only postpone the outcome. A poet once said that pleasures deferred are only doubled. I trust that is the case this time."

Esme tossed her head, eluding his grasp, and replied with defiance. "I had no idea you were pressed to such ends to get a woman in your bed, duke. What a turn-up for such an accomplished libertine," she jeered. Esme refused to quail beneath those dark, hot eyes that promised reprisal for her incautious words.

Before she could utter any more insults, he drew her once more into his embrace, gentling her resistance effortlessly with his expert kisses.

"You will enjoy it once you have abandoned these foolish shrinkings. You were made for a man's bed," he promised. His lips wandered enticingly down her face from her forehead to her throat with ruthless mastery. Esme had never realized how sensitive that part of her body was before. Then he claimed her mouth in an intrusive kiss. What had begun as an assault on her senses turned slowly into a beguiling breach of her defences. His tongue darted into her mouth teasingly, making her long for more. She found herself melting under the hot tide of desire he evoked. Encouraged by her response, his hand crept inside her gown to fondle the warm, aroused flesh there. He touched her softly, then more urgently. Esme tried to steel her body to resist his insidious skill, but somehow she could not summon the resolution to tear herself from his arms. She must not let this happen. What was wrong with her that she could allow him to have his way so easily? With a violent shrug, she tore herself from his arms, and faced him, her cheeks flushed and her bosom heaving.

"Have you no decency, no compunction at seducing a woman who despises you?" she asked desperately.

He smiled, raising one eyebrow sardonically. "A gallant try, Esme, but we have come to far along the path to turn back now. You have put me to a deal of trouble, my girl, for which you will now pay—willingly or no. Come, don't make it more difficult for yourself," he urged, passion now overcoming him as he looked at her with a desire he no longer attempted to mask with cajolery. "We are wasting time."

Suiting his action to his words, he picked her up, easily quelling her attempts to struggle. He then carried her over to the bed, releasing her against the pillows and following her down, his hands and mouth silencing her objections.

Grasping both her flailing hands in one of his, he raised them above her head and pinioned them there while with his other hand, he slid off her gown and bared her body to his gaze. Then, after a moment of running his eyes over her, he opened his robe. He subdued her thrashing body with his knees, anchoring her to the bed, rendering her immobile as he lowered himself onto her. She felt his naked arousal and tried again to avoid his mouth, but he kissed her with easy mastery.

Finally, her writhings impotent, she quieted from sheer exhaustion. His hands and mouth, exploring her secret places, gentled, inducing lassitude and warmth. She knew she should continue to struggle, but it was beyond her. She could not fight the delicious sensations he brought to life within her. Her body stiffened with shock and pain as he thrust into her. He paused for a moment and his kisses turned coaxing and beguiling, arousing an unexpected heat, and then he continued.

After a moment, as the pain receded and the tempo increased, Esme realized with shame that an exquisite sensation was gathering within her, the tension unbearable. Suddenly, an explosive release brought unimagined pleasure. Then she was spiraling downward, her limbs relaxing, and she fell back almost unconscious from the force of the emotion which he had engendered.

Neither of them had spoken a word during the tempestuous encounter, but now he raised his head from its resting place on her breast and looked searchingly into the wet eyes that gazed back at him in confusion and humiliation.

He had breached her every defence without once losing control himself and for that, as much as the eventual outrage, she could not forgive him. She turned her face away, but he would not be denied, and forced her to look at his probing eyes.

"It will be better next time. I regret hurting you," he said gently, as if he could not help himself. Looking at her tear-soaked cheeks and those accusing eyes, a pang of compunction assailed him. What had he done?

She shuddered and replied faintly, "There will not be a next time. You over-estimate yourself, sir."

He smiled a bit grimly, and released her, giving a shrug. "I seem to, or perhaps I underestimate you. And my name is Hugo. Certainly after what has passed between us you need not be so formal." He rose from the bed and stood looking down at her for a moment, a deep scowl darkening his features. Obviously his seduction of her had not pleased him, and she could only feel a weariness and disgust that she had submitted so tamely. Esme was too honest to disguise the fact that she had not fought for her virtue with the passion she should have exerted. Some of her disgust was with herself, but she would not give him the satisfaction of knowing that.

"Well, you have accomplished your purpose, duke. If it was not as enjoyable as you hoped, I can hardly be blamed. You are a brute and a bully. Whatever your famed abilities as a lover, I find you sorely lacking," she jeered, hoping her bitter words would hide the real tumult of her emotions.

"You are a most provocative wench," he growled, unwilling to believe she had found his seduction of her so dreadful, but aware of an unexpected regret for his impetuous act. From the first moment he had met her he had determined to have her, and now that he had fulfilled his aim, he wondered why it gave him so little pleasure. What an unusual girl she was. He had expected tears and protestations, and what he had earned was scorn and disgust. His only recourse was to leave her to reflect on their recent intimacy, and realize that she was now committed to being his mistress. And a reluctant mistress she would be—very unflattering, but no doubt deserved. He had no intention of letting her go. Closing the front of his robe, he turned away and strode toward the door. Before leaving her to her suppositions about their relationship, he had one last warning.

"We will dine in about an hour. I think you will find some suitable gowns in the wardrobe, although, I much prefer you without your clothes," he mocked. Then he left her with an ironic bow and a soft, "Thank you."

Left alone at last, Esme railed at the fate that had delivered her into this lecher's hands. She denied any other feeling, and finally decided that she would not cower here in bed, but would meet him cooly over the supper table and lull his suspicions until she could make her escape from this frightful situation. Up to now he had managed everything to his own pleasure, but he would soon see she was not some tame puppet to be coerced for his gratification. She would escape from this damnable place and from her captor, and he would rue the day he had ever set eyes upon her.

The loss of her virginity concerned her less than she would have believed, but her fury at the ruthless way in which she had been used would not be easily forgotten. She examined herself wryly in the glass, noticing her flushed cheeks and bright eyes, ashamed that she appeared so radiant after what most girls would consider a disgusting and brutal interlude.

At least the duke had gained little pleasure from his conquest, and now that it was done perhaps he would find a rebellious mistress not to his taste. Knowing she had no recourse, she towelled the evidence of their encounter from her body, then opened the wardrobe and gazed at the selection of gowns within, repelled that the man had prepared for this eventuality with such forethought. She reluctantly took out a stylish cream-colored silk gown, trimmed lavishly with lace. Matching satin slippers slid onto her feet easily. How damnably experienced the devil was at ordering female clothes! He had certainly prepared with some pains for this shocking interlude.

She brushed her hair with long furious strokes and bit her lips with vexation. Here she was decking herself out like some doxy, but what choice did she have? She could hardly appear naked at the supper table. But this was just one more score added to the list of transgressions she was accumulating against her ravisher. The duke would pay for treating her like a piece of merchandise, and he would find the payment humiliating if it was the last thing she did on this earth. She looked at herself in the mirror with a certain approval. No man would reduce her to a cringing, apologetic fool. If anyone would do the cringing it would be the duke. She laughed grimly. That was a picture she found most unlikely. With a toss of her head, she left the room for the uncomfortable tête à tête which loomed before her.


Three days later, Esme sat brooding in the drawing room of the manor house which had become her prison. She pondered her options. Had her relatives learned about her abduction and had they notified the authorities or made any push to discover her whereabouts? Did they think she had gone willingly to some rendezvous with a lover? And Robert. Could he suspect the duke was behind her disappearance? She gave a rueful thought to her cousin's state of mind. Far better that he thought she had been spirited away by highwaymen than to learn she had become the duke's mistress.

For that was what she had become. Each night he returned to her bed, trying to beguile her with his skilled lovemaking, and each night she found herself responding in a manner that disgusted her with its wantonness. He quieted her objections easily and every hour that passed she felt more confused by the emotions he evoked.

During the day he had ridden with her, allowing her no attempt to scout out the countryside. She had seen no other houses or farms, nor caught even a glimpse of a possible rescuer. The house was well-staffed with servants who would prevent her escape, even if she could elude the duke. Her only surcease was her sketching, and even on these expeditions he accompanied her, surprising her with the knowledgeable interest he took in her work. Her anger at his casual possession had not diminished, but his only reaction to her occasional outbursts had been amusement.

She walked to the windows, which gave onto a stone courtyard, and wondered where he had gone today. It was the first time he had left her to her own devices. He had left soon after breakfast only telling her that he regretted leaving her but had some important business to conduct.

She would not signify that his leavetaking was important and forebore questioning him about his destination.

"I am grateful that I will be spared your attentions, sir. And I can only pray that your absence will be extended," she replied haughtily.

"And that I come to some dire fate upon the road," he added, laughing at her refusal to reveal her curiosity. "Would you be unhappy if another woman was the object of my absence from your side, my dear?" he asked blandly.

"I can only hope that is the case and that she will keep you so occupied that you will forget all about me, if she doesn't put a dagger in your black heart," Esme responded darkly.

"I am the most faithful of men when my affections are

94

engaged, Esme. You can be sure that I will rush back to your side with all dispatch, for I have not finished with you yet, my termagant." He grinned at her with maddening poise. "Until this evening, then," he said and gave her a bruising kiss. She rubbed her hand across her mouth in disgust, but he only laughed and left without further baiting.

She had no idea where he had gone or when he would return, but if she were to effect her escape she must act promptly. She had ordered a horse, knowing that a groom would accompany her, but hoping somehow to elude him. As she watched from the window, she saw the man bring the animal, a chestnut mare, to the entrance of the house. She had dressed in her riding costume that, like all the clothes the duke had ordered for her, was the epitome of fashion—a bottle-green hussar-styled outfit. She had been pleased to notice that her own clothes had been returned to her and she had found her reticule. Within it was a tidy bundle of notes. She wondered why her money had not been impounded. Could the duke have overlooked such an obvious threat? She had the money securely tucked into the pocket of her riding skirt now. She fingered it, reassuring herself that it had not disappeared. When Baines entered the room, she was sitting quietly awaiting him, hoping to dispell any suspicion that she was panting to leave the premises.

"Your horse is waiting, madam, and your groom. The duke suggested you might enjoy a ride. We are quite isolated here and there are many acres for you to roam, for we are far from any civilized folk," he suggested, his tone heavy with warning. He was telling her most politely that she would have little chance of encountering anyone who could help her escape.

"Thank you, Baines," she said as haughtily as she could. The man had obviously been given his orders, and although he treated her with all deference, she knew he had insured that her escort would be vigilant. The duke would countenance no laxness in his arrangements, but that only put Esme on her mettle. Somehow she must manage to elude her gaolers.

The May morning was sunny and beguiling as Esme and her attendant rode down the driveway toward some low-forested hills in the distance. The groom was a surly type, low-browed and menacing, riding a spirited gelding that could easily outpace her mare, she feared. He guided her unobtrusively on the path he intended her to follow, but made no conversation.

After a brisk half-hour's canter, Esme was despaired of finding any way to avoid his watchful eye. Finally they approached a knoll that topped a thickly wooded area and Esme signaled that she wanted to dismount and rest a while. The man grudgingly assisted her down and tied the horses to a nearby tree. Esme walked a few feet away and looked down upon a deserted scene, green fields, newly planted. Did that mean there must be a farm nearby? And if so, there must be tenants. Probably in the duke's service—but she must not be so faint-hearted.

A stiff breeze had blown up and she took off her plumed hat with a sigh of relief, trying to gain some enjoyment from the pastoral scene that stretched below her. The groom waited nearby, watching her with a steely eye, and some impatience over her interruption of their ride. She took out a small handkerchief from her pocket and wiped her brow daintily, then inadvertently dropped the cambric square and saw the breeze waft it away, finally bringing it to rest on a bush some fifty yards distant.

"Oh, my handkerchief. Could you retrieve it, please," she asked the groom pleadingly.

He frowned, but could not deny a simple polite request, and left the horses to scurry on her errand. The moment his back was turned, Esme leaped up and ran to the horses, jumping quickly to the back of the gelding, and releasing her mare's reins, giving the horse a sharp crack across her rump. Then, spurring her own mount, she galloped away, noting the man running toward her too late to halt her progress or retrieve a mount. With no horse available, he could not follow her. She felt exhilarated to have put herself beyond his reach, although she had no idea where she was traveling or if she could reach a road before she was captured. She raced down the hill and across several heavily wooded acres, the wind whipping color into her cheeks. Whatever the outcome of her mad dash for freedom, for the moment she was alone and for the moment, at least, mistress of her destiny.

# Chapter Ten

For the first time since the duke had stopped her coach en route to Hampshire, fortune blessed Esme. Although the forest and fields surrounding the mysterious hunting lodge had appeared solitary and endless, after a half an hour's brisk riding she found a lane that led to a village. At the local inn she learned that a mail coach was expected hourly and she was able to purchase a ticket. She had given little thought to her ultimate destination, but during her frantic ride, had decided suddenly that she would not try to return to London or Hampshire. She could not face either Robert or his parents under the circumstances. First she must find a bolt hole, and then she would write them of her safety.

The stage was bound for Reigate and from there she could make her way by stages to Tunbridge Wells, where her old nurse ran a small boarding house. Dear Bessie would offer her sanctuary, she knew. She had always kept her contacts with Bessie since her nurse had left her parents' house to marry a neighboring footman and the two had gone into service in Kent. Bessie's husband, Tom Evans, had died from fever after ten years of a happy married life and his widow now managed a boarding house for a stern landlord. Tunbridge Wells had fallen from popular favor when the Prince Regent had transferred his attention to Brighton, and it was doubtful that she would be discovered in the fading watering place.

When she wished, Esme could assume as haughty a manner as any duchess, and she had no trouble in staring down the landlord of the inn where she left her horse, promising that someone would eventually retrieve it. If the man, a severe silent type, wondered at the sudden appearance of a lady of quality at his small inn, which was quite off the beaten track, a generous stipend and curt replies to his cursory interest quieted his questions.

Esme entered the coach with fears of pursuit still heavy on her mind. She could not have ridden more than ten or fifteen miles from the hunting lodge, and she knew her pursuer would not be dilatory in seeking her.

To her relief there were only two passengers on the Reigate stage, one a hearty farmer's wife going to visit her daughter who was expecting a baby, and the other a sour, attenuated man who looked like a solicitor's clerk. The man paid little heed to Esme but Mrs. Given, the farmer's wife, was an open-faced confiding soul, thoroughly involved in her coming grandchild and only too happy to discuss the baby's arrival with anyone who would listen. She prattled on for quite twenty minutes without asking Esme any questions about her own reasons for traveling in such a shabby manner and without luggage. Esme had no difficulty parrying her few questions, only informing Mrs. Givens that she was on a visit to an old family retainer. As the woman was much more interested in delving into the more horrific tales of child-bearing, she was easily dissuaded from discovering Esme's own plans. The man looked annoyed and disgusted at Mrs. Given's artless confidences, but appeared to notice little about his traveling companions. As the miles lengthened, Esme's fears of discovery lessened. Nodding graciously at Mrs. Givens' remarks was able to turn her mind to her revenge on the duke.

Surely now that she had removed herself from his dominance he would forget this interlude. She was ashamed at her own part in their brief liaison, not from any prudish reactions to the loss of her virginity, but due entirely to her own response. She realized that if she had stayed longer she might have succumbed to his intoxicating attraction, and she hated herself for this weakness.

There was no denying that the devil had made her initiation into womanhood a far less terrifying experience than it might have been. But he was a skilled seducer, although he made no attempt to lure her with protestations of love. He had craved her body, that was all. And much of his determination to subdue her had no doubt been sparked by her own disdain and disinterest in him. Her pride had forced her to treat him with scorn and disgust, but she had to admit he was not just the idle lecher she had at first suspected. He had made every effort to see that her pleasure equaled his and she could not deny that her physical response had surprised her.

His conversation was knowledgeable and witty. He knew a great deal about art and in spite of herself Esme had been tempted into telling him about her passion to create a masterpiece. He had seen her portrait of Harriette and flattered her with his understanding of what she had tried to portray. If they had met in other circumstances, she might have found his address and his grasp of an artist's problems and aspirations fascinating, but due to his arrogance and ruthless possession of her, she had closed he ears and mind to his beguiling discussion of the art world.

She had to concede there was more to the man than just his obvious attractions, but she could never forget the coercion and indifference to her own desires which had led to her downfall in that damnable hunting lodge. Well, she refused to pine over what had happened. She must just get on with her life and her painting. She had quite decided how she would reward him for his casual abduction, but that would have to wait until she reached Bessie.

She took a late afternoon stage from Reigate to Tunbridge Wells. Fatigue was overcoming her, but fear of pursuit spurred her to put as many miles as possible between her and the duke.

When he learned of her disappearance, he would probably shrug his shoulders and forget her. At any rate, they could not have remained in the seclusion of his hunting lodge for much longer. No doubt he would return to London and pursue a more willing paramour. But still she would feel more secure in Tunbridge Wells.

Late in the evening the coach arrived at The Bird and Bottle, a busy inn on the outskirts of the town, and Esme hired a hackney to convey her to Bessie's lodgings. She only hoped her old nurse would welcome her without too many questions, for the journey had been tiring and fraught with apprehension. She need not have worried about the warmth of her reception, despite the late hour and the months since their last visit.

"My dear, Miss Esme, whatever are you doing here at this time of night. Come in, come in. You looked fagged to death," Bessie greeted her with affection. She was a plump, hearty type with rosy cheeks and a countrywoman's brisk, comforting manner. She had married late and must now have been in her middle fifties, but to Esme, she appeared unchanged. Esme sank into her nurse's smothering embrace with gratitude, and tried to make an explanation of her strange arrival.

"Now enough of that. Your story can wait until you have had a warm bath and some victuals. Fortunately, my best room is going begging and I can make you quite comfortable, my dear," Bessie fussed, shepherding her charge upstairs without more ado. "Whatever made you travel in such a hurly-burly manner without a maid, and no luggage. Well, all that can wait. Trust Bessie to take care of you now, my lamb," she soothed, guiding Esme into a comfortable bedroom furnished simply with a solid-looking bed and bright, clean linen.

Esme, by now so weary she could hardly hold her eyes open, allowed herself to be cosseted, bathed and fed, then fell into bed. Sleep claimed her almost immediately, all her jumbled thoughts at rest for the moment.

Esme awoke the morning after her precipitate flight feeling much more the thing. After Bessie fed her a lavish breakfast,

101

she settled down to do some hard thinking about her future. She was confined to the house, since her dusty riding costume had been whisked away by Bessie, and she was forced into wearing a disreputable old chenille dressing gown which her nurse had proffered with many apologies. Esme knew she must write to the Cranfords and assure them of her safety as well as make provision for her clothes and painting equipment to be forwarded to her in Tunbridge Wells.

For some time she had been aware that she must make some difficult decisions about her life and this latest crisis in her affairs had only strengthened her determination to leave the Cranford's menage. She had attained her majority and could manage her own life now, even if her decision proved displeasing to her uncle and aunt. Although she dearly loved Fannie, and looked upon Robert with sisterly affection, she felt no such warm ties to the Earl and Countess of Cranford. They had done their duty by her, but had never really welcomed her into their household. For this, she did not blame them, knowing that her interests did not match theirs. Aunt Mildred had hoped, perhaps, to discharge her reponsibility by persuading Esme into a proper marriage, but that was now out of the question. Even if no one should learn of her abduction by the duke, and she doubted that he would want his shocking behaviour made public, she could not in all honesty accept the suit of some proper gentleman. Not that she was inclined in that direction; putting herself at the mercy of even the least demanding of husbands did not appeal to her.

Suddenly a frightening thought sprang to mind and interrupted her reflections. What if she were pregnant! She was not so naive as not to consider this might be the outcome of the duke's possession. Well, if that should occur, she would deal with it as best she might, although she prayed she would not be called upon to suffer such a fate. She liked children, but an illegitimate offspring would be a difficult matter. She laughed ruefully. She need not expect any support from the duke. He was not the type to welcome any such evidence of his

102

lechery. She had a small inheritance and hoped to make more money from her paintings. She was even prepared to offer lessons to a few talented students. Not for a moment did she consider appealing to Hugo Carstairs for assistance, although he was the cause of her situation.

No, she had an idea for dealing with that gentleman and it would hurt him where he was most vulnerable, in his pride and consequence.

Her letter to her relatives was a masterful combination of assurance and deception. She told them she had been abducted by highwaymen but was able to make her escape and was now sheltering with her old nurse. She regretted the inconvenience and worry her disappearance had caused them, but hoped they would now be relieved and understand her intention to remain with Bessie for some time, and keep her direction a secret. She did not want any further interruptions to her painting. She asked them to send her clothes and painting gear. She thanked them for her care of her and sent her love to Fannie and Robert. She wrote a businesslike letter to her solicitor, also informing him of her change of residence and ordering him to send her funds to Bessie's address.

Rising from her desk with a sigh of relief, she knew she had made the right decision. Actually, what had appeared at first to be a shocking climax to a hitherto blameless life might turn out to be a blessing. But that did not signify that she would be content to let the duke off without a just punishment. She would begin immediately on that revenge.

Esme might have settled her life to her own satisfaction, if unable to banish from her mind all disturbing memories of her recent reluctant association with the duke, but her relatives were not to receive her news with such complacency. Whatever the Cranfords felt about their niece, and they certainly had not taken her presence in their rigid household without some degree of irritation, they were not callous. When

John the Coachman returned in a state of excitement and fury from his abortive journey to Hampshire to tell him the news of her abduction, they had responded with horror and dismay, awaiting some request for ransom, but fearing the worst.

Robert had been beside himself, insisting on riding out to the area of the outrage and scouring the surrounding countryside for some clue to Esme's disappearance, but to no avail. The Cranfords hesitated to call in the Bow Street runners, fearing scandal, and their irresolute behavior antagonized their son beyond bearing. Fannie was loud in her reproaches and genuine fear for what had befallen her cousin. As several days passed without news, the Cranfords began to have doubts about the supposed kidnapping, after posing several hard questions to John and the footman who accompanied him.

"It is passing strange we have received no demands for ransom," Aunt Mildred said at the family conference, the latest in several, which she called one evening almost a week after Esme's disappearance. "Perhaps the wretched girl was not really abducted but arranged to vanish, regardless of the inconvenience and pain it would cause us," she complained.

She had never liked Esme, having despised her parents for their loose, heedless ways, and finding the girl herself a disruptive influence in her well managed household. Esme had not displayed the proper gratitude for their guardianship, Mildred thought, nor had she behaved as a respectable young woman in a reputable family should. As a child she had been introspective and unwilling to follow the path the countess had directed. Then, too, there was her appearance, a threat to Fannie's own abilities to attract a husband, although the countess had to acquit her of deliberately trying to win beaux from her cousin. She was nevertheless far too attractive and maddeningly indifferent to her looks. Mildred Appleton, who had married for position and wealth the man her parents selected, had never understood Esme's indifference to the rules of polite society. To her horror she had heard from

Robert that the girl had been wanton enough to paint a portrait of that notorious demimondaine, Harriette Wilson, a woman whose name should never be mentioned in proper drawing rooms. That Robert would have association with such a woman was a question he did not choose to pursue. Now she had endangered Fannie's chances on the Marriage Mart by this strange disappearance. Mildred, Countess of Cranford, was too certain of her own worthiness to feel guilt for not loving or understanding her niece, and she felt a sneaking relief that the girl had now been removed from her son's orbit.

"It is early days yet, Mildred," the earl said, interrupting her thoughts. "But I cannot understand why we have heard nothing." He was well aware of his wife's feelings for his niece, and although he himself had always found the girl amiable, he recognized that she was not of the usual stamp. A man not given to examining his motives or emotions, he craved acceptability and had strict notions of conduct, which Esme had cheerfully ignored, despite his admonishments. But he felt annoyance that he could not resolve the problem of her abduction.

"John said that he believed the highwayman was a gentleman," Robert interjected, worry clouding his brow. "Could she have been kidnapped for some purpose other than ransom?" Robert asked.

"What are you implying, Robert?" his mother asked, watching her son with apprehension. He paced back and forth across the room, reluctant to air his fears before his unreceptive parents. He knew how they would view his doubts. But he could not restrain himself.

"Well, you know she was being pursued by that wretched rake, Sir Guy Wentworth. He might have decided to capture her. And then there is the Duke of Milbourne," Robert offered tentatively, unable to repress his suspicion that some man had wrested Esme from him. He had been appalled to learn of her various deceptions, her painting of Harriette's portrait, which he had discovered on an evening to the demimondaine's house with a group of rowdy friends. *Arethusa* had struck a chord, and he affirmed his suspicions by asking Miss Wilson some leading questions while she was relaxed from the freely flowing wine. If she had hidden her painting, what else had Esme kept from him?

"Really, Robert, that is ridiculous! Esme, whatever her faults, is a lady of breeding. She would not encourage such men, and they would hardly risk their reputation with such an action," his father objected, frowning at his son and giving him a warning glare. How dare the boy make such a suggestion in front of his mother and sister, who must be shielded from the immoral behaviour of sinful men!

"I did not say she encouraged them, only that they were inordinately interested in her," Robert said sulkily.

"Their interest would not take such a form," the earl stated repressively. But secretly he wondered if Robert might be in the right of it. The girl was certainly appealing, and who knew what she was capable of behind their backs? Certainly this business of Miss Wilson's portrait showed she was a secretive, unmalleable chit, with no fit understanding of what she owed the relatives who had cared for her.

"How can you make such judgments about Esme, a dear, wonderful girl, who might be suffering the most dreadful fate while you prose on here," Fannie objected loyally. She was disgusted by her parents' and Robert's innuendoes. Of all the Cranfords, only Fannie seemed to really feel sorrow for Esme's fate and she despised their efforts to shield themselves from the scandal her abduction would induce.

As they argued and conjectured, coming to no decision, their fulminations were interrupted by the butler entering the drawing room with a letter on a silver salver.

"This has just come for you, my lord, by special messenger," he said sternly, proffering the letter.

"Oh, it is news of Esme! I just know it!" Fannie squealed in delight, and watched eagerly as her father carefully unfolded the missive. He read it, frowning over Esme's carefully worded

106

letter, not willing to disclose the contents until he had thoroughly digested the news. Such deliberate hesitation infuriated Fannie.

"Well, father. What is it? Is Esme safe?" Fannie implored, twisting her hands in impatience.

"Yes, your cousin says she managed to escape her abductors, and is now safely ensconced with her old nurse in Tunbridge Wells, where she intends to remain. As she reminds us most ungratefully, she is now her own mistress, and wishes to pursue her artistic dabbling without the distraction of proper surveillance and inclusion in the home which I have provided for her, either here in London or in Hampshire," the earl said rather pompously. Now that the immediate fear for Esme's safety had disappeared, he retreated behind his usual manner—of a man misjudged by his family and peers, worthy and respectable. It was a combination of fussiness and austerity.

"She can't stay in Tunbridge Wells. What will people think?" Mildred Cranford asked, her concern for the family's reputation paramount.

"Well, my dear, we can hardly force her to return," the earl pointed out in a long-suffering voice, hiding his relief that he would no longer have to entertain this cuckoo in his nest. "As she points out, she is her own mistress, and has enough money to live quietly and paint, if that is what she wants to do. If we think she is showing an unnatural attitude toward her relatives, we must hold our peace. A thankless child is a burden we are forced to accept."

"I think you are hateful, abandoning Esme in this callous way!" Fannie cried.

"We are not abandoning Esme, Fannie. She is abandoning us," her father said smugly. "We don't want a scandal."

"Why should there be a scandal? And don't you want to learn of her misfortune, how she escaped her abductors, and what she endured to elude them?" Fannie persisted.

"I suppose she will tell us in her own good time," Robert

said sourly. "I think I might ride to Tunbridge Wells and learn of her adventure," he added thoughtfully. He was suspicious of how casually Esme had tossed off her frightening experience. Any other girl would have carried on at great length, thrilled to be the object of such a malign circumstance, prepared to play the role of victim or intrepid heroine to the hilt. But not Esme. She was completely matter-of-fact about it. Could she be hiding something? Robert was determined to get the real story.

"Well, I hardly think that is necessary, Robert, but you will do what you wish, I suppose," his mother conceded with ill grace. Robert's fascination with his cousin should not be encouraged, but the countess was wise enough to know that trying to prohibit him from visiting Esme would only whet his interest. Her only comfort was that she doubted that Esme viewed Robert as an acceptable parti.

"Oh, do go to Tunbridge Wells, Robert! Perhaps I can accompany you. I yearn to know all the details of Esme's horrid encounter, and how she evaded her captors," Fannie exclaimed, much to her parent's displeasure.

Her mother dismissed Fannie's plea impatiently. "I hardly think that will be convenient, Fannie. You have several quite important engagements." Really, the girl was so naive, so resistant to guidance, a legacy of her cousin's willfulness. It was just as well that Esme had made arrangements for her future that would remove her from daily association with her cousins. "Now, I must see about packing Esme's belongings. She will be needing her clothes and other necessities," the countess said, eager to seal Esme's permanent departure from her household.


Hugo Carstairs learned of Esme's disappearance upon his arrival back at the Surrey hunting lodge as dusk was falling. He had been to London to see about a house in Great Russell Street where he intended to install Esme. She would be away from the fashionable haunts of her relatives and near the artists she found so appealing, and very available to the duke when he wanted to visit her. He was prepared to furnish her with a generous allowance, suitable servants, a carriage, and introductions to those in the art world who would further her career. From the little he had seen of her work, he was most impressed with her talent. In his arrogant, careless way, he was willing to allow her scope to improve her gift—as long as she was ever available for his needs.

Hugo was not quite the cruel, insensitive man he seemed; merely a spoiled and selfish one. He had been both intrigued and delighted by Esme's reception of his love-making. Once the shock of her initiation had dissipated, she had proved to be an exciting partner. She had responded with a passion which had more than gratified him and seemed to give her equal satisfaction. And she had appeared to accept his offer of a more permanent relationship with an amazing docility. She had not once suggested that he do the honorable thing. He laughed a bit cynically, remembering how many other women had pleaded for just such an outcome to the fleeting pleasures of the bed.

He should have viewed that facade of obedience to his desire with more misgivings, but he had been lulled by the force of his own passion, which possession of her had not satiated. In fact, he had anticipated long leisurely weeks of delving into the independent spirit that lay beneath that casual acquiescence. He wondered now at his obsession for the girl, his severe irritation that she had removed herself from his orbit. It was quite a blow to his consequence that she had fooled him so thoroughly, listening to his plans for their joint future with that compliant face while plotting to seize the first opportunity for escape. Probably, it was good for his self esteem to be treated thus, but Hugo did not appreciate the moral of the story. At first he had expended his rage and frustration on the hapless groom responsible for Esme's flight.

The poor man had trudged the weary miles back to the lodge, ashamed at being duped in such a fashion, and fearing the wrath the duke would visit on him. On learning that his master had not yet returned, he tried his best to retrieve his error and rode immediately to the nearest village. He learned that a strange lady, obviously of quality and dressed in a riding habit, had boarded the stage for Reigate. His only recourse was to return to his stables and await the duke's return.

After roundly cursing the man up and down, the duke himself rode off after information, but was no more successful. Leaving his household to pack up and return to London, he followed the trail to Reigate. No amount of largesse, which he passed about carelessly, could secure him any definite news of the mysterious lady. Several stages had left Reigate that late afternoon for various destinations, but no hostler or publican could single out Esme among the passengers.

Determined not to be balked, Hugo himself returned to London, believing that Esme would seek her natural refuge: the Cranfords. He had no difficulty in learning that she had not arrived at the Mount Street mansion. He sent his disapproving secretary down to the Cranford estate in Hampshire, but that too proved to be unproductive.

By now in a fury over Esme's flight, he vowed to make the chit pay for all the trouble she had caused him, not the least of which was the sobering thought that she had so disliked the idea of continuing their association she had fled him at the first opportunity. He would get her back and she would pay for such a slight. He would woo her so adroitly that she would be panting with love for him, and then she would see who would suffer the insulting rejection.

His secretary, Charles Leigh, disapproving of this latest lecherous episode in his employer's chequered career. He could not help but secretly applaud the woman, who had given the duke a much-deserved set down. Of course, when he learned the name and status of the duke's latest amour he was even more shocked to think that Hugo has so far forgotten what was due to propriety as to have abducted and seduced an innocent girl. This time, his employer had gone too far, and

Charles reprimanded him with a severity that astounded them both.

"Your Grace, you cannot have thought what repercussions such a flagrant affront to every decent rule of society would induce. You will be branded a lecher, a satanist and every harsh word. And you will be denied entrance to even the few drawing rooms which now receive you," Charles scolded. Although his own temerity surprised him, his sympathies were all with Miss Sedgewick. It was past time for his employer to be brought to brook for his transgressions.

"I have never heeded the strictures of the *ton* before," Hugo replied, amused by his secretary's efforts to put him on the path to rectitude. "So why you should think that these foolish matrons and their rules should weigh with me now surpasses my understanding. Can you have nurtured some idea, after all this time, Charles, that I might redeem my sins by some benevolent action? Shame on you, dear boy."

"I thought you might have spared some thought for Miss Sedgewick's plight," Charles persisted, intent on using this opportunity to emphasize the infamous conduct that had given him such pain. "You have placed her reputation in jeopardy, aside from any personal unhappiness you may have caused her. She has been forced to flee her relatives' home, deny herself any of the pleasures of society, and no doubt will be treated as an outcast by all who should view her with respect." Basically Charles admired and liked Hugo, and believed that he could be turned from his heedless lecherous ways.

"It is because I am concerned about Miss Sedgewick's future that I am wracking my brains—and wearing out my horses—trying to ascertain her whereabouts, Charles," Hugo replied wryly. He would not admit even to his secretary that he was worried Esme might bear his child. He was chilled by the thought that such a disgrace might drive her to some precipitate action. It was enough to make him wish he had never embarked on this damnable abduction.

"Well, it appears you must call upon the Cranfords and ask

111

them outright for news of Miss Sedgewick," Charles said resolutely. "You have tried every other avenue, including bribing their servants, to no avail, so why not do the obvious thing?"

Hugo frowned. He was not anxious to expose himself to the Cranfords, especially Robert, who might suspect his involvement in Esme's disappearance. Not that Hugo would be afraid of Robert challenging him, but remembering Esme's affection for her cousin, he knew that if he should injure Lord Weirs in a duel, it would not improve his chances with the lady. But at this point it was the only avenue open to him.

"Sometimes, Charles, you show flashes of brilliance that almost make up for your tedious moral prosing. I will follow your instructions this very morning." Hugo grinned, noting sardonically that Charles was really enjoying his discomfort. *Obviously the boy thinks it a fitting punishment for me, and no doubt it is,* Hugo conceded. This whole affair had become far more troubling than he had ever expected.

A punctilious call upon the Cranfords resulted in no divulgence of Esme's location. Even the artless Fannie, although all confusion and blushes, when adroitly questioned by the infamous Duke of Milbourne, kept the secret, if indeed she knew it. And the earl and countess gave him short shift, implying that Fannie, certainly, and even such pillars of rectitude as they themselves, were besmirched by receiving a known libertine in their drawing room. If only they knew, thought the duke to himself. The Cranfords politely accepted his inquiries for Esme, and would only say she was making an extended visit to the country. On his request for her direction they raised their eyebrows and refused in a very chilly manner. He had to take his leave without learning anything of import. Robert, who might have been even more suspicious of the duke's interest in his cousin, was not present at the interview.

With his obvious source for knowledge of Esme's bolt-hold denied to him, Hugo did not despair. The Cranfords obduracy only heightened his determination to seek out the girl. Lately his usual haunts and dissipations bored him, and he found, to his confusion, that he spent much too much time recalling the hours he'd spent with Esme. He craved her companionship, her conversation, her arguments, her sarcasm, her gallant acceptance of the ruthless way he had used her. He must locate her, for a number of impelling reasons.

# Chapter Eleven

"It was kind of you to deliver my bits and pieces in person, Robert. I regret the inconvenience," Esme told her cousin. She received him in the shabby parlor of Bessie's house in Tunbridge Wells with some anxiety. He looked fine-drawn and harried, far from his usual ebullient self. His cravat had been tied hurriedly, not at all like the intricate mathematical he favored, and his Hessians lacked their usual high gloss. She deeply reproached herself for the worry she was causing him and the pain she must inflict, for she sensed that Robert could not be dissuaded from pressing his suit.

Robert passed a hand through his hair in consternation. He did not quite know how to proceed, but his mind was made up. Although he believed Esme was in no state to hear his proposal, he would wait no longer.

"Esme, this is all a hum, about the highwaymen," he stated baldly. "What really happened en route to Hampshire? All John the coachman would say was that you were held up and forced at gun point to accompany some rogues, who spirited you away while he was helpless to prevent your abduction. The damn coward! He should have made a push to rescue you."

"I would not want John's blood on my hands, and he is quite correct. I had no recourse but to follow the brigands' orders," she said calmly. She hoped to soothe her suspicious cousin. If he learned the identity of her abductor, he would immediately call the duke out. Although Robert was a passable shot and quite courageous enough to face his opponent across the greensward, she wanted to prevent any such reckless attempt to protect her honor. In any case, he was too late, but that knowledge she must keep from him at all costs.

"So how did you escape the black-hearted rogues?" Robert persisted.

"When we stopped to change horses, I was able to make my escape, hide in the woods, and then make my way here with some difficulty," Esme answered, choosing her words carefully. "But let us not prose on about my exploits! All has turned out well. I am only sorry that you and your parents were put to such worry and inconvenience."

Robert's eyes narrowed. There was some mystery here and he was determined to root it out. "John implied that the highwayman was a gentleman. Have you no idea who he was?"

"He was well-spoken," Esme conceded, then hesitated. She did not want to pursue the matter. "But I have no idea who he was or what he hoped to gain by such a reckless deed," she lied, dropping her eyes from Robert's searching gaze. How she hated deceiving him, but she must protect him from the duke, and must conceal the outcome of that disastrous abduction.

From long experience, Robert knew his cousin could not be coaxed into confidences. But he had a deeper purpose for this interview.

"Esme, this recent affair proves that you need a protector," he said, continuing hastily when she seemed about to interrupt him: "You must hear me out. You know how deeply I care for you. I wish you would give me the right to shield you from further outrages."

He crossed to her side, and took her hand. "I want to marry you, Esme. If you dislike London, we could live in the country, removed from all society, which you take in such distaste. We have always got on so well, you must see the sense of it."

Esme sighed. How she hated to hurt Robert, who had always

been the dearest of friends and the most kindly of cousins, but even if she returned his feelings—and she did not—it would never serve in light of her recent embroilment with the duke. "Dear Robert, it will not do, you know. I do not love you as a wife loves a husband."

"But I love you, Esme, and after we are wed, I would do all I could to persuade you to return that love. I will not compel you until you are ready, and I will not interfere with your painting." Robert did not understand her passion for art, but he was willing to accept the demands of such a discipline if it would gain him what he so ardently desired.

"Robert, you know you would hate living removed from the fashionable world, and you deserve more from a wife than a tepid affection. Please do not continue with this, for I so dislike causing you unhappiness."

Desperate, seeing the prize slip from his grasp, Robert would not surrender his fondest hopes so easily. "I care less for the world than you think. At least consider what I suggest unless—" He paused, frowning. "Unless there is someone else?"

Esme would have grasped that excuse, but she was too honest to deceive him. "No, Robert, it is just that I feel marriage is not for me, and you have not really had time to consider all the alternatives. You deserve better, a girl who would value you, return your love," she said gently. "And your parents would not look kindly on our union. They look for you to make a brilliant match," she teased lightly, but there was much truth in her objections. If she'd truly cared for Robert, that obstacle would not weigh with her, but she would not make a convenience of him.

"If you would return home, we could go on as before, and you might become accustomed to the idea," Robert pressed desperately.

"I have decided to remain here with Bessie, and continue my painting without any distractions, and you are a distraction, Robert." Esme smiled to take the sting from her words. "Now let us discuss this no further. My mind is made up," she concluded firmly, tiring of the interview and regretting the sorrow she was causing. "Let us talk of other matters. How is Fannie? And are Aunt Mildred and Uncle Egbert in good health?"

"Fannie was all in a dither over your adventure, and I had the greatest difficulty in dissuading her from coming to see you. Mother thought it best that she not," he informed her sulkily. He stubbornly wanted to continue his avowals.

Esme, now thoroughly wretched over the situation she felt she should have prevented, tried to soothe his irate spirits, but with little success. When he finally took his leave, promising that she had not seen the last of him, she had acquired a throbbing headache and the nagging realization that she had not handled affairs adoitly. She had no recourse but to turn down Robert's suggestion. She wondered passingly if she would have succumbed to his insistent proposals if he had continued to badger her. She was exhausted by all this emotion and yearned for solitude to begin her painting.

Bessie, aware of her charge's malaise, kept her distance, and by the next day Esme had recovered her poise, relieved to have put the unhappy interview with Robert behind her. Now, if only her relations would understand her decision, she could get on with her life. But she feared she had not heard the last of Robert's demands, nor of the Cranford's efforts to fulfill their responsibilities. Perhaps she could turn their sense of propriety into disgust if her scheme to wreak revenge on the duke prospered. She set to work with a furious determination.

Robert's sudden excursion to Tunbridge Wells had not gone unnoticed by the duke, who had employed minions to watch the Cranford menage. He quickly learned Lord Weirs's destination and wondered at the visit. The unfashionable spa appeared a strange object of Robert's interest. In due course, he learned tht Esme had sought refuge in a shabby boarding house off the Pantilles, a promenade laid out some two centuries before. How typical that Esme would secrete herself away in this dated refuge of the blue stockings, the duke thought. She had no use for the gaieties of Brighton or Bath, no doubt believing these popular watering holes sinks of vice. Well, she would not escape his attentions so easily. He had a reckoning to settle with the haughty Miss Sedgewick.

Not a man to examine or criticize his own motives, Hugo found himself tormented by memories of Esme. He thought, of course, of their hours in bed, but other aspects of the lady loomed in his mind quite as frequently. He wondered at his stubbornness in wishing to confront her when she obviously wanted to put him out of her life. Was her appeal due to her rejection of him, to her sudden escape from their liaison? Would he have tired of her if the affair had been allowed to run its course? He had no answers to these questions, but they nagged at him like a throbbing toothache. He laughed. It was hardly flattering to be compared to a toothache, but perhaps Esme would find it amusing. Her humor was one of the qualities he found so entrancing. In that, as in so much else, she was so different from the usual females who engaged his interest. Well, he would seek her out and discover if she still held the same fascination for him. He ordered his carriage and prepared to depart for Tunbridge Wells.


Esme had now settled down, if not happily, at least with some degree of contentment, in her former nurse's household. She had vowed to never again become embroiled with demanding men. She worked hard at her painting, but relaxed in the afternoons by exploring Tunbridge Wells, which offered some unexpected delights. After several hours inspecting the library, the fine houses lining the promenade, the Church of King Charles the Martyr, and other points of interest, she decided to sample the waters, which had brought the spa early fame.

The mineral spring that supplied the restorative waters was located on the north-eastern side of the Pantilles. One sunny afternoon she repaired to the building housing the mineral drink. She had not expected to see a fashionable crowd such as the group which patronized Bath. She did not want to encounter any *ton* leaders who might pose her awkward questions. For the most part the company was thin, a sprinkling of dowdy matrons, farmers' wives in town for a day's shopping and gossip, and some officers from a regiment posted nearby. No one paid her the slightest heed, and her artist's eye contented itself with observing the passing throng.

She approached the pump that supplied the restorative waters with some misgiving, reading with amusement the claims for the drink's powers. The plaque announced that the waters would prove beneficial for gout, rheumatism, tropical skin diseases, anemia, and nervous and digestive orders. Since she suffered from none of these ailments, she wondered if she should be so bold as to submit herself to what would undoubtedly be a noxious draught. As she was debating, a young man in red regimentals approached her timidly, and suggested he might pour her a glass. She was a bit taken aback, but he appeared harmless, open-faced and stalwart, a far cry from the starched-up beaux she had rebuffed in London.

"Do you think I might benefit, sir?" she asked lightly.

"Not at all, but as you are here, it is an experience which should be endured. You appear to be in the best of health, so I shouldn't think the waters would harm you," he said, delighted at her friendly acceptance of his efforts. Suiting his action to his words, he poured her a glass and watched as she drank it with a small shudder.

"Not at all agreeable," Esme remarked, handing him back the glass. "But I have done my duty."

"May I be so bold as to introduce myself ma'am?" the young man asked, eyeing Esme with shy pleasure. "Lieutenant Oliver Wells. I am with the Tenth Foot stationed nearby."

Looking at the young man somewhat askance, Esme decided he appeared a bit lonely, and as she was not one to follow conventions, she nodded at him cheerfully and returned the compliment.

"I am Esme Sedgewick, and grateful to you, sir, for my introduction to the waters." She smiled at him for he reminded her of an eager puppy-dog, anxious to ingratiate himself.

"May I prevail upon you to stroll about the rooms with me, Miss Sedgewick. It would quite impress my fellow officers," he said with a certain naivete.

"Am I the object of some soldierly wager, sir?" Esme asked, pretending to be quite annoyed but in reality enjoying Lieutenant Wells' tentative efforts at acquaintance.

He looked properly shocked at such an idea. "Of course not, Miss Sedgewick. What a rubbishy fellow you must think me. It is only that there are so few agreeable females to talk to in this town. And soldiers are not always welcomed by respectable folk, you know. I hope I have not offended you!"

"Of course not, lieutenant. I absolve you of all wicked intentions and would be pleased to accompany you," Esme declared.

Really, she was becoming almost a recluse and a bit of harmless chat with a personable young man could raise her spirits. She accepted his arm, and as he marched her proudly about the room, he confided something of his circumstances. He was the only son of elderly parents who lived in Shropshire on a tidy little estate. His father, after some persuading, had bought him his colors, and although he found army life quite to his taste, he missed his home and family. He had enrolled too late to participate in the rout of Napoleon at Waterloo, a fate he much regretted, and hoped to win glory on some future field. But events did not promise much, he confided.

Esme suspected that he was but two or three years older than herself, if that, but she felt aeons his elder, weighed down by her recent experiences. His ingenuous conversation and delight in her company was a stimulating tonic after the cynicism and ill-natured gossip of London drawing rooms. She responded to his gambits with gentle raillery. She did not return his confidences, being content to listen to his own plans and problems. He was an attractive boy, with a shock of well-trained brown hair, eloquent blue eyes, and an engaging air of candor. Within a few minutes they had become fast friends and she accepted his offer to escort her home, promising that they would meet again.

Delighted by the warmth of her response, he suggested timidly that he would be honored to take her out in his curricle if she could be prevailed upon to spare him some time.

As they neared Bessie's house, Esme laughingly agreed to his invitation, believing that a tool around the town would be a happy respite from her labors. So intent was she upon her new acquaintance that she barely noticed the dark carriage pulled up before Bessie's door. Bidding Lieutenant Wells a gracious farewell, she entered the house, content with her afternoon's outing.

She was startled by Bessie's appearance from the back apartments. "There is a very fancy gentleman awaiting you in the parlor, Miss Esme. Very starched-up, he is, and claims that you are old friends," Bessie announced with a frown. .

She had been quite taken back by the consequence of her visitor, who had refused to give his name, but had been insistent upon awaiting Miss Esme. Bessie had not been brave enough to demur.

"Shall I turn him away?" Bessie asked, seeing a frown darken Esme's face. But before Esme could answer, the door to the parlor opened and the Duke of Milbourne, imposing and obdurate, interrupted their whispered conference.

"Ah, there you are, Esme. I thought I heard your voice." Hugo greeted her urbanely, but she could tell by his tightened mouth and hard eyes that he was in a rage. Esme herself was too startled to be angry, but she felt irritation and some other, undefined emotion bubbling beneath her outward composure. She would not expose Bessie to any further worry. She must deal with this unexpected contingency herself.

"Thank you, Bessie. I will see the duke in the parlor. You go on with your work and we will talk later." Esme reassured her old nurse calmly, seeing the confusion and upset this august visitor had caused in her normally tranquil household. "Of course, if that is what you wish, dear. You will excuse me, Your

121

Grace," Bessie said with a quaint dignity, and took herself off.

Esme sailed through the door the duke was holding politely open, girding herself for the coming unpleasant interview. But if Hugo Carstairs expected a cringing victim, he was mistaken, she vowed. Her back was straight and her chin resolute, even if inside she felt an unpleasant sensation. She turned to face her unwelcome visitor, her face composed.

"You have disturbed Bessie, Duke. And I see no reason for this vexatious visit." She refused his indication of a chair by the fireside. She would not listen to his arguments.

"I'll give you *vexatious*, my girl. How dare you run off the moment my back was turned?" Hugo growled, his impatience and annoyance forcing him immediately onto the offensive. "You can just pack your bits and pieces and come back to London with me right now. I have spent a great deal too much time and effort over your affairs."

Esme smiled, amused despite her anger. "No one asked you to concern yourself, duke. My life is my own to deal with, and that dealing does not include you. My flight should have proved to you that your intrusion into my life was not to my taste. What has already passed between is best forgotten. You behaved in a despicable and arrogant fashion which should not go unpunished," she said severely, noticing for the first time the harsh lines around his mouth and his drawn appearance. The results of temper, no doubt, for she could not believe he had worried about her safety.

She braced herself for an explosion of temper but the duke, surprised her. He leaned against the mantel, apparently relaxed, and contemplated her with raised eyebrows.

"You really are the most amazing woman, Esme. Your constant mercurial moods never cease to please me. I expected furious outbursts or weeping accusations but I receive instead a cool set-down. How enterprising you have been. My poor groom has still not recovered from the way you duped him." He again indicated she should be seated, and she again refused. "Really, my dear, I am quite fatigued from all my detective work, and good manners preclude me sitting while you remain poised for another flight," he mocked.

Esme repressed a smile with difficulty. Really, he was the outside of enough acting as if this meeting was nothing more than a polite reunion between casual acquaintances. Still, what was to be gained by thwarting him in this small duel when a much more important contest was at stake? She sat down carefully in a slipper chair, and he took a more substantial seat opposite her. She waited for his next words but he remained silent, looking at her with a very disturbing gleam in those hard dark eyes.

"I have never noticed that polite manners caused you any concern, Duke," she said with some asperity when the silence had extended from some uncomfortable moments. She did not appreciate that look.

"You wrong me, my dear Miss Sedgewick. I am a pattern card of propriety when the occasion warrants," he asserted suavely.

"Unfortunately, those occasions never seemed to arise in our relationship," Esme retorted. This fencing had gone on long enough. "Why are you here? You can be in no doubt that I want nothing more to do with you."

"I thought you might perhaps have some interesting news for me," the duke answered. His eyes narrowing as they roamed over her body in a most suggestive and intimate manner, recalling memories Esme did not want to entertain.

She laughed scornfully. "And you have come to make provisions for any bastard that might be the result of our irregular union. How thoughtful!" Esme's voice shook with outrage and disgust. How dare he make such a suggestion! "Well, be of tranquil mind, sir. You have no need to worry. And if that regrettable result of your abduction of me had occurred, I would cope with the matter without any recourse to your charity."

"You wound me with your harsh words, Esme. I am really most concerned for your welfare," he replied, not at all disturbed by her reaction.

"Your concern would have been better exercised before you

kidnapped and raped me, Duke! I am not some little doxy from London stews who will cringe and beg for your patronage. I hoped never to see you again and your effrontry in seeking me out passes all bounds."

"I hardly think I deserve such a reception of my perfectly equitable offer to protect you. If I regretted my precipitous action, it is now too late for apologies, but I confess I found our interlude in Surrey completely charming," he parried, pleased that he had aroused some response.

Aware that this distressing interview had moved beyond her control, Esme was determined to make her position quite clear.

"You may believe, in your conceit, that my reluctance to fall victim to your manifold charms is just a ploy to spur you to further excesses, Duke, but I promise you are mistaken. Now, I think we have said enough on this disagreeable subject, and you must take your leave." She rose to her feet in a fury to be gone from his dynamic presence. His unexpected arrival, when she thought she had successfully buried all memories of those passionate nights in Surrey, had shaken her. How dare he pursue her here where she had regained some of her composure and tried to establish her life on a respectable basis. If he had professed love, made humble apologies for his cavalier actions, she might have entertained granting him forgiveness, but such behavior was so foreign to the duke as to be laughable. He cared little for her, but a great deal for his own power over her.

"Come, Esme, there is no need for all of this melodrama," he said. "I want you to return with me to London. I have secured a very delightful house for you. You can study and paint and have a thoroughly enjoyable time, untrammeled by the restrictions of polite society, so hampering to an artist. Of course, you would be under my protection, but that could only be an advantage," he finished outrageously.

"Your effrontery is beyond belief. You abduct me from my home and family, ruin my reputation, then casually suggest a position as your mistress would be quite acceptable to me. You are not only a lecherous cad, Duke, but I find you utterly repulsive." She was astounded at his bold, matter-of-fact terms. But what else had she expected? Even if she had been pregnant, she would never consider such a solution to her dilemma—yoked to this rake in a shocking union, unblessed by law or church. He had a poor opinion of her morals and her breeding if he thought she would succumb to such shabby lures. Even an honorable offer of marriage would not have compelled her to put herself in his power. He had no sensitivity, no finer emotions, but cared only for the satisfaction of a passing fancy. Many women might find his offer flattering but Esme treated it with justified scorn, never admitting even for a moment was she tempted by the great attraction between them.

"You are a tiresome girl. I might be forced to abduct you again," the duke mocked, pretending indifference to her tirade. But underneath his cloak of indifference he found he was vastly disappointed—perhaps even hurt. He had hoped their absence from each other might have induced some softer emotions in Esme, some desire for a meaningful union. He had never felt so frustrated and helpless.

She treated his threat with the contempt he was beginning to realize she sincerely felt, and somehow this raised a compunction in him that was most uncomfortable.

"You will have great difficulty in succeeding, but thank you for the warning. I will take proper measures to protect myself," Esme said. "I realize that any object of your attentions must be thrilled by the honor!—but you must accept my rejection. I find you haughty, ruthless, selfish and hedonistic, without one redeeming quality. And now you must excuse me." Conscious that she had had the last word, and eager to capitalize on her triumph, Esme sailed regally from the room, half expecting him to protest. But he let her leave in silence. A brooding expression darkening his face, Hugo had been brought to a standstill by her refusal.

# Chapter Twelve

Within a few days after her disturbing interview with Hugo Carstairs, Esme had completed the painting that had possessed her since her flight from his hunting lodge.

She stood back from the canvas and tried to view it objectively. It was a large scene, powerful in its conception and shocking in its execution, obviously painted while the artist was in the grip of a violent emotion. Before a turbulent blue-gray sky heavy with menacing clouds, the figure of a dominant man, dressed in black, stood alone. Hanging from his hand was a bloody whip. Cowering before him was the indistinct figure of a woman, her ragged draperies not concealing her welted back, her blond hair unbound and flowing over her scarred shoulders. There was no mistaking the saturnine features and imposing figure of the duke, although the woman's identity remained mysterious. A violent and disturbing picture, which deserved the title Esme had given it, *The Tyrant*.

It was so different from any of her previous work, she hesitated to sign it with her alias, "Arethusa." But she realized that Joseph Gorton would be more apt to accept the work with that signature, and so she took her courage in her hands and scrawled her pseudonym across the bottom of the canvas.

She frowned, knowing this painting was the best she had ever done, and wondering at the passion that had inspired it.

126

Somehow completing the picture had exhausted all her rage and left her with a haunting sense of dissatisfaction. Although the painting had been a catharsis, she now felt drained and empty of all emotion. Now that it was finished, it must be displayed or her revenge would not be accomplished. But would it accomplish its purpose, the humiliation of the duke? And then would she finally be able to put the whole unfortunate episode behind her? She tossed her head and turned away from the painting almost in disgust, refusing to give it any more attention.

Carefully cleaning her brushes and pallette she left the room Bessie had assigned to her as a studio, determined to relax. Lieutenant Wells was coming to take her for a ride and she anticipated their expedition with some pleasure. She would postpone dealing with troublesome decisions for a few days, she thought, unwilling to consider the next step that might involve her in situations she was loathe to face.

Almost a week had passed since the duke's interview with her, and she had heard no more from him. She persuaded herself that she had at last convinced him she wanted nothing more to do with him. Now that the painting was finished, she ought to plan her next move. Should she return to London, find a suitable dwelling and continue her painting? The Cranfords had not invited her back to their household. And in any case, she had decided that she could not inflict her presence on them, in view of what might happen when the picture was displayed. She laughed a bit grimly. She might be overestimating the impact of *The Tyrant,* on a sophisticated public. It might cause little stir and then her carefully calculated revenge on the duke would go for naught. Well, for the moment, she would postpone any thought of the consequences. She needed a respite from all this angry emotion.

Lieutenant Wells, arriving to escort Esme on the promised drive, did not comment on her air of weariness and languor, but he could not fail to notice it. He was too kind and well-bred to press her about her worries, so he contented himself with her company. He was an undemanding cavalier, good-humored and pleasant, striving to entertain. And the weather co-operated with his mood. It was balmy and soothing, warm enough to make their journey to the curious sandstone rocks a few miles beyond the town an enjoyable outing. He had provided a picnic tea, and beyond the high rocks they found a secluded grove, perfect for their al fresco meal.

Esme removed her chip bonnet. She sighed gratefully after finishing the sandwiches, fruit and light wine Lieutenant Wells offered. Casting off her own troubling thoughts, she smiled kindly at the young man, and thanked him prettily.

"This is kind of you, Oliver, to banish my megrims with such a delightful outing. I have been working too hard."

"I did not like to ask, Esme, what has taken so much of your time. Your landlady informs me you are an artist, and I have suspect you have been painting away, involved in your art. I have never known an artist before, at least not a female, I mean . . ." He sensed he sounded stupid, implying that ladies could not take dabbling seriously. But Oliver believed that Esme was no amateur.

Esme was not annoyed. It was a reaction she quite expected from such a naive young man. Indeed, she would have been surprised if he had taken her work seriously.

"There is no reason for you to understand, Oliver. You have never seen any of my paintings, so how could you judge. But I don't want to talk about it today. It's much too relaxing here. Tell me more about your plans for the future."

"Well, there is a rumor that the Tenth Foot will be posted to London. I hope not. I would miss you sorely, Esme," he confessed, his open face wreathed in frowns.

"I might be going to London myself," she said, then regretted her confidence. She did not want to lure Oliver Wells into thinking their friendship might deepen beyond casual affection.

"Oh, that would be capital! Do you have family there?"

128

asked, then cursed his curiosity. Esme never talked abut her background or what she had done before turning up in Tunbridge Wells.

"Yes, but I do not plan to join them. I hope to rent a suitable accommodation—a studio—where I can continue my work without the interruptions family life imposes. I am a sad trial to my relations, for they wish me to be a more amenable proper female, who will follow the proprieties," she explained.

"But you would not live alone," he asked, shocked by her abandonment of all notions of conduct.

"No, I am hoping that Bessie will accompany me. She was my nurse and I am vastly fond of her. I missed her exceedingly after the death of my parents when I went to live with my aunt, uncle and cousins." She hadn't intended to tell him so much, but Oliver was such a disarming young man, so gentle, so obliging and unthreatening.

"Well, of course you know best, but it is quite unusual for such a young and attractive young woman to live alone."

"Yes, well, I am an unusual young woman," Esme laughed at his expression.

"You need a husband, someone to protect and shield you," he blurted out.

"I will never marry, Oliver. Husbands are too demanding. Artists cannot contemplate the domestic joys as can more normal folk," she explained gently, realizing where his protestations were leading.

"That might depend on the husband," he insisted stubbornly. Then realizing that she was in no mood for his avowals, which he was at any rate too timid to press, turned the conversation to London and the wonders it offered. Esme, only too happy for the distraction, quizzed him on his introduction to the city. They happily compared notes about their experiences. But the conversation had decided her. She no longer hesitated as to her future.

Upon returning from the outing, Esme decided to approach Bessie with her plan. She invited her old nurse into her own parlor and breached the subject gently.

"Are you quite happy here, running this boarding house, Bessie?" she asked, looking affectionately at the woman. Bessie had lost her husband after too few years together and she had never been blessed with the children her maternal soul must have craved. She rarely complained, worked hard, skillfully tended to the needs of strangers. Esme yearned to offer her some surcease.

"Well, it's not what I would have chosen, perhaps, Miss Esme, but we must accept what the good Lord brings," Bessie replied cheerfully, her button-bright eyes curious. She was not an introspective woman but she sensed that Esme had some notion in her head concerning her. She continued, knitting her brows as if forming her thoughts into some coherent pattern was difficult. "I must admit I don't take to serving strangers, and most of them that comes here, are not quite what I was used to—not quality, you see. I missed you, Miss Esme, and your parents. We had a good life back then, even if your ma and pa were a bit rackety in their ways. A nicer pair never lived—so considerate and caring they were." Bessie sighed.

"Would you like to come and care for me in London, Bessie? I must return to the city to continue my art lessons and my work, and I would prefer not to return to my uncle and aunt's house. Their mode of living is not mine, although I am most grateful to them for their past kindnesses." Esme saw that her nurse was quite taken aback by this startling suggestion. "I am thinking of renting a small house, and you can have matters much more your own way. We will get some help, someone to do the rough and all," she promised. "But how are you situated here? Could you leave with little notice?"

"Lawks, Miss Esme, the old codger who owns this place might have trouble finding another poor soul to do his bidding, but that would not weigh with me. I owe him little, miserly curmudgeon that he is, serves him right," Bessie said, her face brightening. "I would welcome the chance, you know, my dear, but I fear I am no sort of chaperone for you." She was

130

suddenly conscious of the proprieties as she looked at the lovely young girl opposite her. Miss Esme was a caution, always unexpected, not eager to follow the path her birth and position had marked out for her.

"I don't need a chaperone, Bessie dear. I am not planning on leading a social life. What I need is a friend and companion and no one could fulfill that role better than you," Esme said warmly.

"Well, then, I would be pleased to come," Bessie responded, suddenly caught up in the excitement of this new prospect. "You will be wanting to start off soon, I expect, so I will just send a message to Master Ormsley today. He's the landlord here. Not that I care what he thinks. I have been tied to this place for three years, and worked well for him and been honest besides, which is more than he deserves."

"I had no idea you had such a hateful employer, Bessie! You should have applied to me before."

"Well, we can forget about all that now, thank the Lord." Bessie rose to her feet. "And now I will bestir myself to get on with our packing. The sooner we leave the better. And Miss Esme, you know I will do my best to make you comfortable." She spoke a bit shyly, as if embarrassed to display the affection and warmth she felt.

Esme stood and gave Bessie a hearty hug, much relieved and heartened by her grateful acceptance. With Bessie behind her, she felt that her new life would offer untold comfort and reassurance. And she needed a great deal of both just then, for her audacity in striking out on her own would not go unremarked.

Before the week was out, Esme and Bessie were on their way to London. The shocking picture was wrapped and crated, accompanying them. Bessie had not seen the portrait, for Esme feared any questions from her discerning nurse about the work. Bessie had not queried her about the duke, although

131

Esme suspected she was curious, but respected her charge's reticence. If she thought the duke responsible for any harm coming to Esme, she would have castigated him roundly, although she had been mightily impressed by his hauteur and imposing person. Esme was determined that the duke would be banished from her life now and kept her own counsel. But she took Bessie fully into her plans for their new household.

They spent a few days at the Clarendon Hotel in London while she made the preparations for their new home, inviting Bessie's suggestions and criticisms on inspection tours of several dwellings. Bessie accompanied her to her solicitor's office, and sat by silently while that prim reputable man explained Esme's financial position and, although disapproving, assisted her with the house inquiries. Finally, they decided upon a small cottage in St. John's Wood, as far from the fashionable haunts of society as possible. Mr. Fullerton, the solicitor, pointed out to her rather austerely that it was not a very respectable neighborhood, as several noblemen had installed their mistresses in cottages orné nearby, but this did not deter Esme. If he only knew she smiled to herself, *I am in just the company I deserve.*

She had already endured one painful interview with her aunt and uncle, who, upon learning of her new home, had taken it upon themselves to protest more because it threatened their own position in society than because they cared for Esme's comfort, she thought. But she had brushed off that confrontation with adroitness, and politely but firmly countered all their objections. Her interview with Joseph Gorton was more productive. He had been taken aback by the portrait but agreed to show it without revealing the artist's identity, and he had tactfully made no allusion to the inspiration for the work, such a departure from her usual subject matter.

He needed no urging to place the portrait in the window of his gallery, where it quickly caught attention. Esme had wanted *The Tyrant* to attract viewers but even she was surprised at the notoriety the painting quickly gained. A few days after moving into the new quarters in St. John's Wood,

Esme read in the *St. James Chronicle:*

A certain Bond Street gallery is currently exhibiting in its window a brutal scene whose central figure bears a striking resemblance to a certain nobleman of very high rank. Can this be a true portrait of the notorious Duke of . . . . .

Well, Esme thought, that should provide the *ton* with a juicy tidbit for the salons this week. And also cause the duke no little embarrassment if not humiliation. Would he realize the artist's identity?

She had painted the picture in a burst of rage and passion, hoping for just such a reaction, wishing the duke to be wounded in his amour propre, for she had no other method of paying him for robbing her of her chastity. That the scandal might rebound on her head she had considered and then decided that it was of no account. She had already made her decision to withdraw from society.

Now that she was safely established in St. John's Wood with few knowing her location, she had little fear of reprisal. She was prepared to withstand whatever attempts the arrogant Hugo Carstairs made to bring home to her the iniquity of her revenge upon him. That the Cranfords might be damaged by any discredit which connected them with the artist was regrettable, but Esme was not in good charity with her relations at this point, except for dear Fannie, whose loyalty, alas, might be tested.

Now that the deed was done she admitted to a nagging sense of shame at her part in such a bitter revenge. Exposing the duke for the villain he was brought her far less satisfaction then she had expected. Tossing her head with vexation, she threw the journal from her. Enough of this. She must get on with her life and the devil take the man.

Lady Jersey was among the first to recognize the significance of *The Tyrant*. She immediately spread this delicious tidbit of gossip among her intimates, which comprised most of the leading figures of London's haut monde. Imperious, spiteful, and somewhat ill-bred, Lady Jersey's ironic sobriquet was *Silence* because of her babbling tongue. This latest *on dit* was too scandalous not to bruit about with all rapidity. She confided her suspicions first to one of her bosom bows and fellow patronesses of Almack's, Princess Leiven, over the tea cups, secure in the knowledge that the report would soon be all over London.

"And Dorothea, what could Milbourne have done for this unknown artist to have drawn such a cruel portrait?" Lady Jersey asked, her eyes sparkling vindictively.

Princess Lieven, who had a sneaking admiration for the libertine Hugo Carstairs, protested. "I can't believe he would actually have taken the action shown in the painting. He is a dreadful rake, with a most fearful reputation, but surely not sadistic, my dear Sally!"

"I understand the artist is a woman, which makes the whole affair even more curious," Lady Jersey confided, enjoying this budget of rumor to the utmost." Alvaney told me. He always discovers the latest secrets."

"Really, how peculiar! Could she be a spurned light skirt? It's not Hugo's style to dally with respectable girls," the princess mused.

"But don't you remember the terrible scandal about the Earl of Grafton's daughter the year she made her come-out?" Lady Jersey purred, for she never forgot a transgression, or the hint of one. "He was supposed to have seduced her in the Devonshires' summer house and then abandoned her. She was whisked to the country and married forthwith to a dull country squire, as I remember."

"Cora Romilly was a flighty piece. It might have been the duke or a score of others. She was as bad as Caro Lamb," Princess Leiven pointed out. But she could not deny that Hugo Carstairs was no saint when it came to the female gender.

Lady Jersey reached avidly for another rock cake, her appetite whetted by this wonderful scandal. "Well, this portrait puts him quite beyond the pale! He will be ostracized from every decent drawing room despite his handsome looks and fortune."

Princess Leiven looked at her companion with some disgust, for she did not share her eagerness to destroy the duke's credit.

"Oh, do be careful, Sally. Hugo Carstairs is a formidable man. I would not want to make an enemy of him. And I doubt if he cares two pins for his reputation, but he could ruin yours," she warned.

"My position is unassailable, and if Hugo Carstairs wants to play the victim, he had better change his ways forthwith," Lady Jersey informed her companion, not at all pleased by her rebuke. She had an inordinate pride in her own power to make or destroy reputations, and Hugo Carstairs was no favorite of hers. He had laughed at her too often, and for that there was no forgiveness. She quite enjoyed thinking of the humiliation in store for that reprobate. But she was determined to get to the bottom of the matter. Why had the picture been painted? What did it signify and who was the artist who hated the duke so violently? The matter would occupy her pleasantly for days to come.

In the Cranford drawing room the recent events were not viewed with such vulgar enjoyment. Robert had been the first with the news of *The Tyrant*, hearing the speculation at his club and rushing around to see the picture and interview Mr. Gorton, from whom he had received small change. But his suspicions were confirmed by the signature, "Arethusa," and he quizzed his sister Fannie vehemently. Not having the good sense to confine his questions to a private confrontation, he challenged her before their parents one evening.

"Fannie, with what name does Esme sign her paintings?" Robert asked his sister over the coffee cups.

The young woman, having heard the *on dit* in a roundabout way, was flustered by her brother's perspicacity. Yet she was prepared to protect her cousin. Twisting her hands in a fever of embarrassment, she tried to equivocate. "I am not sure, Robert. Sometimes she does not sign them at all."

"Does the name *Arethusa* mean anything to you?" he persisted, staring at her with determination and noticing her flushed cheeks and general distrait air.

"I don't think so. Wasn't she some kind of Greek nymph?"

"Really, Robert, I do not think such questions are fit for your sister's ears," the earl reprimanded, his ideas of mythology very shaky but certainly salacious. "And why should this picture have any connection to your cousin?" he added crossly.

"Because I think she painted it, and that means she has some reason to dislike the duke. There is no doubt in anyone's mind that the central form is his," Robert retorted, his anger overcoming his prudence.

"Are you implying that Esme has had some irregular relationship with the Duke of Milbourne, Robert?" his mother asked, shocked. "She would never be so bold or so lacking in propriety to confess her authorship of this outrageous portrait!" she said a moment later as she considered the ramifications of such a circumstance.

"I, for one, have always doubted that Banbury Tale about the highwayman. I think the duke may have abducted her and seduced her and this is her way of exacting revenge," Robert muttered, beginning to wish he had not blurted out his suspicions.

"I can't believe it! I can't believe any of it, and I will have no more of these slurs on your cousin's respectability!" his mother protested, but her brow furrowed as she thought back over Esme's behavior during the past weeks.

"Esme cares nothing for respectability," Fannie said, then covered her mouth with her hands, realizing what she had revealed. The last thing she intended was to bring disgrace upon her dearly loved cousin.

136

"That is quite apparent, Fannie," her mother answered in quelling tones. "If Esme has so forgotten her duty and her upbringing as to bring this disgrace upon us, I for one will have nothing more to do with her. It is the outside of enough that she has repaired to that ghastly little cottage in St. John's Wood and is living unchaperoned in the most shocking way. But if she is responsible for this scandal, we must completely disown her," Lady Cranford insisted decisively. "And I am not surprised she should behave in such an intolerable fashion. What this will do to your chances I shudder to think."

"I have no chances, mother, as you well know, and I will not abandon Esme!" Fannie declared bravely.

"Do not speak so to your mother, Fannie," the earl said. "Apologize at once." He rounded on his wife, prepared to shift the burden of this embroglio onto her shoulders. "This is what comes of taking your sister's daughter into our household, madam!"

"I am sorry if I offended you, mother, but I think you are being very unfair," Fannie offered sullenly, then turning to her brother. "And you, Robert, who have so admired Esme, how can you turn on her in such a fashion?"

Robert, having stirred the hornet's nest to no purpose, was now ashamed of his ill-considered words. "I only want to discover if there is any truth in these damnable rumors that some irate woman has held the duke up to ridicule and ruin."

"The man is a libertine and a rake with no reputation to ruin, but the mere coupling of Esme's name with his is enough to bring her, and us, into disrepute. This must go no further, Robert," his father warned. "As for you, Fannie, you are to have no concourse with your cousin. She has seen fit to abandon all decency by leaving this household, where she was treated with kindness and brought up in respectability. She must suffer the consequences. She is no longer my niece and will not be received here. That is my last word on the subject."

But it was by no means the last word, and Fannie continued to protest his decision and urge Esme's cause. Robert, aware that his role in this family decision was far from admirable, said little, his jealousy and suspicions warring with his genuine affection for his cousin, whom he now suspected was lost to him forever.

*Chapter Thirteen*

Hugo Carstairs, the object of all this scandalous discussion, had earlier decided to adopt a pose of haughty amusement. On entering White's the day after the picture appeared in Gorton's window, he had been inundated with coarse jokes by some of his acquaintances.

Lord Alvaney, one of the *ton's* most august leaders, hailed him with a suggestive leer. "Well, Carstairs, I always knew you were a dog, but I had no idea you could inspire such—er, artwork!"

Hugo looked at the stout, fashionable figure with a raised eyebrow. "You flatter me, Alvaney. I'm afraid I am not nearly so—imaginative in my dealings with the gentler sex as the artwork you refer to would suggest. Much too fatiguing, my dear man," he said with some languor, settling himself at the card table and indicating that he would join the players in a round of faro.

"A case of mistaken identity, then?" another beaux suggested, not willing to incur Milbourne's anger, but titillated by the *on dit* that the notorious Hugo Carstairs was the center of yet another scandal.

"Not at all. It seems the artist used me for the central figure, possibly unaware that society would view it all too literally," Hugo explained pleasantly, but his questioner did not like the look in his dark eyes.

"Quite, quite, I understand. Shameful that you should be caricatured in such a dastardly manner," the man backed down hurriedly. "Shall I deal?" he added to distract any more probing questions.

"What are the stakes?" Hugo asked calmly, indicating that the conversation no longer amused him. However, Sir Guy Wentworth was among the players, and he could not resist the opportunity to repay Hugo for the episode in the Leivens's garden.

"I understand that the artist is a woman, Carstairs," he murmured. "That does strengthen suspicion that she is some light-skirt you treated badly."

"I hardly think that the talents of the light-skirts either of us honor with our protection run in such artistic directions. It is quite an artist who produced such a powerful canvas," Hugo said, eyeing his tormentor with careless indifference. "And few of the muslin company that I have adopted have any reason to complain of my treatment, unlike others here, I warrant," Hugo said, looking sardonically at his accuser. Wentworth was known for his lack of generosity to those who had suffered his attentions. Sir Guy flushed. Well, Hugo Carstairs might turn the affair away with casual ease, but he was convinced there was something havey-cavey in this rumor and he would take steps to bring the villain to account. He would not be stigmatized by this aristocrat, humiliated before his fellows. Hugo turned away, signaling that the discussion was at an end, and threw out his counters. There were few in the assembly who wished to pursue the matter, whatever the conjecture, and no more was said about *The Tyrant* that evening.

Despite Hugo's studied air of indifference to the scandal which was whirling around his head, he was not ignoring the situation. He had already purchased *The Tyrant* from Joseph Gorton, anticipating the Prince Regent by a few hours. The gallery owner reluctantly had signified that he would remove the picture and deliver it to Hugo's house, but the duke had shrugged and insisted the compromising canvas remain in the gallery for the motley to view. He intended to submit the picture to the Royal Academy, and had already apprised the president of that august body, Benjamin West, of his plan.

He secretly applauded Esme's revenge, for he was convinced that she had painted the picture, and he did not want the subsequent scandal to rebound on her head. She was the victim in this affair, and for the first time in his heedless life he was ashamed of his selfish concern with his own gratification. He had taken her against her will and she had used the only means at her command to redress matters between them. Her courage and disdain for public opinion was evident, but he would see to it she didn't suffer for it. Beneath that confident intransigent air lay a vulnerable, fragile girl who had exposed herself to the wounding judgment of the society to which her birth and breeding entitled her. And the fault was his alone.

He had discovered by now where she was living, and had decided to offer her the one sure recompense for his villainy. If she were his duchess not even Lady Jersey would snub her. His motives for offering matrimony did not bear examination. He was willing to pay his penance, but beyond that thought he was not willing to go. Damn the chit, she had thoroughly overset his life. At least as his duchess, she would be under his control, to some extent, and once they were wed, he could have some peace from the torment he now endured. It never crossed his mind that she might refuse him. So he set off for St. John's Wood in a calmly determined frame of mind.

Esme received him cooly. If beneath the aloof facade she displayed, her heart was beating madly with emotion, she would not d splay her fears to this arrogant, ruthless man who had carelessly altered her life. She had made no effort to dress well for the meeting, wearing an old blue muslin gown of extreme simplicity, but the faded color and shabbiness of her costume only accented her vulnerable haunting air.

"I thought you might have me thrown from the premises," Hugo said warily, with an ironic smile.

"I don't think that would be possible, even I had a man available to attempt it," Esme countered, loathe to relax. He filled the small parlor with his dominating presence, and she looked at him askance, hoping he could not sense her trepidation. She neither trusted him nor liked him, but he engendered strong feelings in her, which she did not dare admit to herself. She hoped to hide successfully from his discerning hard eyes.

"Quite right. You must have known I would bring you to account over that striking picture which is titillating the *ton*, my dear. I realized quite soon who the artist was. Your talent is exceptional. Quite a blow to my self-esteem, but that was what you meant it to do. Actually, I find it an unusually brilliant execution, worthy of the best in the land." He complimented her suavely, watching the blush rise to her cheeks with satisfaction.

"You deserve even more condign punishment, sir. Did you hope to escape retribution for your disgusting assault?" she railed, angry that he could pierce her armor with his sarcasm. But she knew she had revealed herself. She had not meant him to know she had painted the picture, but of course he had discovered it.

"Disgusting?" he questioned with a suggestive smile. "I found our encounter many things, but hardly disgusting, Esme." His eyes roamed over her body and lingered on her breasts with a hot glow.

Esme turned away, walked to the window, unwilling for him to see the confused emotions he aroused with his reminder of their intimate past. She stared unseeing at the street beyond the draped windows, hoping she could hang on to her composure, but his words had stirred a torrent of memories. Why did this ruthless man dominate her thoughts? She had believed that by painting the picture she had exorcised him from her mind, but now she found it wasn't so.

142

"How did you find me?" she asked bluntly.

"You could not hide from me, Esme, no matter how you tried. I would find you. And the publicity of that picture demanded that I take some action to redeem your reputation in the eyes of the world. Perhaps that was what you had in mind," he explained cooly, as if recompense for kidnapping and seduction could be tidied neatly away.

Esme's fears were swamped by a flood of anger. How dare he explain his brutal disruption of her life as a mere peccadillo that could be easily explained and arranged to his satisfaction. She turned to face him, her fists clenched in fury. How she would like to batter that smooth face.

"And just how will you manage that, Duke?" she said sarcastically.

"I will marry you," Hugo replied, then cursed to himself. That was not how he had planned to propose, but the woman overset his every good intention. Surely she could see that this was the only answer. She should be grateful that she had won from him a concession he had never intended to offer any female.

Startled, Esme felt no appreciation of the honor. She would not be wed to retrieve her reputation. Or was it concern for his own consequence which had led him to this pass? Why did this unexpected offer of marriage cause her such disappointment? Had she expected a passionate avowal of love and devotion? The august Duke of Milbourne was probably incapable of such human emotions. No doubt he wanted her in his power, so he could dominate her with his physical magnetism and punish her for her rash revenge in exposing him to the *ton*. Well, she would not be such a fool as to consent.

"You must be mad to think I would consider putting myself in your power, sir," she said meeting his eyes fearlessly. "You have done your best to ruin me, and I have repaid you in kind. Now we are quits, I think."

If Hugo was startled or disappointed, nothing in his demeanour showed any evidence of it. A tense silence stretched between them, and Esme held her breath, not knowing what to expect from this man, who maddened her, intrigued her and threatened the safe sane life she planned to lead.

"You deceive yourself, Esme, if you think we are finished with one another. I could force you to marry me, you know, but I have compelled you once and would be loathe to do it again. You will find yourself in a very invidious position if you are so determined to lead a reclusive life. Society will condemn you, shun you, even insult you. As my wife you would be spared such abuse," he explained, for once completely in earnest. He wondered at his own efforts to persuade her, why he felt it so important to obtain her consent.

Esme, taken aback by his sincerity, looked at him searchingly. Had she misjudged him? Was he truly seeking to redress the wrong he had done her? Or was it just that he could not bear having his will thwarted? If she consented she would be once again a victim, and this time there would be no escape. Aside from her understandable fear of submitting to his dominance, there was also her conviction that as his wife she could no longer pursue her painting. As his duchess she would have duties and responsibilities that would take all her energies. Then there was his past. She could never trust him. Fidelity and devotion were not qualities which she associated with the Duke of Milbourne.

Her only defence was scorn. "I hardly think that marrying the notorious Duke of Milbourne would retrieve my reputation from ruin. Besides, you and I are badly suited. I would expect more than you are willing to give and you would expect a subservience and acceptance of your rakish ways I am not willing to extend," she concluded thoughtfully. If he had professed a passion of love for her she did not know how she would have responded, but his matter-of-fact proposal of marriage as a stop to convention made her feel unaccountably low.

"God, you are stubborn," Hugo growled, crossing to her and

taking her in his arms. He looked down into her shuttered face with a frustrated scowl. "What is there about you that rouses my worst instincts, I wonder?"

"My reluctance to fall at your feet in gratitude, no doubt," Esme retorted with spirit, though his overwhelming presence, the clasp of his restraining arms was making it difficult for her to think rationally.

Before she could protest he pressed a hard kiss on her resisting lips. The hot tide of desire his embrace roused in her enfuriated Esme. He could so easily lull her into acquiescence with his lovemaking, and she despised her reactions to him. And he knew how she felt, the devil, she noticed as he released her.

"You may deny what we feel for each other, Esme, but your wayward body betrays you. You have not seen the last of me," he promised. "But I will leave you now to think over my offer. Do not take too long. I might change my mind." He grinned at her, knowing how to spur her to indignation. But he swept from the room before she could order her thoughts and give him the scathing set-down he deserved.

Oh, he was a cunning rogue! Esme fumed, abandoned and flushing from his caresses. Well, she would not submit even if she had to marry the next man she met. She fled to her bedchamber to mull over the recent conversation and decry her own spinelessness.

It was unfortunate that within hours of Hugo's departure Oliver Wells should call upon Esme, for she received him with such warmth that his hopes were raised by the pleasure she evinced upon seeing him.

"Why, Oliver, I did not expect to see you again so shortly. How did you find my address and what are you doing in London?" she asked him, smiling at his eagerness.

"I told you before you left Tunbridge Wells so abruptly that our regiment had been posted to London, and I was able to wring your address from Mrs. Evans's former employer. See how diligent I am in pursuing our friendship? I hope to see a

145

great deal of you, Esme, while I am in London."

"You are a true friend, Oliver, and your presence here will add immeasureably to my stay." Esme smiled. How kind and uncomplicated Oliver Wells was with his obvious delight in her company. He was no threat to her serenity or the reclusive life she had adapted. She welcomed him with more cordiality than she would have extended if she had not been smarting from her recent interview with the duke. And Lieutenant Wells, not knowing the reason for her effusive greeting, decided he would put his chances to the touch at the first opportunity. His admiration for Esme was not untinged with awe. The thought of winning such an exceptional wife quite raised his spirits. He left her, after exacting a promise to allow him to escort her to the theater, with a great deal of satisfaction.

But if Esme thought she had effectively routed the duke, she could not have been more mistaken. Two evenings later at the Drury Lane performance of "The Provoked Wife," to which Oliver escorted her, she looked up from their seats in the stalls to see Hugo Carstairs enter a box above them. He stood broodingly over the company, and Esme drew back, sheltering behind Oliver's stalwart figure. At first she thought he was alone, but she saw he was soon joined by a jubilant crowd, among them a striking brunette, obviously one of the muslin set, who hung on Hugo's arm and moved enticingly against him.

Esme's lips tightened, and she averted her eyes. He was hardly pining from her rejection, she thought sarcastically. He had returned to his old form, lavishing his attentions upon the type of female he preferred. She would not admit the pang of hurt she suffered from the sight of Hugo Carstairs obviously enjoying himself. After all, it was no more than she expected. Esme hardened her resolve never to contemplate the future he had suggested. She forced herself to concentrate on the stage and on her companion, but it took the utmost effort to drag her eyes away from the performance in the box to the far less absorbing one on the stage.

In the interval, Esme acceded to Oliver's suggestion that they walk about and survey the scene—a fashionable one, for the play was popular. Almost immediately Esme regretted her decision. As they promenaded, they passed that doyenne of the fashionable world, Lady Jersey. In the past, Lady Jersey had been quite civil to Esme, but tonight she looked at her in the most haughty way and extended only the curtest of nods before turning away. No doubt Aunt Mildred had made known her niece's shocking decision to leave the safety of her home and live alone. Esme had placed herself beyond the pale. She smiled ruefully. No more than she deserved, no doubt, but the chilling rebuke and other cold stares did not weaken her determination to stick to her chosen path.

Her discomfort, however, was soon heightened by a casual meeting with the Cranfords and Fannie, as she and Oliver were about to return to the stalls. Her uncle and aunt greeted her with austerity, but Fannie was all affection and delight. Perforce Esme had to introduce her companion, and she could see that Aunt Mildred did not view the introduction with pleasure. Poor Oliver Wells was not an acceptable parti. Esme was convinced her aunt believed that here was even more evidence of the wisdom of ostracizing Esme from any contact with her cousin. But Fannie would have none of it, and peeping shyly at Lieutenant Wells, received the introduction with naive gratitude.

She pressed Esme to tell her news, and was lavish in her protestation of regret that they were together no longer. But even Fannie could not help but notice her parents' aloofness, and the group soon parted with assurances from Fannie that she would call upon Esme soon in her retreat. That won a scowl from her father, whose unbending dignity would not allow him to reprove his daughter in public. It would have been an amusing encounter if Esme had not regretted the unhappiness it undoubtedly caused her cousin. Fortunately her uneasiness was not increased by any untoward meeting with the duke. She

147

prayed he had not seen her in the audience, but her prayer was not answered.

The following day, while she was absent on a visit to Somerset House, Bessie informed her that the duke had called and delivered personally a huge bunch of roses with a note.

Your escort last evening did not prove as successful a red herring as you wished, dear Esme. I anticipate our next meeting with pleasure. Hugo

The heavy strokes of the distinctive scrawl did nothing to calm Esme's nerves. What would it take to discourage the man? And if she was completely honest, did she want to discourage him? She had found him invading her dreams, reminding her of those passion-filled nights they had spent in Surrey. But she would root out those disastrous feelings, for they could lead nowhere. Some whim, some belated remorse had impelled him to offer her marriage, but it was not the type of union that would bring her contentment, and she would not sacrifice her peace of mind, her work, for a few exciting nights of lovemaking. He could not give her the fidelity, the domestic tranquility she needed. Far better to look elsewhere for a husband, if that was what she craved. The strain of these conflicting emotions and sleepless nights took their toll on Esme. Her eyes became even more haunted, her figure thinner as she wrestled with her demons.

A welcome distraction was Fannie's continuing friendship, for she visited Esme in St. John's Wood despite her parents' disapproval and Robert's assumed indifference. He had taken his rejection hard but masked his wounded pride by ignoring Esme and believing she had deceived him. He threw himself into a round of frivolity that restored his self esteem, and raised the hopes of several fetching young women. He won quite a reputation as a dashing man about town whose heart was never endangered.

Oliver Wells, encouraged by Esme's enthusiastic reception

of his overtures, spent every free moment at the St. John's Wood house, often joining Esme and Fannie in expeditions to look at pictures, and taste the more humble excitements of London. Fannie relaxed in his undemanding company and lost the shyness which had made her debut in fashionable society so tormenting. But, however courteous and amiable was Oliver's manner toward Fannie, it was Esme who engaged his affections. Still, he hesitated to put his chances to the test, and Esme continued to treat him in a open, sisterly way that he hoped would deepen into a more lasting feeling.

The three were sitting in Esme's small parlor one afternoon discussing an expedition to the Tower. Fannie had never visited that imposing pile and Esme felt she would enjoy the treat.

They were interrupted by the sudden appearance of Hugo Carstairs, who had deliberately ignored Esme for some days after the delivery of his roses. He had smiled ironically over Esme's stiff little note of thanks. He was too clever to try to win her by lavish gifts and constant attention, but he had in no way surrendered his desire to marry her. Just why he was so determined to compel a reluctant bride, he had not resolved. The scandal over the picture continued to engage the *ton* but the first shocking impact had lessened as other delicious gossip supplanted *The Tyrant* in interest.

"Come, Esme, don your bonnet and shawl. We are off to visit Joseph Turner," Hugo insisted after a cursory greeting to Oliver and Fannie.

"But I am already engaged this afternoon, duke," Esme said in what she hoped were quelling tones. Hugo appeared not to be impressed.

"Nonsense, an interview with Turner is far more important than any appointment you may have made," Hugo replied, overriding her objections in his usual ruthless manner. "I am sure your companions can spare you for the afternoon."

Esme, who had always wanted to meet the Royal Academician, was tempted. She had recently viewed his "Crossing the Brook," a dramatic painting of a Devon landscape, and the work had impressed her with its color and power. But she disliked surrendering to the duke's high-handed arrangements. Fannie, however, forced her hand by urging her to pay no mind to their previous engagement.

"Please do not consider me, Esme, if you wish to meet Mr. Turner. I know how much you admire him. We can visit the Tower any afternoon," she offered shyly, for Hugo Carstairs' overwhelming presence awed her. She felt most uncomfortable when he turned his dark eyes upon her poor, insignificant self.

Oliver, wanting to prove his interest in her work, despite his annoyance at the duke's intrusion, joined his assurances to Fannie's. "I will escort Lady Weirs to the Tower, Esme, so you will not be denying her the treat. We will give you a full report!"

Esme laughed, and relented. "That is most obliging of you, Oliver! But please do not continue to call Fannie by her imposing title. I can see it embarrasses her. We are all friends and a little informality would not be amiss."

As the duke wheeled his curricle through the rural lanes toward the heart of the city, he was very much aware of Esme at his side. She looked incredibly fragile in the warm summer day, her complexion pale and her attempts to appear poised and aloof unavailing. She made few concessions to style; her driving dress of cerulcean silk faced with white was crisp and neat, but hardly in the first stare of fashion.

"You are behaving most unfairly toward that young man, Esme, and your efforts to convince me that he is an object of your interest strain credulity," Hugo said, noticing that his gibes had met their mark. A betraying pulse fluttered madly at her throat.

"Oliver Wells is a most amiable young man who has proved a good friend to me," she reproved primly, inwardly furious that the duke had seen through her maneuvers. "I am quite fond of him."

"Nonsense. You are using him as a shield to protect

yourself. He is much more suited to your pleasant plain-Jane cousin."

"I do not need protection. I am quite able to fight my own battles!" Esme retorted.

"Well, amuse yourself with the cub if you wish, but sooner or later you'll grow very bored, my dear," the duke warned, as they turned into Pall Mall.

She tossed her head defiantly but would not be drawn further into the fray.

"I am quite eager to meet Mr. Turner," Esme said to change the subject. "Thank you," she added awkwardly. It went against the grain to show gratitude to this rogue.

"I will claim my reward at a more opportune time," the duke replied lightly.

Esme looked sharply at him but could not decide whether he was serious or not. Certainly, he was all gallantry as he assisted her down from the vehicle and escorted her through the portals of the Royal Academy.

"I must warn you that Turner can behave in a most farouche manner. But I am sure he will be quite taken with you," Hugo said as they mounted the steps toward a large studio. "He has seen *The Tyrant* and is most impressed."

How like Hugo Carstairs to remind her of the controversial painting just as she approached Turner, Esme thought, scowling. He really was an unaccountable devil and she had no idea why he was going to all this trouble to woo her after the scandal she had engineered.

Reported to be completely uneducated, with sensual and sordid appetites, Joseph Mallord Turner had a rough manner but a surprising sense of humor. He was small with crooked legs, a ruddy complexion and a prominent nose, his appearance redeemed by merry blue eyes. Gossip had it that he hated teaching but was compelled to accept students for pecuniary reasons. He did not like showing his work, but it seemed that today, in a jovial mood, he was prepared to make an exception.

He greeted them in the workroom which was ringed with his

work sketches of cathedrals interspersed with a few striking water colors, his preferred medium, Esme believed. "Ah, your Grace, you have brought this talented young woman to see my paintings! I am honored," he said graciously.

"This is Miss Sedgewick, or 'Arethusa' as she wishes to be known—the artist reponsible for *The Tyrant*." The duke's dark eyes glinted with amusement as he introduced the unlikely pair.

"It is a pleasure to meet you, sir," Esme said, ignoring Hugo's reference to her controversial painting. "I am a great admirer of your work." She smiled shyly at the little bantam cock, who preened under her flattery.

"And I of yours. Of course, I have seen *The Tyrant*, and recognized a certain resemblance to our friend, here, but your landscape has a precious quality that does not lend itself to the drama of the scene," Turner replied. "More color, my dear, more color," he criticized.

Esme, eager for his advice, pressed him to be more explicit, and he emphasized his point by drawing her attention to his various works, ranged haphazardly around the room. Soon they were deep in a discussion of primary color, light, and various types of tempera. Hugo looked on with a satisfied air, leaning gently against a wall. After about a half-hour of this professional talk, Esme recalled that she had monopolized enough of the famous artist's time and protested that they must make their farewells.

"It is decided, then, that you will accept Esme as a pupil," the duke put in.

"It would be an honor to teach such a talented young woman," Turner agreed.

"And none of your infamous conduct over the easel, Turner. Save your amorous instincts for your models," the duke warned, casting an admonitory eye on the artist.

Esme was shocked at Hugo's implication. "Not every man shares your proclivities, sir!" she said tartly.

But Turner only laughed heartily. "Your little pigeon will be safe with me, Duke," he promised, "although I must admit you are putting temptation in my way. You are a beautiful woman, but I do not poach, ma'am," he said with the air of a connoisseur.

"Of course, I will pay your fee, sir. I only hope it is not beyond my means," Esme insisted, a bit worried. She did not notice the warning glance the duke, standing behind her, gave the artist.

"For you, my dear, I will charge nothing. It would be an honor to teach you. Turner insisted mendaciously, knowing the duke would be generous. Before Esme could correct Turner's assumption that she was under the duke's protection, Hugo had whisked her away from the studio and out to his curricle.

"I suppose I must tender my thanks, sir, for your introduction to Mr. Turner," Esme said grudgingly. "I understand he is loathe to take pupils, and I am grateful for the chance to study under such a master."

"You see, we can deal quite well together, Esme, if you would only put your trust in me," Hugo answered smoothly, raising an ironic eyebrow at her. He was not unaware of her irritation at owing him any gratitude and it amused him.

"Trust you to lure me back into your bed, you mean. Are you trying to blackmail me, sir, with this favor?" Esme answered smartly, seeing the way the conversation was leading.

"Not at all, my dear, only proving my devotion. I have said from the beginning I am all admiration of your talent and want only to further your career," the duke insisted, drawing his horses to a halt in front of her address. "I hope you have not forgotten my honorable offer of marriage," he reminded her, his tone guileless.

"I have not. Nor have I forgotten the reason you made it or the fact that I refused it."

"Oh, well. I will have to persevere. Incidentally, I must go out of town for a few days. If, upon reflection, you should regret your refusal, you may reach me at Grosvenor House. In the meantime, you might rough out another shocking portrait of me to titillate the *ton*. You are quite good at it."

Esme tossed her head, and stepped out of the curricle, with as much dignity as she could muster. "I will not invite you in, sir, as you will not want to keep your horses standing. Goodbye," she said with a finality in her tone that brooked no argument.

But the duke did not seem impressed and laughed at her stiff demeanor before taking his leave.

## Chapter Fourteen

While Esme was thrilled at the opportunity to take lessons with the gifted Turner, she wished she did not owe her lessons to Hugo Carstairs. The burden of gratitude added to the confusion of her feelings for the enigmatic duke. In fact, her reactions to the duke on every suit were a melee of justified anger, suspicion of his motives, and an unaccountable inability to forget their tempestuous liaison in Surrey.

It was as well he would be absent from London for a space. She needed the time to sort things out, not the least of which was the duke's astonishing marriage proposal. Could it be that Hugo feared she was pregnant? Perhaps he wanted an heir. Most men did, and ordered their affairs to comfortably arrange this contingency without in any way dampening their pleasures. Damn all men, Esme concluded. Shaking off her malaise and her lowering conviction that her life would never return to its calm even tenor, she turned to her easel. At least that solace never failed her, and in fact, she was painting with more enthusiasm and skill than ever before.

Having banished all thoughts of men and spent several gratifying hours with her paints and brushes, Esme sat down to dinner that evening quite in charity with herself. The peaceful productive hours had restored her sense of humor and her natural serenity. But her hard-gained composure was soon to be rudely disturbed.

About nine o'clock, when she was reading quietly before the fire, she heard a thunderous knocking at her door. Surprised, for she had few visitors but Fannie and Lieutenant Welles, and neither was expected, she warned Bessie not to open the door. The disturbance continued. Loathe to attract the attention of her neighbors, she finally went to the door herself. With Bessie clucking her disapproval, she threw it open to find a disheveled and very drunken Robert on her doorstep. He staggered into the hallway, ignoring her protests, intent on having his way. In one glance Esme realized he was badly foxed. His cravat was askew, his hair wildly tumbled and his speech slurred.

"Couldn't wait, had to see you. You must hear me out," Robert muttered, swaying unsteadily.

"Oh, Robert, what a state you are in! Come into the parlor," Esme ordered, frowning. Obviously her cousin was in no condition to realize the impropriety of calling on her at this late hour.

She pushed him determinedly into the parlor and indicated that he should be seated. He looked around groggily, not aware of his location, only of his companion, whom he leered at wolfishly.

"You will not turn me away, Esme. You must listen to me. I don't care a rap for the parents. I will make you my wife. Can't have this gossip continue. You are the talk of the *ton*," he muttered, staring at her with an unfocused gaze.

"Never mind that now, Robert. Try to compose yourself," Esme suggested gently.

"It's all over the clubs that you are that rakehell Milbourne's mistress, and I won't have it. I am going to challenge the devil!" He staggered to his feet, then sank down at Esme's, and grasped her unwilling hands.

Esme could barely restrain her impatience. "Don't be such a sapskull, Robert! Bessie, bring some coffee," she said to the hovering Bessie, who was much shocked by Lord Weir's appearance and news.

Robert, shaking his head to clear away the brandy, persisted with drunken stubbornness. "You don't understand. You are too innocent. You are the butt of all the worst gossips in town. The parents are furious and vow to abandon you, but I don't care a rap for that, or for the duke. I will marry you and restore your reputation."

Esme sighed. His news was not completely unexpected. But her first and most pressing task was to soothe Robert and prevent him from making some hideous mistake. She knew the duke had fought several duels, and was no doubt a notable hand with a pistol, no match for Robert at all. Robert was looking around the room with bleary eyes as if he expected to see his rival cowering behind the furniture.

"Where is the rogue? I will face him now!" he declared, staggering to his feet.

"Don't be ridiculous, Robert. You are making a real cake of yourself. I thought better of you," Esme reproved him sharply. Really, it only needed this. She was wondering what to do with the drunken man, so pathetic in his attempts to play the righteous defender. A guilty pang prevented her from taking him to task as he deserved. Before she could reassure him, Bessie entered the room with a tray of coffee, clearing a table and putting down the pot and some cups and saucers.

"Whatever are we to do with the poor lad, Miss Esme? He's foxed, he is," Bessie said, standing with her hands on her hips and looking disapprovingly at Robert.

"It's all right, Bessie. You can leave my cousin to me. He is a trifle overset, but I will bring him round," Esme assured her nurse. Esme shepherded her firmly to the door, then returned to her cousin's side, and tried to offer him the coffee. He pushed it away pettishly, and grasped her hand, covering it with impassioned kisses.

"I don't care if you have been the duke's mistress, Esme. I love you and your only recourse is to marry me. We will go to Dorset and all these vicious rumors will soon subside. You must marry me. To hell with the tame tabbies who would destroy you!"

"Robert, we cannot discuss this now. Come, you must try to order your senses. Do try some of this coffee," she urged, but he ignored her pleas, continuing his tirade until all of a sudden he collapsed back on the settee, and fell into a stupor.

Esme looked at him with compassion, but also with irritation. This was a fine turn up. What could she do with an unconscious man, deep in his cups. She took a light blanket from the end of a sofa and covered him gently, then tiptoed from the room. He would have to sleep it off and perhaps in the morning she could talk some hard sense into his befuddled head.

Really, men were impossible, so selfish, so egotistical, so ready to believe that every woman must be honored by their attentions. Then she reproved herself. She must restrain her annoyance with Robert. They had shared too much for her to treat him cruelly now.

She could not return the love he felt, and some day he would be grateful she had refused him. No doubt his "love" was spurred by her rejection, she thought. If she had welcomed his advances, he would not have been so intrigued.

Esme was completely unaware of her power, of that remote air of hers that maddened men to conquer the citadel. She knew she was not unhandsome, but thought little about her looks, and could understand neither the duke's nor Robert's passionate desire to possess her. Much of the haut monde's preoccupation with the games of love, the flirtations, the hyprocisy, the mannered attitudes proscribed by society baffled her and she wanted no part of it. She believed that marriage was not for her.

She had never felt the stirrings that Fannie attributed to a finer feeling, but she could not deny that the duke's potent masculinity, his expert initiation of her into the pleasures of the bed, had more than disturbed her. Before his determined assault on her senses she had been puzzled by the lure that love held for other women. And even now, after her ruthless

158

introduction, she was inclined to dismiss her wanton emotions as a weakness. In fact, she spent entirely too much time thinking of Hugo Carstairs, wondering about his motives for offering her marriage, and even idly imagining what her acceptance would bring. But that was not love as she understood it, only the shameful physical craving of the body. She must not consider joining her life to such a man, who would dominate her and threaten her hard-won independence. Once he had mastered her, while she would be in thrall to him, no doubt he would be bored by her devotion and turn elsewhere for his satisfaction. She could not bear that. But she did not examine why that prospect was such a bleak one.

Shrugging off her malaise, she looked at Robert sleeping off his alcoholic stupor and returned to the problem at hand. In the morning she must persuade her cousin to abandon his hopes and somehow she must do this kindly and without damaging their old relationship. Really, men were so romantic. It was women who were the realists, having to cope with the results of male idiocy, while bolstering the poor fools' egotism. Very trying and time consuming, Esme mused, shaking her head. She would not become yet another sighing victim of their heartless indifference to the women they conquered.

At last Esme left the parlor to repair to her own chamber, where sleep eluded her for quite a while.

The next morning, showing no effects from her troubled night, Esme greeted a sullen Robert over the breakfast table. Bessie had managed to restore his physical being somewhat, but obviously he was still feeling aggrieved and misunderstood. Esme refused to sympathize, but greeted him brightly if sternly over the coffee cups.

"I suppose you are not feeling too spritely this morning, Robert, but that is the price you must pay for your dissipations of last night. I only wish you had found some other place to sleep off your excesses," she said in a matter-of-fact tone.

Looking at his hostess, who was gowned in a fetching yellow silk morning dress, Robert had the grace to feel some shame, but he had not abandoned his intention.

"You will have to marry me now, Esme. I have compromised you by spending the night in your parlor, even if I was all unknowing of the honor." He reddened under her cool considering stare.

"Robert, I fear you are not in a condition to accept my complaints, but I cannot lose this opportunity to speak plainly to you," she said in a sisterly manner, which quite overset him. She continued, "I have not been compromised because I do not accept those silly rules of your society. And in any case, I am already beyond rescue, leading the life of an artist."

"If you married me, your respectability would be restored," he argued stubbornly, refusing to see the force of her arguments.

"But that is not the kind of marriage I want or that you deserve, dear Robert. Some day you will look back on this interlude as a youthful experience, when you have met and won the heart of a girl who can give you the love you deserve. I am not that woman, Robert. Believe me, I have nothing to offer you but cousinly affection."

"I could make you love me," he insisted, passing a shaking hand through his hair.

"You cannot compel love, Robert, and you are in no state to be upsetting yourself with these silly arguments when you are suffering from a headache and a queasy stomach," Esme said sensibly. "You must take yourself off home and restore yourself."

"I know what it is. You are besotted with that rake Milbourne! But he will never marry you and you will be abandoned like all his other women!" Robert said, his mood turning ugly with his thwarted desire.

"We will not discuss the duke, Robert. And I do not care for your tone. I have done nothing to deserve such treatment from you, and I did not appreciate your arriving here last night in such a condition. I have been very patient with you, due to my real affection for you, but you are straining the bounds of civility," Esme said sharply, out of patience with her unwelcome suitor.

"You are the reason I was so up in the boughs," he muttered, but spoke half-heartedly, for he knew he had behaved badly.

"That is no apology, but I will forgive your transgression if you take yourself off now and forget all about your foolish behavior. There must be no repeat of last night." She restrained her amusement at his chagrin with difficulty. What a little boy he was.

"Oh, all right. I will leave, but you have not heard the last of this. Everyone in London believes you painted that portrait of the duke, and all the gossips are entertained by the reason for such an unflattering picture. You are the butt of every scandal monger in town," Robert protested, feeling very hard done by.

"You exaggerate, Robert. And even if what you claim is true, it in no way alters my determination to refuse you and send you home. That is my last word on the subject. I will be pleased to see you again when you have come to your senses." Esme sailed from the dining room, tired of the whole matter. Perforce Robert, feeling ill-used and guilty, had to take his departure in the lowest of spirits.

Later that day, Esme discovered that Robert had not exaggerated the rumors titillating society. She stopped by Hatcherd's book store in Picadilly to buy a particular collection of prints she wanted, and encountered the Princess Leiven and Lady Annabel Poole, whom she knew only slightly. Both ladies were inclined to shun her, but their avidity over the latest gossip prevent them from cutting her off entirely.

"Good afternoon, Miss Sedgewick," the princess greeted her haughtily. "What a surprise. I understood you were in hiding."

Esme replied cooly, "Not at all, Princess Leiven. I have taken a house in St. John's Woods." She would not dignify the princess's curiosity by any further explanation. But she hadn't reckoned on that lady's determination to discover the truth of

161

the rumors exciting London society.

"Ah, yes. I understand you have retired to paint. I had no idea you were such a serious artist," Princess Leiven said spitefully.

Esme averted her head and said nothing. She would not try to justify her actions, but she wondered how much the princess and her friends really knew. She was turning away, hoping to avoid any further questioning when Lady Annabel Poole, entered the conversation.

"I understand that you are a good friend of the Duke of Milbourne, Miss Sedgewick. Can you possibly be the artist who painted that shocking portrait, *The Tyrant,* that has everyone agog?" Her tone was insinuatingly warm, contrasted with her limpid blue eyes, which were hard and cold. Lady Annabel had her own reasons for pressing the inquiry, for she did not like the suspicion that had occupied her mind for some days past, after she had viewed the painting.

"I believe the artist prefers anonymity," Esme responded cooly, refusing to lie, but appalled that her connection with the painting should become common knowledge. Her first thought was that the duke had revealed the secret. It would be his own revenge for her treatment of him. She would not cower before these two august personages as if she was some timid victim of their savage spite. She wondered what Lady Annabel's interest was in the affair, but she suspected that the lady's concern was for the duke. There had been some gossip at one time about the lovely widow and the duke, she remembered vaguely.

"I believe you have been most foolish and indiscreet, Miss Sedgewick. You will be the one to suffer if the rumors are true," Lady Annabel warned, convinced there was some basis for her suspicions that this girl was involved with the man she had hoped to secure as a husband.

"I have no idea what you mean, Lady Annabel. Now you must excuse me. I have a pressing appointment. Good day, Princess Leiven." Esme returned the scornful glance Lady Annabel bent on her, knowing she could not remain here to be quizzed by the arrogant woman. Both women looked avidly after her as she left the shop with her back straight and her chin set.

Once outside the shop, she hurriedly summoned a hackney and sank into it, trembling with rage. How dare these women question her as if she were some fallen tweeny. She owed them no account of her life, nor was she interested in their assessment of her character. Her disappointment and anger at the duke raged as she rode toward St. John's Wood. She had always known the man was a cad. He professed to want to marry her but he was not averse to airing their infamous relationship to every gossip in London. Well, she would ignore the tattle, and furthermore, she would see to it that the duke no longer played any part in her life.

## Chapter Fifteen

In blaming the duke for unmasking the artist who had painted *The Tyrant* Esme lay all her troubles on his shoulders and was blind to other possibilities. If she had been thinking with her usual good sense she would have considered Robert, who was indeed the perpetrator. Unable to control his sense of grievance, he had blurted out the news while foxed at White's.

He had discovered Esme's secret by rummaging through the paintings still stored in Mount Street, confirming his worse fears. From the beginning he had not believed Esme's story of the highwaymen's abduction or her fortuitous escape. Brooding over the significance of *The Tyrant* had convinced him that the notorious duke was Esme's lover, either by force or her assent, and that he had installed her in the St. John's Wood house under his protection.

Even after recovering from his night of dissipation, and Esme's reserved treatment of the situation, he still sulked over her rejection of his magnanimous proposal. He had determined to rescue her from a life of shame and retrieve her reputation but all he had done was ruin his chances of ever making her his wife, and worst of all he had emerged as a figure of ridicule in her eyes. It was insupportable!

He had no memory of his revelations at White's but he was soon to be informed on that score. On repairing to the club that evening in a gloomy frame of mind, he found the members discussing little else.

Lord Alvaney, that dandy and leader of the smart set, buttonholed Robert the moment he stepped into the place.

"Well, Weirs, you have let the cat loose among the pigeons. Not good *ton*, my lad, to discuss a lady, particularly your own cousin, when you are under the hatches. You have set all the gossips buzzing!" Although not above a bit of salacious gossip himself, the plump gentleman respected the stringent codes of society. While he enjoyed being at the center of a shocking tale, he had a certain standard of behavior and Robert had transgressed it.

Robert reddened under this criticism, knowing he had made a cake of himself. Worse, he had exposed Esme to the very notoriety from which he had hoped to save her.

"I seem to have said a great many things that I now regret, and which I have no reason to believe are true," Robert apologized, seething under Alvaney's knowing eyes.

"A word of advice, my boy. Ignore any questions and just say you were too foxed to remember what you said. By far the best way," Lord Alvaney said kindly, and turned away, but then, struck by another thought he added, "I understand Carstairs is out of town, but if this idea of yours about your cousin is all a hum, or even if it's true, and he takes exception to it, you will find yourself in an unenviable position, Weirs. If I were you, I would take a repairing lease for a few weeks and hare off to the country."

Nodding amiably, Lord Alvaney drifted over to a gathering of his cronies, leaving Robert prey to bitter doubts. He was not a coward, but he had placed himself in a difficult position and he could see no way of extricating himself.

While Robert was cursing his drunken disclosures, another lady with a deep interest in Hugo Carstair's future, had decided that she must enter the lists and rescue that gentleman from the dilemma in which he found himself.

Lady Annabel Poole had in her first Season married an

elderly but very wealthy peer. He had conveniently met his death on the hunting field before she could provide the much desired heir. She had been left the bulk of the fortune, while the nephew who inherited the title received little income to support it and found himself in hard straits. He would have liked to see the lady find a new husband, which would make the money revert to him, but she had been rather dilatory in choosing a new mate.

In fact, Lady Annabel had set her sights on the Duke of Milbourne, but had been unable to bring him up to scratch. She conceded now it had been a mistake to surrender to him, for he soon lost interest in her, and began to pursue other matrons, who were conveniently tied to legal spouses. But Lady Annabel, who did not underestimate her assets—and they were considerable for she was a gazzetted beauty in the much admired golden-haired blue-eyed mode—had not given up her efforts to gain a duchess' coronet.

In this endeavor she had an ally in the duke's sister. Lady Hansford judged Annabel to be the perfect remedy for her brother's rakehell ways. She had the breeding, the entrée to the best circles, the dower funds, and a sophisticated approach to marriage. She would turn a blind eye to the duke's excesses as long as she was treated civilly, a not uncommon arrangement in the circles they both frequented. And the duke could hardly fail to find Annabel attractive. But Lady Hansford had another, purely selfish and maternal reason for urging Annabel Poole on her brother. Her eldest daughter, Elizabeth, would be making her come-out within a few years, and the girl's chances would be vastly improved if she were launched under the aegis of the Duchess of Milbourne.

So Emily, Lady Hansford, was more than willing to put her head together with Annabel over a plot to lure the duke into matrimony. She would have been quite shocked to learn that he had already initiated plans of his own along that line. If Annabel suspected as much, she was careful not to suggest such a possibility to his sister.

It was unfortunate that Hugo Carstairs had chosen this interval to absent himself from town. He had wisely wanted to give Esme a chance to miss him and reflect on the advantages of accepting his proposal. To his surprise, he found himself missing her, and rather keenly. He realized now how vital her acceptance had become to him. It had never occurred to him that she would not eagerly assent, and her unequivocal refusal had thrown him off balance. Now, at his estates in Somerset, he examined his motives and was forced to admit that the chit had somehow entwined herself in his life and become necessary to his happiness. He laughed cynically to himself. How fitting that he who had for years adroitly escaped the snares of title-minded mamas and their debutante daughters, should now be ensnared by the one woman who cared nothing for his title nor his wealth.

Unaware that his sister and Annabel Poole were scheming to settle his future for him, Carstairs continued to rusticate. He prided himself on being a conscientious landlord, inititiating agricultural reforms and keeping his tenants' farms and cottages in good order. He paid more than quarterly visits to his estates and listened carefully to complaints and saw to it that his bailiff honored his promises. This visit also included a conference with his housekeeper at which he hinted that Milbourne Abbey might soon have a chatelaine. Hugo wanted several rooms redecorated, among them a possible site for Esme's studio.

While Hugo was thus occupied, Lieutenant Wells had decided to put his chances with Esme to the test. He had a very humble opinion of his own worth, but he felt he could delay no longer, for he feared some other man with much more of this world's goods would seize the prize. He set the stage for his proposal with some care, escorting Esme on a pleasant ride to Richmond, selecting a day that augured well for the outing. His gentle courtesy and respectful admiration was very soothing, and Esme was inclined to look kindly on the young officer.

After Robert's outrageous behaviour and the duke's

arrogant manipulation, Oliver Wells appeared as a safe harbor. The scandal which she had induced with her painting of the duke, had brought her more suffering than satisfaction.

Lately she had found it impossible to work, and the two sessions she had endured with Mr. Turner had deepened her malaise, for he was not the most patient nor the most encouraging of tutors. She could have coped with this if she had not been so disturbed by the general tenor of her life. That Hugo Carstairs was at the bottom of her unhappiness she refused to admit.

Now as she looked at Oliver Wells's open frank countenance, at his guileless blue eyes, she reflected upon what an uncomplicated and worthy young man he was. As they disembarked from his phaeton and walked slowly down the green paths surrounding the palace, Esme felt at peace for the first time in days. Looking at the sylvan view, she wondered if she had made an error in settling in London. A cottage in the country might have been a better choice, although she would have missed the stimulating environment of the city's museums and galleries, and the opportunity to study with Mr. Turner. While she was musing about perhaps making a change, escaping from all the diverse personalities who interrupted her serenity, she did not notice that Oliver was screwing up his courage for a momentous announcement.

"Shall we stop and rest here for a moment, Miss Sedgewick? There is a matter of great importance I must discuss with you," he said gravely, indicating a convenient bench under a large leafy oak tree.

Esme, startled from her dreaming, looked a bit apprehensive as she sank gracefully onto the bench, loosening the ribbons of her green silk bonnet and letting her hair blow in the light breeze.

"You have such lovely hair. In fact, you are altogether the most beautiful lady I have ever known, dear Esme! I have been trying now for days to gain the courage to ask you to be my wife, and I can wait no longer." Oliver reddened as he blurted out this ingenuous proposal.

Oh, dear, Esme thought to herself. Why did all these unsuitable men keep proposing marriage? I must let Oliver down gently. He is such a likely lad, and would make an exceptional husband for the right girl.

"Oliver, it is most flattering to think that you would choose me for a wife, but I am afraid, dear friend, that we would not suit. I am a managing, self-absorbed female, with little interest in domestic ties. You need a far more obliging girl who would defer to you, follow the drum or preside over your home in the country with charm and ease. Someone like Fannie, for instance. I am unable to do any of those things, and although I admire and like you, I feel none of the emotion you should evoke from the girl you honor with your proposal." Esme thought she had expressed herself well. The suggestion that Fannie might suit, which had only just occurred to her, was a master stroke. Still, she knew her answer could not please him.

"I realize I have neither the position nor the address to win such a paragon as you are. And I will not pester you with unwelcome attentions. But I want you to know that if I can ever serve you in any way, I would be honored to do so. Living alone as you do, prey to the unwelcome approaches of unsavory types, you need the protection of a man. Even Oliver Wells, for all his kindly intentions, was not above seeing her artistic choices—her rejection of society—as unseemly. But at least he failed to badge or hector her as Robert had done, or sneer and condescend in the mode of Hugo Carstairs. Really, Oliver was worth two of these selfish, opinionated men.

"I cannot marry you, Oliver. I am not sure I can marry any man. Do forgive me!" Esme put her hand over the young man's.

"You are an angel, Esme. Of course, we will continue to be friends. I am not such a nodcock as to sulk and threaten all kinds of foolishness," he replied gallantly, earning Esme's increased respect and approval.

Without any embarrassment, they continued their outing,

and when Oliver eventually escorted her back to St. John's Wood they were in complete charity with one another. Esme promised to accompany him to Anstley's Amphitheatre on a subsequent evening.

On removing her bonnet and shawl, she was greeted by Bessie with the news that she had missed two callers: Fannie, who had looked quite disappointed to learn that Esme and Oliver had departed on their outing, and Emily, Lady Hansford, whose equipage had quite impressed Bessie, but whose name was unknown to Esme. Before many hours had passed, however, she would learn a great deal more about Lady Hansford than she welcomed.

The next day Esme returned from her lesson with Mr. Turner in a more cheerful frame of mind. The session had gone well; he had guided her to a more brilliant use of color, his own particular forte. The summer day added to her good spirits and as she traveled toward St. John's Wood in the hired hackney she felt that finally she had banished the demons that had oppressed her lately and made a firm decision to not let the distractions offered by such men as the duke interfere with her real mission, to paint.

She instructed the coachman to drive past Gorton's gallery. Her mood improved further when she noticed that *The Tyrant* had been removed from the window. Now, perhaps, that misguided act of revenge could be forgotten, along with the man who had inspired it. She wondered fleetingly who had purchased the painting, but knew she would find out the next time she spoke to Joseph Gorton to discuss the payment. For now she was eager to return home.

On entering her house, Esme was greeted by a very flustered Bessie.

"There is a grand lady awaiting you in the parlour," Bessie chattered. "She says she is a Lady Hansford, and quite starched-up she is, too. Now don't get yourself in a pucker. If she tried to give you the rough side of her tongue, you just call me and I will sort her out. The idea of behaving in that hoity-toity manner!"

"Strange. I saw no equipage outside the house," Esme mused as she smoothed her ruffled hair before the glass in the small entrance hall.

"She sent it away to come back in a half an hour, and that was some time ago. Didn't want to keep the horses standing, I suspect. Her kind always cares more for cattle than people. I hoped she would take her leave before you arrived. She called yesterday, too. Mark my words, the harridan means to cause trouble," Bessie finished in a sibilant whisper.

"Well, the least I can do is discover what she wants with me. Perhaps it will be a commission for a picture, and if that is the case, we are behaving in a shabby fashion lurking out here discussing our visitor!" Esme pointed out.

Esme entered her parlor with dignity.

"Good morning, Lady Hansford. I am Esme Sedgewick. I understand from Mrs. Evans that you are anxious to see me. I regret that you have been kept waiting, but I was not expecting a caller today."

The lady sat immobile on her settee and stared unnervingly at Esme.

"So you are Esme Sedgewick, the notorious *artiste* who has held my brother up to ridicule before the *ton!*" Lady Hansford's lip curled.

Hugo Carstairs's sister! Esme recoiled with embarrassment, then straightened, determined not to be quelled by this rather severe woman. Esme wondered how much the woman really knew of her relationship with Hugo. She doubted very much that Lady Hansford was in her brother's confidence. Was it just prurient curiosity that had brought her here or was she prepared to offer some insulting inducement to break off what she must believe to be a shocking affair?

From a cursory glance, it was obvious to Esme that Lady Hansford shared her brother's arrogance and short temper. Her close-set dark eyes held no warmth and she sat bolt upright, as if contact with the furnishings might despoil her.

She wore an unattractive magenta silk riding dress, high in the neck and most unsuitable for the warm day.

"I hardly think it is your business to call unheralded and make such disparaging remarks to a stranger," Esme said cooly.

"How dare you take that tone with me!" Lady Hansford huffed. "I know all about your relationship to the Cranfords, who took you in after your rackety parents were killed, but that does not entitle you to be received by decent people after your outrageous conduct. Your aunt and uncle have failed miserably to inculcate the minimum standards of behavior in you. I do feel for them—such scandal you have brought down on their heads!"

"I cannot see how my behavior is any concern of yours, Lady Hansford. I find your attack on my parents, my character and my art completely uncalled for. And I don't believe your brother would welcome your interference in this matter."

At the mention of the duke, Lady Hansford bridled, her sallow complexion reddening in fury.

"Indeed, madam. It is on my brother's behalf I have subjected myself to this offensive interview. You may believe, because of your birth and connections, that you can lure him into regularizing your immoral relationship, but you shall not succeed. He is aware of his duty to his family and it does not include marriage to a doxy! I have come here to warn you that I will not allow this marriage. I will see to it that you are barred from all decent society. Hugo will despise you," she railed, her anger overcoming her last vestiges of prudence. Esme's defiance infuriated her.

Esme laughed gaily, hoping the effort it cost her, was not apparent to her enemy. "Really, Lady Hansford, you are making a cake of yourself over nothing. I owe you no explanations, and I doubt very much if the duke cares a farthing for your opinion of me or of him. We have nothing to say to one another." Esme crossed to the door and threw it open, hoping that her unwelcomed visitor would take the hint.

"You have made a bad mistake, my girl, in treating me in such a fashion," Lady Hansford blustered, uncertain and humiliated. Somehow this woman, whom she had believed to be little better than a light skirt, had thoroughly routed her. She had been prepared to offer the jade some inducement to abandon her association with the duke, but she had the sense to see that would not be accepted. Helplessly, she had to abandon this crusade to save her brother from making another disastrous misalliance. "I have done my duty," she continued. "Now I will take steps to see that you suffer for your sins!" Rebuffed and embarrassed, her only recourse was a scornful glare as she swept from Esme's presence.

Watching Lady Hansford board her carriage, Esme wondered if she had been at fault during the interview. Why should she take the blame for a situation that had been brought about by the duke's own selfish arrogance. Lady Hansford's unfortunate call only hardened Esme's heart against the perpetrator of her unhappy circumstances.

# *Chapter Sixteen*

After a week, Hugo posted back to town full of purpose, as yet unaware of the events that had cast a rub into his plans. He paid his first call on Esme, hoping to find a friendly reception.

But Esme, feeling that every humiliation, disruption and rebuff she had experienced in the past weeks could be traced to the duke, was in no mood to greet him with charity. His sister's visit had further strengthened her determination to banish her tormentor from her life once and for all. So her demeanor when she marched into her parlor to greet him was far from encouraging.

"You are looking a bit fine drawn, my dear. Can it be that you have missed me?" he drawled as he bent over her hand.

"No, I have not, your Grace. In your absence I have suffered insults in the clubs, set-downs by my relations, and a dreadful visit from your sister," she raged.

He raised his eyebrows at this tirade. "Can we not at least sit down and discuss this budget of troubles before you continue to rake me over the coals?" he asked, indicating the sofa.

Esme glared at him, but found herself obeying his command. She was careful to chose a narrow slipper chair as far from the intimate settee as possible.

There was no denying Hugo was an attractive devil. He was dressed today in the most formal and correct garb, a midnight-blue superfine coat cut by that master Weston, cream kersey pantaloons, and a snowy cravat tied in the intricate mathematical style. As usual, he wore no jewelry other than a simple signet ring, and the buttons of his coat were of the most restrained sort. He followed the dictates of Beau Brummel in his dress, rather than those of the dandy set, for he needed no false aids to his imposing and muscular figure.

As Hugo's appearance registered, Esme could not help recalling those few tempestuous nights in Surrey. Neither Robert nor Oliver Wells had ever inspired such a response from her. She put this down to Hugo's superior expertise. Surely there was no other possible reason for her continual remembrance of their brief liaison, even to the point of losing sleep at night.

Hoping that her emotions were not mirrored in her face, she decided that it behooved her to adopt a cool, reasoning attitude rather than a shrewish display of temper which no doubt merely amuse him.

"I see it was a mistake for me to give you the opportunity to brood over my misdeeds, but I had a noble purpose in visiting my estates," the duke teased, not at all put out by her inimical silence.

"I am sure your estates are no concern of mine, Your Grace," Esme returned sharply. She would not be cozened into a better frame of mind.

"On the contrary, if you become my Duchess, they certainly will be. And I thought it behooved me to put in train some new furnishings for what will become our nuptial chamber," he said blandly.

"Our nuptial chamber!" Esme gasped.

Hugo waited for a moment, watching her from beneath his hooded lids, noticing with pleasure the rapid rise and fall of her bosom beneath the severe blue silk gown she was wearing. Well, Hugo thought with a curious pang, at least he had stirred some reaction beyond anger and irritation. "When I last suggested we might deal well together as husband and wife, you

175

seemed more insulted than pleased, but now that you have had some time to absorb the idea, I must plead my case once again. Is is the perfect solution to all your difficulties. Just think! You will be able to thumb your nose at society, if that is your wish. And you will have a most exciting and appreciative bed partner, who will hope to recapture all the delights we enjoyed on our first forays into passion." He smiled ironically at Esme's confusion at his blunt reminder of those nights in Surrey.

But before he could assume a certain satisfaction, she rushed into speech. "I might remind you, Duke, that such a solution would not be necessary if you had not behaved like a cad and a libertine in the first place. And even if I were inclined to treat your offer seriously, you are hardly a suitable husband. As a lover, you have—I admit—a certain undeniable appeal, but for any more lasting relationship I fear you would be a dismal failure. I would not want a husband who would stray before the month was out, and no doubt you would be quite quickly bored with me within that time. Perhaps you feel a measure of guilt for abducting and seducing me, but that is hardly a basis for marriage. I am surely not the first respectable virgin you have seduced. Do you appease your conscience by offering each of them marriage?" She gazed cooly at the negligent figure who lounged opposite her with the maddeningly smug expression. Even if she were dying of love, she would not give him the satisfaction of accepting him, Esme concluded, her reasoning somewhat muddled. Suddenly it seemed most important that he should realize he could not always have his way, although she had a niggling suspicion she would regret turning him down in such a summary fashion.

His dark eyes narrowed, and he looked at her in a manner she found most unnerving. "Now that you have expressed yourself so forcibly, and relieved all that emotion, perhaps we can consider the matter in a more prosaic light. Such an excess of emotion is so fatiguing and apt to cloud the issue." He protested in the mildest of tones, but Esme suspected that his

176

bland words disguised an anger as great as her own. She had pricked his self esteem, and he would not countenance that. "I don't want to marry you. And I won't! You can hardly drag me to the altar," Esme protested, wondering if he would do just that, in order to get his own way, ignoring any of her objections or feelings.

"Really, Esme, you are behaving in a very tiresome manner. I suppose you would acquiesce with more amiability if I confessed to an undying love, to the passion which transports poets, if I professed that my life would be ruined if you refused me. I doubt if you believe such fustian. I need an heir, and I have had enough of casual affairs. We suit very well, share an interest in art, and are compatible in bed."

"I'll thank you not to make further reference to that episode, Duke. It is most unchivalrous of you to do so. There is only one reason for marriage, and we do not have that." Esme's voice shook with emotion.

The truth was, she was closer to accepting his far-from-empassioned proposal than she would ever have thought possible. Only the thought of a union based on mere physical desire restrained her. He would own her body and compel her with the force of his expert, if soulless lovemaking. No doubt he would get her with child, abandon her in the country, and return to his hedonistic pursuits in town. She knew she could not endure that, although she could not have explained why. Far better to marry a lesser man who would respect and protect her, provide domestic tranquility. A society marriage—one undertaken to protect her reputation, to provide an heir—was not a choice that appealed to Esme. She would be sacrificing her piece of mind, control of her life and her art, her very independence.

Suddenly that independence seemed a bleak comfort to Esme, and she longed for the peace that had been hers before this ruthless rake invaded her life. Frowning, she rose to her feet, unaware that her face revealed her hard-won decision to Hugo.

"So you would choose to continue your nun's life in this retreat," he said tightly. "To while away a few innocuous hours with tame pups like your cousin Robert or that callow young officer whose been dangling after you. How long can you live like that?—you, a woman made for passion. And you are that; I have seen it in your painting and I have experienced it first-hand, although you would have me forget that. Well forgive me if I do not intend to live a monk's life. I will pursue my pleasures elsewhere."

"Yes, I hope you will do exactly that," Esme said in a shaking voice. "Good day, Your Grace."

As the Duke passed her, he suddenly stopped and swept her into his arms. He kissed her brutally, then released her with an ironic bow.

Esme turned her back on the sight of him leaving her house, her hand pressed to her swollen lips. Tears of indignation, humiliation, and loss rendered her helpless. Suddenly she saw Bessie's appalled face before her.

"My poor lamb, what has that dratted man said to you, to leave you in such a state? Come, now have a nice lie-down, and Bessie will fix you a cup of tea," the woman clucked, steering Esme toward her bedroom. Although feeling both ashamed and hopeless, Esme allowed herself a small smile. Bessie thought a cup of tea and a nice lie-down could solve all of life's problems.

The duke did not have recourse to a cup of tea and a nice lay-down, but tried to banish an equal sense of loss in the time-honored masculine fashion of downing as many glasses of brandy as possible and ending the evening with some roistering fellows at Kate Hamilton's establishment. There, as a valued customer, he was received by her lady birds with flattering eagerness, but found himself unable to summon up any interest in the delectable lovelies offered up for his amusement.

He awoke the next morning with a dreadful head and the memory of Esme's beautiful face to taunt him. This put him in a black humor, causing his secretary and staff to tiptoe warily about the house in Grosvenor Square. Finally, he took himself off to call on his sister, Lady Hansford, for if he could win no satisfaction from Esme, he could at least inflict his anger on a more accessible victim.

If Esme believed that she had at last settled the business of Hugo Carstairs to her satisfaction, this belief was not shared by Lady Poole. If she were to wring a proposal from Hugo she must deal with Esme Sedgewick, for the gossip about the pair had now assumed serious consequences. The *on dit* in the clubs was that Hugo Carstairs was fairly cuaght and by the most unlikely sort of woman.

The beau monde loved a mystery, and there was certainly a great deal left unexplained in the relationship between Esme Sedgewick and the outrageous duke. Lady Annabel wanted to gnash her teeth when she was twitted over the defection of her former cavalier by such spiteful gossips as Lady Jersey, but she assumed a bland mask of indifference and turned the comments aside with a careless laugh. "Oh, that's just like Hugo, always breaking hearts. It's rather amusing but not of any consequence," she tossed off airily.

Inside, she was burning with rage. Hugo had not answered a note she had sent around to his house. If Hugo Carstairs was at last considering remarrying then his choice of bride would not be Esme Sedgewick, if Lady Annabel could prevent it. After some thought, she summoned her cousin, Gerald Beaumont, to an interview.

She looked with some approval on the engaging young man as he entered her drawing room. Yes, he would do very well, for he was well nigh irresistible to the fair sex. Tall, slender, blue-eyed, with a shock of wheat-blond hair and a tanned face, he had proved the ruin of many a female. His reputation was nearly as fearsome as Hugo Carstairs's, but he lacked Hugo's considerable assets. He was always in dun street, and even now had just returned from a repairing lease in Devon after a particularly bad run of luck at the tables.

"Ah, beauteous Annabel! You are in fine fettle, as always. And what do you want with my humble self?" He greeted her with an audacious smile as he bowed over her hand.

"Why should I want anything, Gerry? Can I not just enjoy your company?" Lady Poole raised a haughty eyebrow in reproof. She needed Gerry but had no illusions about him. She would have to go carefully. He could be led but not driven, and even for a healthy allowance, he might balk at her plan.

"I have a little chore that should be quite simple for a man of your talents, Gerry, and I am willing to pay handsomely if you can bring it off. But it will require some subtlety." Annabel frowned at him. Gerry needed careful instructions, for he could overset the cleverest ploy on a whim or through an excess of boredom. Despite being always in perilous financial condition, he could still cozen his tailor and bootmaker into providing the latest rig. Today he wore a garnet coat with silver buttons, a splendid embroidered waistcoat, and pantaloons of the most subtle cream. His half-boots were polished beyond criticism, and his jewelry was in the best of taste.

How he managed she did not know, or care. But he might be able to solve all her difficulties and in the end, be instrumental in securing the Milbourne coronet for her. Esme Sedgewick must be routed and Gerry would be the means.

## Chapter Seventeen

Emerging from her lesson with Joseph Turner the day after her disturbing interview with Hugo Carstairs, Esme felt in somewhat better spirits. While she was painting and discussing art with the eminent artist she was able to banish from her mind the disturbing erotic pictures of a different sort that remembrance of Hugo brought her.

She paused for a moment on the busy avenue, searching for a hackney to convey her to Bond Street where she intended to indulge in a splurge of shopping. She did not notice the ruffian who approached her until the man had grasped her arm and attempted to tear away her reticule.

Struggling, she tried vainly to escape, the man's fetid breath and rough handling threatening to overcome her. But before the man could rob her, he was wrested away by a tall gentleman, who gave him a flush facer, which sent him to the ground cowering.

Gasping with relief, Esme looked up at her rescuer gratefully. She saw a tall, smiling gentleman with startling blue eyes gazing at her with concern.

"Has this villian harmed you in any way, ma'am?" he asked, evidencing more than concern in his look of obvious admiration.

"Oh, no, sir. Your intervention was most timely," she

assured him. He smiled reassuringly, and turned to deal with the man, who had taken the opportunity to stagger off from the pair.

Esme, was profuse in her thanks to her unknown rescuer. "How providential that you were passing, sir. That man intended to rob me," she said, settling her shawl around her shoulders with a slight shudder.

"What can your relatives be thinking of, ma'am, to allow you to travel unaccompanied on London's streets? You are a temptation to any villain who might be roaming about looking for just such an opportunity," he chided, but his eyes showed admiration rather than censure.

"I am my own mistress, sir," she answered with simple dignity. "I have been making this journey for some weeks in safety. One does not expect varlets of that type to be roaming in such respectable haunts. I was taken quite by surprise. I am Esme Sedgewick, and may I know the name of my rescuer?"

"Gerald Beaumont, at your service, Miss Sedgewick, And now that we have introduced ourselves may I escort you wherever you were bound?" he asked engagingly.

"Alas, I am bound for the shops, and I cannot think that would appeal to you, but if you would be so kind, you can summon a hackney for me," she asked, smiling up into his guileless blue eyes. He was certainly a handsome fellow, well-set-up and dressed in the latest rig, a well cut black coat showing off his shoulders. And his tanned face spoke of a healthy outdoor life. His name meant nothing to her, but perhaps he was a country man, up in the town from his estates.

"You could not be so unkind as to turn me off when we have only just met. Come now, do allow me to escort you. I assure you I am most skilled at advising on ladies' furbelows," he pleaded with an irresistible air. "I claim this privilege as a reward for rescuing you."

Esme laughed, amused by his cozening ways. "Oh, well, since you insist, I will have to submit. You are a most persuasive rogue," she protested.

"Thank you, Miss Sedgewick. You have brightened my day. I was anticipating a very dull visit to London, but your kindness has persuaded me I must have a guardian angel watching over me," he replied, shepherding her into a carriage which he had hailed with expert assurance.

Shaking her head at his audacity, Esme allowed herself to be helped into the conveyance and they were on their way. She wondered a bit at her acquiescence. It was unlike her to be so easily persuaded.

Some hours later, over a delectable luncheon at Gunters in Berkley Square, she teased him over his knowledgable acquaintance with ladies' fripperies. He had taken the most flattering and assiduous interest in her purchase of trimmings and ribbons in the Pantheon Bazaar and then advised her with wicked amusement on a fetching bonnet she had seen in a milliner's window in Bond Street.

Now that their acquaintance was firmly established, Esme had decided he was a most obliging gentleman with none of the heavy-handed gallantry nor annoying flirtatious ways of the fashionable men about town. She refused to compare him with Hugo, for she had decided that the sooner she abandoned thoughts of that disturbing gentleman the happier she would be. Gerald Beaumont was a sophisticated companion with an amusing turn of conversation. She wondered a bit about his background. He appeared to be plump in the pockets, and a man of some experience and taste, but he was not forthcoming about himself. He seemed intent instead on learning all about his companion, which was very flattering to Esme after her recent duels with more obdurate men.

She thanked him prettily for the luncheon and his rescue as they prepared to leave the confectioners.

"Although we have met in such an adventurous manner, I hope I may be allowed to call upon you. I would hate to lose sight of such a fascinating lady. I have never known an artist before," Gerald said as he led her from the shop.

"I could not be so unkind as to refuse such a brave

gentleman," Esme teased, half in earnest. She found his company soothing to her self-esteem. "I will give you my address."

"Perhaps you will honor me by allowing me to escort you to the theatre?" he asked as they once again boarded a hackney. "Kean is appearing in 'MacBeth' at the Haymarket tomorrow evening. Do you enjoy Shakespeare?"

"Oh, inordinately! And I have not seen Kean's MacBeth, I did see him in 'Hamlet,' but it was not so suited to his talents. His MacBeth, however, should prove most interesting. He is a powerful actor. I would be delighted, Mr. Beaumont," she consented, ignoring the impropriety of agreeing to an invitation from a stranger whom she had met in such an unconventional way. She had always given in to impulse, and somehow this man was a tonic to the depression that had haunted her since the episode in Surrey.

He escorted her home but refused her invitation to take tea, and left her with the sally that he was living for the moment they met again.

Gerald sighed with satisfaction as he rode away from St. John's Wood. It had all gone surprisingly well. He had planned the introduction to Esme with skillful contrivance. The robber, a low type he had found with little difficulty in London's stews, had been well worth the guineas he had paid. Now he appeared a fine fellow in the attractive Miss Sedgewick's eyes and he was clever enough to captialize on his advantage.

He could quite see why Annabel feared the lady as a rival to whomever she had set her determined sight upon. Esme was an uncommon type and must be an attractive antidote to Annabel's grasping selfish temperament. He would make it his business to find out who the man in question was. He thought this interlude might prove more than entertaining.

The evening at the Haymarket lived up to both Gerald and Esme's expectations. Kean's "MacBeth" proved to be all that the much-heralded actor's performance had promised, both engrossing and menacing, convincing in every detail. Gerald had secured a box with Annabel's assistance and set out to make his companion at ease with him. It was fortunate that he did not at once notice the gentleman in the box opposite them glaring throughout the latter acts of the play.

Hugo Carstairs had invited a group to the theatre that evening as a way of escaping from his restlessness and his nagging thoughts of Esme. Annabel Poole was among the company and used her opportunity well, trying to beguile Hugo with her considerable charms. Although he seemed distracted and indifferent, she was not discouraged. She had noticed with approval her cousin's attentions to Esme Sedgewick, and pointed out the pair to her host.

"There is my cousin Gerry, across the way, with a most attractive lady. I wonder if he has set up a new mistress. He seems quite *epris*," she suggested slyly to Hugo, noting his furious stare with mixed emotions. It was as she suspected. He found the annoying Esme Sedgewick of inordinate interest. Well, Gerald would prove a formidable rival. There were few women who could resist him when he set out to charm. Why should this annoying soi-dísant artist be any different?

"I doubt that Esme Sedgewick is his mistress," Hugo growled. Damn the girl, he thought as he watched the two conversing lightly, Esme all smiles and agreeableness. She never responded to him that way.

"Oh, is that who she is?" Annabel replied archly, not at all dissatisfied with his reaction. "And why could she not be his mistress? She has a dreadful reputation, as I am sure you know," she continued in an insinuating manner. She was not quite prepared to question Hugo about his own relationship with the girl. He might tell her more than she wanted to hear.

But Hugo, suddenly recollecting himself, was not to be drawn out. "She is Cranford's niece, and her breeding is as good as your own, Annabel, not the sort to be taken in by a ne'er-do-well like Beaumont." He replied smoothly, never taking his eyes from the couple in the box, his expression

185

inscrutable. This was a turn-up, he thought. How had Esme met that bounder? And how did she feel about him? They seemed uncommonly intimate.

"Her breeding may be impeccable, Hugo, but she has been turned away by her relations, I understand, and not without cause," Annabel said, then realized she was revealing more than she intended. She knew that Hugo was the model for *The Tyrant*, or at least that was the *on dit*, but she would not be so foolish as to tax him with that information.

"Is there nothing so vicious as *ton* gossip?" Hugo responded bitterly. Then, as if bored with the topic of Esme's reputation, he rose and suggested they take a stroll before the next act began. Annabel accepted with alacrity, taking his arm in a possessive hold, which he noticed with a lift of his eyebrow. She chattered gaily as they walked, greeting friends, and pretending not to notice Hugo's distrait air. He was searching for some sign of Esme, Annabel knew, but evidently she preferred to remain in their box, beguiled by Beaumont.

Gerald, in fact, had been trying gently to persuade her to venture forth. But Esme had seen Hugo with the luscious Lady Annabel and had no wish to encounter him in the theatre lobby. Several young bucks, obviously Gerald's cronies, visited them in the interval, and she did not like their encroaching manner toward her. Although nothing overt was said, she could not help but notice that they looked her over as if she were a bit of prime blood.

Gerald noticed her frown of displeasure and her aloofness, and hurriedly dispatched his friends, ignoring their avid and questioning glances. If Esme was the subject of gossip, he would protect her from the rumor mongers, he implied. His attentions became even more courteous and gallant. Esme, not aware of his conclusions, haughtily refused to make any explanations, but the evening lost some of its enjoyment. And Hugo's presence in the box opposite did not add to her ease. She had recognized Lady Annabel and concluded somewhat cynically that Hugo had lost no time in finding a replacement

186

for her. For that she should be grateful, but she found herself resenting his cavalier transfer of interest. Certainly if he was sincere in wanting to marry, Lady Annabel was much more suitable for the position of his duchess than was Esme. But although Esme tried to dismiss her unaccountable pique, she was not successful.

The sight of Hugo and Lady Annabel in such intimacy cast a pall over the rest of the play and when Gerald suggested a supper, she pleaded a headache and insisted on going home. As they waited outside the theatre for their carriages, Esme suddenly felt the back of her neck prickling and turned as Hugo greeted Gerald.

"Good evening, Beaumont. Did you and your companion enjoy Kean's 'MacBeth?'" he asked, giving Esme the most cursory glance in which indifference mingled with a certain disdain. She stiffened and returned his enigmatic gaze cooly, her heart pounding.

"Very much, but Miss Sedgewick has a headache, I am conveying her home," Gerald replied easily. "You do know Miss Sedgewick, Carstairs," he ventured tentatively, uneasily aware of strange undercurrents, and noticing Esme's restlessness at the encounter.

"Oh, Miss Sedgewick and I are old friends, or should I say sparring partners?"

"Good evening, Duke. Did you not find Kean masterful?" Esme responded with more assurance than she felt, ignoring his inference. She nodded haughtily to Lady Annabel, who received her greeting with a condescending air.

"The man is a poltroon, but he can act," Hugo replied. "I had no idea you knew Beaumont, Esme," he added, his curiosity overcoming his prudence.

"We met under exceptional circumstances," Esme explained curtly, unwilling to continue this uncomfortable conversation and hoping that Hugo would take the hint. She should have known better.

"You seem prone to exceptional circumstances," Hugo

187

came back outrageously.

"Really, Hugo, what can you mean? You are embarrassing Miss Sedgewick with your barbed remarks," Lady Annabel interjected, annoyed at the allusions Hugo was making.

"I believe this is our carriage. Delightful to see you, Annabel, Carstairs. I will be calling on you soon, Annabel," Gerald warned, to his cousin's discomfiture. She did not want Hugo or Esme to think there was anything more than casual cousinly relations between them, but Gerald seemed remarkably obtuse this evening.

"Such a pleasure and a surprise, Esme, meeting you again," Hugo said casually as Gerald turned to help Esme into the coach.

Esme hurried into the sanctuary of the carriage with Gerald losing no time behind her.

"Really, Hugo, you quite annoyed Miss Sedgewick with your strange manner. I had no idea you were so well acquainted," Annabel pouted, knowing she should keep a still tongue but unable to repress her jealousy.

"Miss Sedgewick and I are more than mere acquaintances, as I am sure you know, Annabel. Surely you are up to the latest rigs and have learned that I am supposed to be the model for her provocative portrait, *The Tyrant*, which has all of the *ton* agog."

Annabel was saved from an injudicious reply by the arrival of the duke's crested carriage. She stepped hurriedly into it, tightening her lips with anger. Then she purred winsomely at Hugo and tried to regain the ground she felt she had lost. She would not be discouraged by Hugo's mocking air. She had not lost him yet.

Gerald was almost as silent as Esme on the ride to St. John's Wood. The recent uncomfortable encounter had cemented his suspicions that Hugo was the man Annabel intended to shackle. Gerald was no coward and he had a tested faith in his own ability to win a woman, but Hugo Carstairs was not a man with whom he wished to compete. He had come to respect

Esme and to rue his involvement in this plan of Annabel's. If he weren't in such desperate financial straits he would tell his cousin to go to the devil. For once in his heedless life Gerald Beaumont suffered some compunction for his careless philosophy. He sensed he had entered dangerous waters, where his insouciant disregard for the well-being of others would not serve him well.

For her part, Esme chided herself for her deep malaise, a feeling of desperate unhappiness which the unexpected encounter with Hugo and Lady Annabel had induced. How could she be such a fool as to care that Hugo had transferred his interest to a woman who would not give him anything but the most cursory affection? The Lady Annabel was a grasping shallow shrew who masked her true character with a bland beauty which ensnared men and left her untouched, Esme concluded spitefully. Then she sighed. What difference did it make? Hugo had lost his desire for her, for desire was all it had been, and perhaps he deserved to be captured by Lady Annabel. They should suit, both cynical, worldly-minded and incapable of any true regard for one another. She should be content with the friendship of men like Gerald Beaumont and Oliver Wells from whom she would receive courtesy and respect, not the possessive passion which was Hugo Carstairs' reaction to her.

Somehow she could not bring herself to rejoice over the conclusion of her affair with Hugo. In compensation for her low spirits, she thanked Gerald for the evening with such feeling that he was convinced he had made a favorable impression on the lady—for which he was uncommonly grateful.

# Chapter Eighteen

"Has your new beau displaced Lieutenant Wells in your affections, Esme?" Fannie asked, unable to suppress her curiosity. She had just met Gerald Beaumont across the tea table.

"Not at all. I am very fond of Oliver, but I find Gerald most amusing. Did you not think he was attractive?" Esme teased her cousin, noticing that Fannie had blushed and seemed uncommonly confused.

"I thaink he is overly fond of himself and a practiced philanderer," Fannie replied sharply. Then recollecting that perhaps her cousin found her new friend more to her taste than Oliver Wells, she apologized. "I do not mean to criticize, Esme, but you surely cannot prefer Mr. Beaumont to Oliver, who is so worthy and devoted." Fannie dropped her eyes. She could not admit to Esme how taken she was with the officer. After all, he was obviously in love with Esme and treated *her* much like a younger sister.

"Oliver is a fine young man, but a bit unsophisticated, don't you think?" Esme offered, eyeing Fannie with a sudden understanding. Could her cousin be attracted to Lieutenant Wells? They were very well-suited, except for a disparity in their positions, but Esme cared nothing for that. She feared that her aunt and uncle would force dear Fannie into an alliance based on prestige and property, ignoring the girl's gentle warm spirit and leading her to great unhappiness. Fannie could never stand up to an arrogant careless husband who left her to her own devices while he followed the usual amusements of society.

"Lieutenant Wells is so kind and comforting. He never criticizes me," Fannie admitted shyly. "I know that often he would prefer to be alone with you, but he never is impatient when I am included in your outings, or makes me feel like a gooseberry!"

"And he had better not. You are a dear girl, and a loyal cousin. Your concern for me is typical of your warm heart, Fannie, for I know your parents, and probably Robert, have chided you unmercifully for not ignoring your disreputable cousin." Esme was touched by the girl's devotion to her.

"As if I would desert you because of a lot of unfounded gossip," Fannie said with some indignation, placing her tea cup down noisily. "Robert is behaving dreadfully, no doubt because you refused him. He is as bad as the parents, implying you are some sort of light skirt intent on luring men into your toils and then ridiculing them. I have taken him to task for his attitude but he never listens to me!"

"Robert had some mistaken idea that we might suit, but it is only a passing fancy. He will recover," Esme said gently, her eyes clouded for she regretted hurting Robert.

"Well, that might be, if he ever abandons that brass-faced creature I saw him driving in the park yesterday, but still he has no call to treat you like a pariah, just because you would not accept him. He's a sapskull, and bound for deep trouble if he doesn't mend his ways," Fannie said with all the frankness of a put-upon sister. "He should go back to Dorset and make a push to wed Anne Harcourt. You remember her, Esme, our neighbor and a lovely girl who has always fancied Robert. She will make her come-out next year and be snapped up by some fortune hunter, no doubt, for she is an heiress as well as handsome. Then Fannie moaned, her own fate overwhelming her, for she had received no offers and her parents were most disgusted with her.

"You will find a husband, Fannie, if that is what you want. I must confess I find this parading of young girls on the Marriage Mart heartless and disgusting. It is so deameaning, treating them like cattle," Esme fumed.

"Well, it's the custom, and how else can we meet men but by undergoing the Season?" Fannie looked at her cousin with admiration. "Not that you seem to have any trouble meeting men, Esme. There is Mr. Beaumont, and Oliver, of course, and even that wretched rake Hugo Carstairs. Do you still see him?" Fannie asked artlessly. She dearly wanted to know how Esme felt about the duke, although she refused to believe the gossip concerning them.

"Hugo Carstairs has no place in my life, and he is certainly not a fit subject for a girl of your tender years to be discussing," Esme reproved sharply. Then, realizing how critical she sounded, softened her tone. "I do not mean to be so mean-spirited with you, Fannie. I am sure you have heard all the talk about *The Tyrant*. There is some truth in the *on dits*, but I cannot explain matters to you. I regret sounding so mysterious, but be assured, Hugo Carstairs is not a factor in my life," Esme spoke with more firmness than truth. She could not confide in her innocent cousin, for she feared losing Fannie's love.

But Fannie, appalled at her own temerity in suggesting that Esme could be at fault in any way, hurried to soothe matters. "Of course not, Esme! At any rate there seems to be some understanding between the duke and Lady Annabel Poole. They are seen together everywhere and an announcement is expected momentarily, I hear. I cannot like her. She is so haughty and pleased with herself. Of course, she *is* beautiful. Still, I don't believe she likes her own sex much," Fannie concluded with a perception Esme found surprising.

"You are no doubt quite right. But she and the duke should be a perfect match, for he, too, is the most arrogant of men, indifferent to finer feelings and completely selfish." Realizing she had said more than she ought, Esme turned the conversation to Lieutenant Wells.

Esme had noticed how well they got on together. Fannie did not show to best advantage among the usual gallants, but with Oliver she was her natural confiding self. Oliver was coming to take them to Astleys that evening and Fannie was eagerly anticipating the outing. Perhaps Esme might plead fatigue, she thought, and let them go alone, although if Fannie's parents learned of the outing, there would be trouble. Well, Esme would do her best. Fannie would find the military life much to her taste, and when Oliver grew tired of following the drum, she would be equally happy in the country. Why hadn't she realized before that was where Fannie's affections lay? Too occupied with her own problems, and too selfish to help her dearly loved cousin achieve happiness, she silently chided herself. Well, this was just the tonic she needed, to play matchmaker to a pair of fine young people, both too diffident to settle their own affairs. Hugo Carstairs would no doubt decry her rosy-eyed view of their future, Esme reflected darkly. But then what did his cynical opinion matter?

Hugo was discovering himself that his cynical views were giving him little satisfaction. The worldly Lady Annabel had begun to weary him, with her prosing and false signs of admiration. Granted, she was a beautiful woman but she had little else to recommend her. He had been a fool to allow himself to be entrapped in her toils again. And Emily was encouraging the match. Any scheme of his sister's immediately set up his hackles. If she thought that her approval set the seal on an alliance with Annabel she was much mistaken.

After his last encounter with Esme he had tried to dismiss her from his mind, arguing that she was an ungrateful shrew who would have made his life a misery if she had accepted his peremptory proposal. Serve her right if she ended up shackled to that puppy Oliver Wells, who would never dispute her will and bore her mindless within weeks of the nuptials. And if she thought that rogue Gerald Beaumont would offer marriage she had much mistaken her man. He wanted a mistress, not a wife, and Esme had made it quite obvious that role was not to her taste. In fact, there was something havey-cavey in Gerald's sudden interest in Esme, and Hugo determined to get to the bottom of it, not examining his own motives or his fury at her preference for a man who was as much a libertine as Hugo himself.

He took himself off to White's where he believed he might encounter the gentleman, while reviling himself for giving in to such a recourse. The blackguard should have been expelled from White's long since for his conduct was reprehensible, Hugo thought, then snorted at his own hypocrisy.

White's was uncommonly full for so early in the day, a situation Hugo viewed with annoyance. Alvaney, "Poodle" Byng and Sefton were already established in the famous bow window that overlooked St. James Street, making their usual acidulous comments about the passersby. But the trio of arbiters quickly transferred their attention to Carstairs as he entered the room.

"Ah, a rare visit by *The Tyrant*," Poodle Byng ventured maliciously, but not in a tone that could be heard by Hugo. He had no wish to challenge that gentleman's mercurial temper.

Hugo nodded formally at the trio but made no push to join them. He sank down into a chair far removed from the men and called for a bottle of brandy.

"Brandy so early in the day? Carstairs must be in a sad state," Alvaney remarked. A portly man, verging on the dandy in his dress, he could put down an encroacher with the greatest of ease, but he had a basically kindly nature despite his foibles. He had always rather admired Hugo for his indifference to the *ton's* rules, despite his own subservience to them.

"He is a veritable ogre," Byng lisped, always ready to criticize. "I find the man impossible." Byng had suffered several times from Hugo's acerbic sneers about his habit of riding through the park with his much-barbered poodle on the

194

seat of his curricle.

Frowning at his companion's comment, Alvaney excused himself. He then strolled over to Hugo, interrupting his reverie.

"Good afternoon, Carstairs. What brings you here so early in the day?" Alvaney sat down in a chair next to Hugo, and received a ferocious scowl in return for his mild question.

"I am looking for Beaumont, and thought he might have favored the club with his presence," Hugo muttered. He had no stomach today for idle conversation.

"Is that young puppy back in town?"

"He was at the Haymarket last evening."

"I thought he was still on a repairing lease at his ramshackle Devon estates. He's a downy one, though. May have come around. Not your taste, I would have thought." Alvaney was curious as to why Hugo Carstairs would be seeking out Beaumont. "Perhaps Lady Poole may give you his direction."

"No doubt, but I prefer to see him here," Hugo said shortly, not liking the reminder of the ubiquitous Annabel.

"There are several bets down about your forthcoming nuptials with the lady," Alvaney mentioned daringly, with a quizzical look at the duke.

"Some fools don't care what they do with their money," was Hugo's harsh response. He took a deep drink of the brandy in his glass.

Deciding that no more news would be forthcoming on the topic, and that his presence was not welcome, Alvaney stood up to take his leave. He could not resist one small riposte. "I understand *The Tyrant* has vanished from Gorton's gallery. Leicester was quite provoked. He wanted to purchase it, no doubt for Prinny."

"I bought the picture," Hugo informed him curtly, but with a look in his eye that challenged Alvaney to go no further.

"Yes, of course. Most sensible," Alvaney agreed, and scuttled away. He did not want to tangle with Hugo when he was in that mood. He hurried to rejoin his companions in the window.

Hugo sunk in the surliest of moods, finished his brandy, and was about to leave the club when the very man he wanted to meet entered the clubroom.

"I want a word with you Beaumont," he said in his silkiest tone, but one that brooked no argument. "Join me in a glass."

Gerald made his way relunctantly to his side. Hugo eyed the man with a cooly measuring gaze. He observed Gerald's discomfort, which only fuelled his belief that the man was up to something.

"How well do you know Miss Sedgewick, Beaumont?" Hugo asked boldly.

Gerald, convinced more than ever that Carstairs was the man whom Annabel intended to win, tried to retain an air of cool indifference, but was not completely successful. He knew too much about Hugo's famous temper.

"I met her on the first day of my arrival back in London. I did her a trifling service—rescued her from a varlet who intended to grab her purse outside the Royal Academy—and she was uncommonly grateful," Gerald said lightly, repressing a shudder as he wondered what the duke's reaction would be if he knew that Gerald had skillfully arranged that meeting to show him in his best light.

"She's a damn independent filly, always embroiling herself in some folly," Hugo muttered, annoyed that Gerald should have been allowed to play the hero.

"But a very attractive one, don't you think?" Gerald suggested with more audacity than sense. He would be wise to tread warily with Hugo, he knew, but he refused to be cowed.

Hugo's eyes narrowed. "She has very little money, you know, Beaumont. I doubt you could afford her."

"Ah, but the lady's charms make a fortune unnecessary!" Gerald replied gallantly, hiding his dismay. If Esme had been well endowed with worldly goods he might have succumbed to matrimony at long last. Although Gerald was a feckless rake, caring little for anyone but himself, Esme had touched some chord in him. He found himself wondering what it would be like to abandon his present style and settle on his estates, try to make them pay and renounce his past. But that way lay madness. No doubt he would soon be bored and hankering for all his old pursuits. Still, he'd wager she would be better off as his wife than as the casual mistress of Hugo Carstairs, for it was inconceivable that the duke had any other intent.

"I do not think the lady is interested in marriage, Beaumont, and if she were, there are others who could offer a more respectable match," the duke replied. If Esme wished for a husband to reform, *he* would offer the better bargain, Hugo mocked himself. He wondered if Beaumont was really serious in his pursuit of Esme.

"Surely you are not entering the lists, Carstairs. I always understood you were not a marrying man. In any case, your affections seem to be engaged elsewhere."

Hugo's lips thinned, and a hard, frightening look entered his eyes. "That is not your concern, Beaumont. And neither is Miss Sedgewick."

Gerald rose to his feet, unwilling to prolong the uncomfortable interview. No woman was worth facing Carstairs across a dueling field.

"My friendship with Miss Sedgewick, although of only the most ephemeral sort, need not cause you worry, Carstairs. I know when I am outmatched," he agreed suavely, bowed and took his leave, inwardly cursing at the poor figure he had cut.

He had learned why Annabel was so set on removing her rival, and before he renounced the whole idea he must confer with her. If he could oblige his cousin, and come out of the affair with his own consequence intact, he would not be averse to seeing the arrogant duke foiled in his plans for Esme, whatever they were.

He felt, for the first time, some compunction for using Esme thus. She deserved better than to be quarreled over by two shameless libertines. A conference with his intriguing cousin was clearly called for and Gerald lost no time in visiting the lady. She received him cooly, but he could sense she was impatient for a report of his progress. Well, she could wait for that. He had some questions himself.

"It was clever of you, Gerry, to secure Miss Sedgewick's company at the theatre the other evening. You work quickly. I am quite pleased with you, and do not rue the money spent on your indulgences," Annabel praised him. He certainly cut a figure any female would find fascinating. If she were not so closely related to him, and determined to wear a duchess' coronet, she might fancy him herself. Not that he was worthy of her, but he must be an exceptional lover. Few men would resist an overture from her, and today she had every reason to have faith in her abilities to attract. She looked elegant in a cerulean blue silk gown, lavishly adorned with lace, the low decolletage showing off her creamy bosom to perfection. Only her blue eyes, agate hard and scheming, revealed her true character.

"She was an easy mark," Gerald revealed, feeling ashamed at discussing the candid and beguiling Esme in such a way. But a man had his way to make and could not always afford the indulgence of a conscience. Whatever he felt for Esme, he needed Annabel's support, almost as much as she needed his, but now he felt in a more secure position to wield power of his own.

"I think you are chancing your luck with Carstairs, dear cousin. He might not be as susceptible to your particular appeal as you think," Gerald informed her a bit maliciously. Annabel's disdain of him had often riled him in the past and he rather enjoyed returning her gibes.

But Annabel was not to be goaded. "If you do your job as you should, I will have no worries," she said, not showing her surprise. She was not at all pleased that Gerald had somehow ferreted out her victim.

Gerald smiled at her discomfiture. "I thought there was something between Esme and Carstairs when we met at the Haymarket, but he has just warned me off in no uncertain

198

terms. I have come from a very enlightening interview with the duke just moments ago," Gerald admitted.

"You mean he told you to stay away from the chit?" Annabel pursed her lips in annoyance, her bland beauty turning almost ugly as she realized that her ploys might not serve.

"Yes, indeed. Whether his future includes the lovely Esme, I cannot venture a guess, but I doubt very much if he is considering asking for your own delightful hand," Gerald said with some spite. Annabel deserved a set-down for her haughty ways. "And even if he were not a serious entrant to the lists, I must advise you that I am not the only man involved with the lady. There is a very respectable, well set-up military officer who appears quite taken with Esme."

"Well, that is very satisfactory, but I should be surprised if this officer could offer you much competition. I am depending on you, Gerald. You might even marry the lady. She cannot expect much in the way of a husband with her reputation, and she might even be able to reform you," Annabel mocked, knowing how Gerald feared being shackled.

"She might indeed," he countered sincerely, to her surprise. She wondered what quality Esme had which seemed to entrance such different sorts of men.

"Well, marry her if you feel you can afford it. I might even offer you an allowance, but whatever you do, keep her from Hugo's attentions. If you cannot capture her as a mistress or wife within the next few weeks, I will have to employ more desperate measures to remove the chit," Annabel threatened, leaving Gerald with a lowering impression that she really intended to remove her rival by any means, even foul ones. He took himself off without more ado, promising nothing, for he had a sudden disgust of Annabel and his own role in her plots.

# Chapter Nineteen

"I have come to take you riding in the park," Hugo told Esme, ignoring the fact that she was obviously dressed for some prior appointment, and looking very appealing, too, in a dove-gray walking dress edged in darker braid. He had arrived as she was preparing to meet Oliver and Fannie at the British Museum, after a visit to Gorton's gallery. She had been both annoyed and surprised when Emma announced that the duke was on her doorstep.

"Your invitation is not only inopportune but foolish. In view of what has passed between us, I thought we had decided that any relationship between us was finished," Esme answered. She did not like the devilish glint in Hugo's eye. He was goading her for some reason of his own.

"You may have decided thus, dear lady, but I had different thoughts," Hugo replied suavely, flicking his crop against his booted legs impatiently as if to signify that he found her remarks foolish and time wasting.

Esme, who could not suppress a spurt of happiness at seeing the duke after so long an absence, would not lower her guard and put herself at his mercy. "Well, in your usual arrogant way you may have hoped to alter events, but for once you will be disappointed," she replied sharply, jerking on her gloves nervously, a mannerism not unnoticed by the duke. He gave an appreciative glance at her austere profile. Gad, she was a fetching female with her sun-streaked blond hair and her tilted gray eyes, which at the moment were shooting sparks of defiance at him. She made all other women seem tame and boring.

"What is this pressing appointment that takes precedence over a ride in the park? It's a lovely day, not at all suited for dull errands or dry business," he cajoled, looking down at her with a disarming smile, which created more havoc within her breast than she wanted him to guess.

"I must visit Joseph Gorton and then meet Fannie and Lieutenant Wells, for we intend to view the Elgin Marbles," she answered pertly. "Though what business it is of yours, I cannot conceive. At any rate, for me to be seen riding in the park with you at this fashionable hour would quite set up the gossips again."

"But that is just what I intend, my dear. Did you think I would so easily be persuaded to abandon you?" the duke responded suavely.

"Abandon me? What do you mean? I refused you!" she sputtered.

"Perhaps my choice of words was not felicitious. I stand corrected. But come, you can rake me over the coals to your heart's content as we tool down Picadilly. I will escort you to Gorton's myself, and then deliver you to the British Museum, although why you should want to see Elgin's pesky mutilated statues I cannot imagine," he mocked, taking her arm and quite dragging her to the door.

"Brute strength is a sure persuader," Esme agreed, surrendering. She could not find it in her power to deny Hugo, although he should be refused for his own good.

"That's a good girl. You really are a most forgiving creature, Esme. I had hoped I could presume on your good nature," he said with satisfaction.

"Have you given Gorton any more scurrilous paintings?" he teased as they drove toward Picadilly.

"If you mean have I painted any more portraits of you, you overestimate your influence on my life, Duke," Esme replied repressing a smile. He was impossible, but no other man made her feel so alive. "I delivered several landscapes to him the other day, and we must bargain over the price, which I loathe doing, but Mr. Turner had steeled me to the task. I cannot thank you enough for persuading him to take me as a pupil, for he has taught me a great deal. I wish I had his ability." Esme sighed, for her session with the artist had improved her work but not her confidence. She still had a great deal to learn.

"I hope he has behaved with respect toward you, Esme. He can be a terror with women," Hugo said. He had hoped that introducing Esme to Turner might be some recompense for what she had suffered at his hands. He realized that her painting was vital to her spirit.

"Mr. Turner has always behaved like a perfect gentleman, well except for losing his temper when I fail to grasp his instructions," Esme conceded with a laugh.

"Can you say the same of Gerald Beaumont?" the duke asked with a searching look at her.

"You must not judge others by your own licentious conduct, Hugo," Esme reproved primly, delighted at the chance to score off him.

"True, it is an unconscionable habit of mine. But what can you see in Beaumont? He has a certain specious charm, but little money and less sense."

"It must be the specious charm, a quality he shares with his cousin, Lady Annabel," she responded, then instantly regretted showing any interest in the duke's relationship with that grasping widow.

"Of course, the Beaumonts all have that ability to charm, and know how to use it, but there is little real merit in using the gifts God gave you. It is what you make of life's problems which is the true test," the duke agreed gently. "Your painting, for example, you might have been content just to daub away at some silly flowers and never realize the strength and power in

202

your talent."

Esme was surprised and pleased at his discernment. Whatever her confused emotions about Hugo Carstairs, she knew him for a connoisseur.

But before she could respond adequately, they had arrived at Gorton's Gallery. The obsequious owner greeted them effusively, masking his curiosity about the aristocrat's possessive manner toward Esme. There was certainly some relationship between the two and Gorton was enough of a pragmatist not to presume, but he sighed for his profits. The duke would see to it that Miss Sedgewick, unworldly when it came to a fair price for her work, was not cheated. And so it turned out. The duke inspected the two paintings of Hampstead Heath, which Esme had submitted to Gorton, and immediately bought one, postponing discussing the crass subject of money until a later time.

"I must inform Leicester of this other one. He will want it and I cannot be selfish," Hugo told the pleased Gorton. "But see to it that you insist on a good fee. Leicester can afford it. Miss Sedgewick has an uncommon talent, not perhaps Constable's quality but a very definite style worth rewarding." Hugo gave his impression haughtily, making Esme smile. She had no pretensions of genius, but Hugo's frankness bordered on arrogance. She had expected no less, and teased him when they had emerged from the gallery.

"You certainly can depress any illusions I have in no mean fashion, Hugo," she said but her laughing eyes showed she had taken no umbrage.

"You are a fine painter, but no Constable or Turner, my girl. I would be less than honest if I pretended otherwise," Hugo replied firmly.

"A fine painter, for a woman. At least you did not demean me by that remark," Esme agreed, accepting that whatever Hugo's arrogance, he did not denigrate her work because of her sex.

"Being a woman has nothing to do with it. But I will not

203

pander to your conceit further today, my dear. Let us by all means tool around to see these execrable pieces of marble, now. I abominate Classic ruins," he said in a disagreeable tone, but his sudden ill humor was not really exercised by Lord Elgin's marbles but by the thought that Esme had an engagement with her military johnny.

"Thank you, Duke, for your patience," Esme murmured, refusing to engage in any more verbal duels. She did not understand why Hugo was behaving in such a proprietary manner, agreeing to accompany her to an appointment he took in such dislike. Could he be loath to leave her to Oliver's mercies? Surely not. And then there was Fannie. Would the duke suspect that Esme intended to give her cousin every opportunity for attracting Oliver, and that her own interest in the young man was really only sisterly? Well, she must just be careful not to show her hand.

If she had not been so apprehensive about the meeting between Hugo, Fannie and Lieutenant Wells, she would have been amused. The young couple were overwhelmed, Fannie red and stammering and Oliver respectful to the point of embarrassment. Hugo, on the other hand, handled the introductions in his most adroit style, looking over Fannie kindly and saying, "I don't understand why we have not met before, Lady Cranford, or may I call you Fannie?" he asked, covering her with confusion.

"Of course, Your Grace," said Fannie. "I suspect you have just never noticed me at balls and routs. And you don't frequent Almack's," Fannie stammered, wondering how Esme could treat this august personage so casually.

To rescue Fannie before Hugo could give his no doubt scathing opinion of Almack's Esme introduced Oliver Wells.

"Ah, yes, lieutenant. I believe you met Miss Sedgewick in Tunbridge Wells, a most dreary water spot, I think. How fortunate you were to have Esme's company to relieve the tedium," he ventured with a straight face, although Esme suspected he had a meaning to his innocuous words.

"Yes, Your Grace. Esme, er Miss Sedgewick, had been so kind as to honor me with her friendship," Oliver said bravely. He, too, found the duke overwhelming, and wondered at his own temerity at offering for Esme when such a top-of-the-trees nobleman obviously was interested in her.

The oddly assorted quartet strolled about the hall looking at Lord Elgin's marbles. Fannie found them a bit shocking, but didn't dare voice such an opinion before the worldly duke. She confined her comments to whispered asides to Oliver. Esme, seeing the two in such easy companionship, was more sure than ever that they would deal very well together.

"Disappointed, Esme?" Hugo mocked, watching her as she viewed the statues with a professional eye.

"Not at all. The execution is masterly, even if time has vandalized the works. But I am not sure Lord Elgin should have removed them from their site. It seems a cruel fate for them to end up in this dusty hall when their glories should be displayed to the citizens of Greece."

"Such a romantic, dear girl. The peasants would probably have pulled them down eventually to build their hovels," was the duke's cynical reply.

"I am romantic about art, and make no apologies for it. But in my personal affairs I am most realistic," she reproved him, in a low tone, not wanting Fannie to hear their conversation. But that young lady was too engrossed with Oliver to pay much attention, and too intimidated by the duke to interrupt their tête à tête.

"I am glad to hear that. It makes my task easier, but somehow I do not see you as an ambitious, hard-hearted female," the duke replied lazily, eyeing her with a wicked smile. Then as if tiring of their duel, he said, "Do you suppose your gallant military cavalier might escort your cousin home? I still insist on the ride in the park, and we have wasted enough time here."

"You are a philistine, not the generous appreciator of art that I believed you to be. Shame on you for mocking these treasures! I am still reluctant to drive in the park. To abandon Fannie, the kindest and most loyal of cousins, would be most ungrateful."

The duke raised his quizzing glass and looked over the young couple with some hauteur. "They seem very well-suited. You had best leave the gallant officer to your cousin, for she seems quite *epris,* and he is hardly up to your weight, my dear. If I did not think it unworthy of you, I might believe you have dangled him before me to raise my jealousy, but then, such a ploy would not be in your style."

Esme could not help but laugh. "You are impossible." But she realized her spirits had risen during their interchange. Hugo Carstairs had the ability to make her heart sing, and even his cynical comments gave her a lift no other man had ever induced. If only matters had been differently arranged . . . she thought with a sigh.

Hugo Carstairs, heartened by her sudden acquiescence, was quick to take advantage of the situation. He called Lieutenant Wells and Fannie to his side, and suggested that they leave the museum.

"I think we have seen quite enough of Elgin's thefts. May I hope that you would escort Fannie home, Lieutenant Wells, as Esme and I have some important business to discuss," he insisted, leaving the officer little choice. He did not approve of the duke's cavalier attitude toward Esme, but she did not object and he was too timid to put himself forward and incur her displeasure.

"I promised mother I would be back for tea," Fannie interjected softly, not wanting to make any difficulties.

"Then, of course, you must go, Fannie dear, but do come by for luncheon tomorrow. I have something of importance to discuss with you. And Oliver, I know your duty calls, but no doubt we will see you before too long," responded Esme, fearing to expose Fannie to any of the duke's searching questions, and Oliver to one of his famous set-downs.

206

So the quartet left the museum to go their various ways, but Esme again demurred about the ride in the park.

"You know that at this hour every gossip in London will be promenading in the park. And when the likes of Lady Jersey sees you tooling me about, there will be an upsurge of all the rumors about *The Tyrant*," Esme warned as the duke handed her into his curricle.

"Just what I intend and what you deserve, my termagant," Hugo said with satisfaction, waiting for her explosion of anger, but she surprised him again.

"I don't understand you, Hugo. Certainly you cannot want all that talk to start up again just when affairs seem to have settled down," she protested, eyeing him with a severe look.

"I will quite enjoy being the object of all eyes," he said taking up the reins in a skillful manner, and avoiding her look.

"You deliberately court scandal, I think. But is it fair to embroil me in your dubious pleasures?" Esme pleaded. She did not like the idea of the *ton* whispering and nudging one another when they saw her so publicly in Hugo's company.

And she was not mistaken. Hyde Park at that hour was thronged with fashionable society promenading, and the couple was soon the object of much conjecture. Hugo, formally nodding to acquaintances, was oblivious to her discomfort as knowing eyes inspected the couple. Just like him, she thought, ignoring opinion and not bothering over her humiliation. Esme's anger, never long in abeyance when she was in Hugo's company, threatened to surface again. But she bit her tongue and faced her accusers proudly. She had no doubt of what they were thinking. Here was the notorious Duke of Milbourne showing off his mistress with his usual arrogance.

Hugo smiled, having a good idea of what she was thinking and waiting for the harsh words to fall on his head.

"You certainly are not playing the role of my inamorata with any pleasure my dear. Please try to arrange your quite beautiful face in more acceptable lines. The *ton* will believe you intend to murder me, not love me," he teased.

"I don't love you. Most of the time I find you abominable," Esme replied through gritted teeth. Then, to her dismay, she watched Lady Annabel and Gerald approach and signal they wished to stop and greet them.

"Why, Hugo, how odd to see you taking the air with all the dandies. Most unlike you," Annabel simpered. Her blue eyes narrowed at the sight of his companion. She nodded coldly in Esme's direction with a murmured, "Miss Sedgewick."

"Not at all. I am trying to reclaim my respectability, Annabel," Hugo replied blandly. He was not unaware of Annabel's proprietory tone, although he did not evidence his annoyance. The couples chatted in a desultory way for a few minutes, Gerald bending every effort to show his admiration for Esme, but Hugo soon put a stop to his gallantries.

"My horses are restive. You must excuse us," he said preparing to give rein.

But Annabel would not release him so easily. "I will see you at the Esterhazys this evening, won't I, Hugo?" she asked in her most dulcet tones.

Hugo dismissed her shortly. "I have other plans." He was not unappreciative of Esme silently fuming by his side, and he found the idea of her jealousy most heartening.

"You should not treat Lady Annabel in such an off-hand manner, Hugo. She is an Incomparable and not used to such rubbishy manners," Esme chided, although her instinct was to give him a resounding blow across his complacent face.

"She is not incomparable to me. I save that sobriquet for you, dear Esme. But you are so obdurate, my heart quite quails," he answered lightly. But his remark had an undertone she could not fathom. Could he be earnestly wooing her, with his heart engaged? For a moment Esme almost felt faint at the idea, but scorned her suspicion. Hugo had his own devious designs and she might wonder about them.

When he at last deposited her in St. John's Woods, she was very cool in her thanks for the outing.

"Adieu, dear lady. I will be seeing you again shortly, but perhaps I will leave you in expectation. So much more exciting!"

He laughed as she flounced through her door. Then he walked quickly down to his equipage and rode off without a backward glance.

# Chapter Twenty

"Oh, Esme, I was so ashamed. Mother and Father behaved so shabbily to Oliver. How could they treat him that way? Whatever they say, I will not obey them!" Fannie wailed, almost incoherent with anger and humiliation.

"Now, Fannie, this won't do. Calm yourself. Here is a handkerchief. Dry your eyes, compose yourself, and tell me what happened," Esme urged. Taking Fannie competently by her shoulders and giving her a reassuring hug, she led her to the sofa and settled quietly beside her, holding her hand in a comforting clasp.

"Mother met Oliver as he was bringing me home from our trip to the British Museum and, in her most haughty manner, implied that he was no fit escort for me—as if he were some fortune hunter or rakehell who had no business pursuing an eligible girl! It was dreadful! Oliver was quite polite, but he turned very red and then pale and I know he was astounded by her put-down," Fannie explained between gulps, and then as if she could not restrain herself: "He has been so kind and patient with me, Esme, never overstepping any bounds! I know he would prefer to be with you. He has never evidenced anything but the most polite interest in me, a kind of brotherly affection, and he doesn't make me feel stupid and unattractive. What could Mother be thinking of?"

Esme suspected she knew very well what Aunt Mildred was thinking, but she was determined not to make matters worse by exhibiting her own anger and dismay at this turn of events.

"Oliver is a perfectly respectable young man with only the most proper attitude, but alas, I feel his credentials are not imposing enough for your parents. They must believe you have a *tendre* for an unsuitable young man," Esme explained bluntly.

Fannie blushed and lowered her eyes as if afraid to confront her cousin, then blurted out her fears. "I know Oliver cares for you, Esme, and if you returned his regard I would be the first to offer you my sincere wishes for your happiness with him, but I believe you do not think of him in that way." Her voice wavered on the hopeful note she could not completely suppress.

"Dear Fannie, I admire Oliver as a friend, but have no warmer feelings toward him. He is a very exceptional young man and I understand is far from a fortune hunter. He is the only son of well-dowered parents in Somerset and could offer you a comfortable country life. I have thought for some time that his affection for you could deepen into a more meaningful relationship, and I have been pleased. He is just the husband for you," Esme insisted stoutly.

"But, Esme, it is you he wants for a wife," Fannie protested, a gleam in her tearful eyes.

"He is experiencing a boy's first infatuation, attracted by my unusual circumstances and the chivalrous thoughts of protecting me. You and Oliver have much more in common, and he is sensible enough to see that eventually. You would make a good wife for him and he would be a kind and devoted husband. He cares for you more than he realizes."

"Do you think so, Esme? I . . . I love him very much. He is so different from the fashionable beaux mother and father keep pushing my way. I suspect they feel they will never push me off except onto a gazetted fortune hunter, who will take me for my money and treat me badly. Lately they have been urging

211

that I see more of Lord Moreton, and he's a widower with four grown children—a nasty man with a lewd eye!"

"They cannot want to give you to that dreadful man," Esme protested, shocked. Did the Cranfords care nothing for Fannie's sensibilities?

"They just want me married and off their hands. But I will not accept Lord Moreton no matter what they do. I will run away!"

"It will not come to that, I am sure. Let me talk to Oliver."

"Oh, Esme, you would betray my feelings for him. I could not endure his pity," Fannie wailed, overset by a new bout of crying.

"Come now. You must be prepared to fight for your happiness. I promise I will not cause you any embarrassment. Now how did you escape to come here? I doubt if your parents are pleased at your continued association with me, and probably blame me for introducing you to Oliver," she said shrewdly. She confessed she would like to challenge the Cranfords in defense of her cousin who did not dare fight for herself. Fannie could easily be coerced into a tragic misalliance in an effort to please her parents, who had never understood or appreciated their daughter. Well, she would not let Fannie be forced into a loveless union like theirs, and certainly not with a man like Lord Moreton. But she must tread carefully and not arouse their animosity and suspicion.

"Now Fannie, I want you to return home and say nothing to rouse your parents' anger. Leave it to me. I will help you sort out this tangle, and I promise you, you will not wed Lord Moreton."

"Oh, Esme, you are so brave and independent. Why could I not be like you?" Fannie looked at her cousin with admiration untinged by envy.

"I am not a paragon, Fannie, dear, and have made several grievous mistakes, but I will not allow you to suffer if I can prevent it and I think I can. Now, you go home and play the meek daughter, and I will notify you when my plans are complete." Esme gave her another reassuring hug. "Appear to acquiesce with your parents' directions for you, and say nothing of your anger about their reception of Oliver. I will sort this all out," Esme concluded avoiding explaining just how she hoped to accomplish this.

"Thank you, Esme. I knew I could trust you to understand," Fannie said, immensely cheered. With Esme enlisted on her side, she felt she could face her parents, even deceive them. "You will not make me wait long, will you?" she pleaded, as she donned her bonnet and prepared to leave.

"No, Fannie. I will put affairs in train immediately," Esme promised, escorting Fannie to the door and signaling to her waiting abigail that her mistress was ready to take her departure.

"Thank you, Esme. You are a wonderful friend and cousin," Fannie replied, giving a watery smile. For a moment Fannie forgot her own fears wondering why Esme had not captured a husband. It must be that she did not want the ties of domesticity, although the spinster's life was not an enviable one, and certainly Esme was far too attractive not to have a number of men clamoring for her hand. Was she in love with the terrible Duke of Milbourne? How disastrous that would be, for even in her naivety, Fannie knew that the duke was not husband material.

After bidding Fannie an affectionate farewell, Esme returned to her sitting room and sat down at the secretary to pen a missive to Oliver. She would discover just how Oliver felt about her cousin and if what she thought were true, Fannie, at least, would gain happiness in marriage, even if such a felicity was beyond Esme's own hope. She wondered, as had Fannie, just what her fate would be if she accepted Hugo's careless proposal. He did not seem so eager. It had been several days since their last encounter.

Oliver was prompt to accept Esme's invitation to supper that evening, arriving a few minutes before the proscribed hour, and appearing to be his usual cheerful self.

213

Esme made no push to introduce the subject of the invitation, chatting easily to Oliver about his military life, and cleverly sounding him out on his estates and parents in Somerset.

"I am finding regimental life a trifle boring, not quite what I expected. I suppose if we were still fighting the French it would be more exciting—useful at least—but guarding the Tower, and the spit and polish of parades is not to my taste," Oliver conceded over the rhubarb tart and clotted cream. "Most ungrateful of me, I know, when my father was at such pains to secure my commission."

"Not at all, Oliver. You seem much more suited to country life. There is so much flummery and hypocrisy in London society, and you are too honest and wholesome to take to the japes and frivolity which concern most young men thrown on the town."

"But you like living in London," Oliver inquired wistfully, not denying her words.

"Not particularly, Oliver. I was brought up in Hampshire, and I love riding and sketching in the country. I stay in London for my art lessons and because the galleries are here. I do my best work in the country. I find its serenity a tonic," Esme confessed, then wondered if she had been wise, for Oliver might regard her preference as encouraging him to make another shy avowal.

"Somerset is lovely, too, and I feel the need to return. My father is ailing and really not up to running our modest estate," Oliver said, wondering if Esme meant she would be inclined to favor his suit. For some reason, he did not seem so eager to press his previous proposal again. Surely he had not fallen out of love with this admirable woman. From the beginning, Oliver had been aware that he was not up to her touch. She was too independent, too involved with her art, and too attractive to men who had so much more to offer, he admitted humbly. Sometimes, too, she made him feel inadequate and young, not qualities which would promise a happy union, for Oliver was

214

old-fashioned enough to expect a wife who would look up to her husband.

"Oliver, dear, I was very honored by your proposal of marriage, but I believe you have had some cause to regret your impetuous words," Esme suggested gently, looking at the candid young man with warm regard. "Be honest. You must know I would not make a comfortable wife for a country gentleman."

"You would make any man a wonderful wife, Esme, but I can quite see that I would not be worthy of you." Oliver blushed.

"A bad wife, but a good friend, Oliver. You must agree that that is the relationship you prefer with me. And I have reason to think that another woman has replaced me in your regard," she offered gently.

"I am not such a rubbishy fellow that I would repudiate a proposal which I once offered in good faith," Oliver insisted, embarrassed and appalled at the direction of the conversation. Did Esme mean she had changed her mind?

"I would not suggest that you are lacking in honor, Oliver, but I believe you are far more drawn to my cousin Fannie than you might be prepared to admit. She is a dear girl and would make you the perfect wife," Esme said carefully. She must discover how Oliver felt about Fannie, if he had realized how much he had come to rely on the girl's companionship and regard.

"She is a wonderful girl, so warm-hearted and such enjoyable company. She has always seemed to like me. But her parents do not approve of me," Oliver admitted with a combination of diffidence and anger. "Lady Cranford made that quite clear to me the other day."

"Aunt Mildred has never understood or appreciated Fannie. Now all she wants is to marry her off, and to a dreadful old lecher, twice her age, who would make her miserable. And I am afraid the Cranfords have the means to compel her, although I believe her affections are engaged elsewhere," Esme hinted.

"They could not do that, compel her to wed a man she detests!" Oliver replied, getting to his feet and pacing the room. He turned and faced Esme. "And who is the fortunate fellow she prefers?" he asked.

"I don't know . . . but I can guess. Who has she spent so much time with during the past weeks? Surely your modesty does not prevent you answering that question."

"You cannot mean that Fannie would accept me, Esme?" he asked, flushed with emotion. "It is true we have much in common, seem to have a meeting of minds, but I never suspected . . ." he stammered in his confusion. The idea did not seem at all repugnant to him, Esme noted with satisfaction.

"She is a girl of simple tastes, who has been very unhappy in the social round her parents have forced upon her," Esme said. "But with the right man she would be a contented and a conformable wife."

"Yes, Fannie has much to give some fortunate fellow. But I am afraid that her parents would never consider me," he mused, as if struck for the first time with the thought Esme had cleverly introduced. Unlike Esme, Fannie had never made him feel gullible, or ineffective. She looked up to him, depended upon him and generally made him think himself a fine fellow indeed. But his stubborn honor would not allow him to abandon Esme. After all, he had offered her marriage. He could not now turn away and decide that another more biddable female suited him better. That would be the behavior of a coward and poltroon, and Oliver despised himself for thinking, even for a moment, that Fannie would make a much more acceptable wife than the glamourous and unattainable Esme.

"Oliver, what you felt momentarily for me was just a brief infatuation. What you need is a wife who can respect you, look up to you, feel that you are the most wonderful man alive. I fear I would be a grave disappointment, even if I returned your affection," Esme explained carefully, not wanting to hurt Oliver's tender feelings, but determined to put forward Fannie's case. "You do not want a goddess on a pedestal,

216

Oliver, but a warm, loving companion, who would be honored to be your wife, run your home, bear your children. Come, now, admit that I am most unpromising material for such a role." Esme smiled as she looked at him, realizing the struggle of his conscience over his real desire.

"Oh, I know you would not have me, Esme, but Fannie deserves better than to be second choice." Oliver replied with a cast-down air.

"She would not be second choice, but the better choice. And if you are thinking of resigning your commission and settling down on your estates, you will need a helpmate."

"The Cranfords would never agree to my courting their daughter. Lady Cranford made no effort to hide her opinion of me," Oliver said, recalling the humiliating interview. "I could never approach Fannie's father."

"It is not Fannie's father and mother you would have to persuade. Fannie must seize her chance for happiness. I will help you," Esme said gently.

"We would have to elope, and that would bring scandal upon Fannie."

"Not at all. You could secure a special license, take her to your parents and be wed in your village church," Esme suggested with a practical grasp of the affair which surprised Oliver.

"I will do it. But first I must appraise my parents of my intention. Father will be pleased if I come home, although he would never urge me to abandon the regiment if he believed I really craved a military life," Oliver confessed. "He's a fine man and I would not want to disappoint him." Oliver blushed as he admitted his fondness for his parents, but that only impressed Esme with his real quality.

"You will know how to manage events sensibly, I am sure, Oliver, and you must put your case to Fannie at the first opportunity. I will leave you alone to approach her when your decision is made. You can rely on my assistance on every suit," Esme said with satisfaction. She had finally repaid Fannie for her cousin's loyal and loving support of her while her aunt and uncle and most of London had spurned and reviled her.

Hugo Carstairs would no doubt find her determination to meddle in Oliver and Fannie's lives amusing, but she cared nothing for his cynical attitude, so typical of the *ton's* concern with prestige and fortune. Fannie's tastes were simple, and she craved affection. Oliver would give her that and much more and, in return, have the benefit of a companionable and loving wife. Yes, she had been wise to spur him to this solution.

Oliver crossed to her and raised her to her feet, giving her an enthusiastic kiss on the cheek. "You are, as I said, an exceptional woman, Esme. I bless the day I introduced you to the waters at Tunbridge Wells!"

"I, too, am grateful, Oliver. I know you will be happy," Esme returned his salute with a warm smile. "And mind you, treat Fannie well, or you will answer to me," she teased.

"You will be our first visitor, to give your opinion of the match, Esme. And you will stand godmother to the heir," he replied, laughing as she gasped at his candor. But as he left her that evening full of ideas for his future, Esme was pleased to see that he had taken on the mantle of a responsible man with much to offer the girl of his choice, unaware that he had been maneuvered gently into the decision.

*Chapter Twenty-One*

With Fannie's future settled to her satisfaction, Esme could not escape wondering about her own. She felt restless, could not settle to anything, and even the hours spent at her easel did not bring any sense of accomplishment or relief. Finally, she admitted to herself she missed sparring with Hugo Carstairs, who had unaccountably disappeared from her life. Had he at last taken her rejection seriously and turned his attention to the more receptive Lady Annabel Poole?

His absence was a constant ache in the back of her mind, and she realized that she cared more for the devil than she had thought possible. She was honest enough to confess to herself that if he had renewed his suit she might have been persuaded into accepting him, for the empty days and nights looming ahead suddenly seemed desolate and lonely. Was she foolish enough to have fallen in love with a rakehell who could never be faithful to any woman?

Ruefully she owned that it must be the case. She loved him. In the silence of her bed, during the sleepless nights, she recalled his tempestuous lovemaking, and yearned for those passionate hours in Surrey. How could she be lost to all sense and decency to wish for a renewal of their relationship? But Esme had never deceived herself, and, too late, she realized that even a solely physical relationship with the ruthless, selfish duke was better than this mindless wanting.

If she had known that Hugo was keeping his distance, hoping for just such a decision on her part, her anger and disgust with herself and him would have returned. But Hugo was keeping his own counsel, determined to conquer the citadel, convinced that Esme would eventually see where her true feelings lay. He ignored the bets laid down in the clubs that within weeks his engagement to Lady Annabel Poole would be announced. If Esme heard the rumors, he hoped it would give her pause, make her realize where her confused actions were leading. But he was neither impressed nor influenced by the marital schemes of Annabel and his sister, Emily.

Emily had called on Hugo early one morning, catching him at breakfast where he was trying to ignore the effects of a night of heavy debauchery. He scowled at her as she sailed into the room.

"Well, Hugo, you do not look at all the thing. All this carousing will be the death of you!" Emily announced.

"Probably," he conceded, pushing aside his dish of shirred eggs, which he viewed with repugnance. Although his dark, saturnine face appeared drawn and tired, his dress could not be faulted. His linen was white and pristine, his well-fitting coat of midnight blue superfine stretched over massive shoulders displaying to advantage the powerful physique he treated with such indifference. He frowned at Emily, wondering why his sister caused him such irritation. She was not an unhandsome woman, having inherited her share of the Milbourne looks, but both her manner and her values vastly annoyed Hugo.

"Hugo, it is past time for you to be indulging in dissipation and riotous living. You should think of your name and responsibilities. You should be settling down and producing a family, an heir to your considerable estates," Emily said.

"I have every intention of doing so, but perhaps, not for your prosy reasons," Hugo replied. He and his sister had never been close, and her obvious disapproval grated on his senses. He knew exactly why she had made this damnable visit. Well, she would get little change from him.

"When are you going to offer for Annabel?" she blurted out, unable to restrain her satisfaction that at last he was heeding her advice.

"That is surely my business, not yours, Emily," he replied silkily, amused at her efforts to coerce him into an admission of his intentions. Poor Emily, so impressed with her consequence and so amazingly prosaic.

"Of course, it's my business. I have some family feeling, even if you seem lamentably lacking in that respect," she said, her temper rising despite her efforts to remain cool.

"Do you believe that Annabel would acquiesce in producing this much-desired heir?" Hugo mocked, amused at her championship of a lady he believed incapable of any deep affection. He knew Annabel for what she was. Her breeding and beauty did not disguise her ambition or her grasping nature. She made an acceptable bed partner, but in every other way she was wearisome, conceited, empty-minded and possessed of the instincts of a whore.

"She would, of course, do her duty. And she would make an exceptional chatelaine for the abbey," Emily persisted. She smoothed her gloves nervously over her fingers, wanting to pursue the matter, but fearing to put up Hugo's hackles.

"I am not sure I like the idea of bedding the luscious Annabel for duty's sake," Hugo responded thoughtfully, remembering some past encounters with the lady.

"Don't be crude, Hugo, You know what I mean. No respectable woman would admit to enjoying that aspect of marriage." Emily looked embarrassed. How could Hugo be so vulgar as to discuss what went on in the bedroom, even between legally bound partners?

"How disappointing the late Lord Hansford must have been. You have my sympathy, Emily," Hugo mocked.

"You are impossible as always. I should have known better than to try to make you remember your duty!"

"Yes, you should have, Emily. When I am prepared to enter

the parson's mousetrap, you will read all about it in the *Gazette*. Until then, you must compose your soul in patience," Hugo answered with an evil grin. How his prosy sister would hate what he intended—marrying a scandalous artist who had no interest in observing the proprieties. Remembering Esme, his spirits rose, then plummeted, wondering how longer she would hold out against him, and their mutual emotions.

"You have exposed Annabel to the most scathing rumor, and she expects an offer. Does she deserve to be treated in such a shabby fashion?" Emily asked baldly, realizing that fencing with Hugo only served to bring out the devil in him.

"Oh, I think Annabel knows exactly what she can expect from me," Hugo replied engimatically.

With that Emily would have to be content.

This conversation, as were many with Hugo, had proved to be extremely frustrating for Emily. She rose to make her adieux, realizing she could not report to Annabel any satisfying conclusion. Still, there was some hope. Hugo was just trying to tease and mortify her, his normal style, but she would not be disheartened. He had not completely denied his interest in Annabel.

"Rest assured, Emily. You will soon be able to welcome the new Duchess of Milbourne, and I hope your other wishes will not be far behind," he promised, smiling at her obvious dissatisfaction with their interview.

"I hope you will inform me of your intentions before I have to read it in the *Gazette*," she concluded as Hugo escorted her to the door with punctilious politeness. "You owe me that, Hugo."

"You must contain your impatience, Emily. And give my respects to Annabel," he replied, smiling at her confusion. He sighed with relief as he saw her sail through the door, annoyance in every line of her tightly corsetted figure. Poor Emily. She had not found life to her satisfaction and could not resist meddling, but she was harmless. And he knew that in the end she would accept Esme, because she would not bear to be

222

excluded from Hugo's patronage, nor denied access to her childhood home. But damn it, if she did not receive Esme with the respect she deserved, Emily would not escape the sharp side of his tongue.

He called on Lady Annabel later in the day, and was not surprised to discover the lady in intimate conversation with Gerald Beaumont.

"How kind of you to call, Hugo! Gerald and I are reminiscing. Let me offer you some wine and we can then have a comfortable coze," Annabel greeted him with a dulcet smile and just restrained herself from preening over Hugo's attentions. She gave Gerald an eloquent look.

"Well, Beaumont, I seem to trip over you wherever I travel. And how do you find the delectable Miss Sedgewick? You seem to live in her pocket these days," Hugo asked blandly, disguising his interest behind polite words. He noticed that Annabel found his question annoying, but it was no more than she deserved. He did not like her blatant pursuit, nor her interference, and he had a good idea that she was encouraging her cousin to pursue Esme. He was determined to discover how affairs really marched between the two.

Before Gerald could respond, Annabel unwisely entered the lists. "Gerald is very taken with the chit, you know, Hugo. Not the woman I would choose for him, perhaps, but he must settle down some day. Like you, he is reluctant to surrender," Annabel teased.

"Oh, am I to wish you congratulations, Beaumont?" Hugo asked, a dangerous light in his eye.

"Miss Sedgewick is an amazing woman, quite out of the ordinary, and I fancy she returns my regard," Gerald admitted uneasily. He did not like the look in Hugo's eyes, but could not restrain himself from challenging the man.

"I think you would be wise to forget the lady, Beaumont," Hugo warned, infuriated by the fellow's cool assumption of possession.

"I am escorting her to the theatre this evening and for a cosy supper later," Gerald boasted, revealing rather more than was politic. "Perhaps I will put my chances to the touch."

"Well, bon chance," Hugo replied with more sang froid than he felt. Now that he had learned what he had feared, he was eager to leave, and within moments had bid the pair farewell, leaving a troubled atmosphere behind.

Annabel took her cousin to task almost before Hugo had disappeared. "Really, Gerald, you were not wise to dare Hugo. Just out of pique he might carry off the lady, and then our plans would all come to naught. You should have acted with more prudence," she criticized, her smooth face flushed with anger.

"Annabel dear, you will mar that lovely face with wrinkles if you keep on this way. After this evening, Hugo Carstairs will play no part in Esme Sedgewick's life. Depend on it," he soothed.

Annabel's rage turned to a sullen pout. "You seem awfully sure of yourself, Gerry. What do you intend for the girl?"

"That is not your concern. But I intend to compromise the lady so that she has no choice. I doubt that Hugo Carstairs wants my leavings," Gerald said coarsely, with a wicked leer.

"You would not go so far as to marry her?" Annabel quizzed, her hopes rising.

"Why not? The lady has some money, and I expect you will frank me if it furthers your ends. I have to take a wife someday. Like most men, I want an heir, even if my estates are sadly encumbered. And I don't think Esme will reject an honorable proposal," he assured his cousin with some arrogance.

"Hugo Carstairs is a formidable rival, Gerry, and no woman would turn down the chance to become his duchess, even to wed you, dear cousin,"

"Women are cautious souls, in my experience, and are inclined to respectability. I doubt that Carstairs has offered marriage," he said with some complacency. "Her name is tarnished, and if she wants to regain her reputation, marriage is the only answer."

"You are a bounder, Gerry, but a seductive one. I fear you will make the girl a devilish husband," Annabel smiled cruelly. "But once you are wed, you need not worry about that."

"How well you know me, Annabel. But I might still surprise you. I find Esme unusual, and I might even be induced to fidelity once I am shackled," he mused, surprised as much as his cousin by his desire to claim the elusive Esme.

"Well, whatever expenses are involved in the task, you can rely on me," Annabel assured him, now restored to good spirits. "But it is still a mystery to me why Esme Sedgewick is so alluring. She is not in the popular style, and has no sense of dress nor of proper behavior." She frowned in puzzlement.

"Yes, well, perhaps, she has other qualities you would not appreciate." Gerald knew that his cousin would never understand Esme's appeal, so different from her own, and so intriguing to a jaded palate.

Once more in charity with one another, the conspirators parted, after Gerald had promised Annabel to report on his success at the first opportunity.


Esme, preparing for her evening with Gerald Beaumont, had no suspicion that she would be enduring anything more than a casual visit to the theatre and an enjoyable supper. She had never made the mistake of taking Gerald's profession of devotion seriously and considered him nothing more than a distraction, an antidote to the nagging feelings of loss thoughts of Hugo inspired. And his relationship to Annabel Poole did little to enhance him in her eyes.

At least she had insured Fannie's happiness, she congratulated herself as she dressed. Tonight she would wear a subdued gown of Italian crepe in a soft shade of rose with little trimming, but with ruched ribbon at the decolletage and hem. Despite Annabel's scorn of her fashion sense, Emse knew her own style—elegant simplicity—and gave little thought to the elaborate toilettes favored by those obsessed with the latest modes. She needed none of the artificial aids to beauty practiced by less well endowed women, for her glowing complexion and huge haunting eyes allied to a striking, if thin, figure were attraction enough.

Fastening her mother's simple strand of pearls around her neck, she gave herself a cursory look in the mirror, then crossed the room to read again the note she had received a few hours before from Oliver.

Dear Esme,

Fannie has agreed to our plan and I have secured leave to escort her to my parents' home, but she insists you accompany us. Since the sooner we put affairs in train, the better, I have suggested we set out on the morrow, and hope this sudden departure will not inconvenience you. We will collect Fannie from Hatchard's book store in the forenoon, and be on our way smartly, hoping to avoid early pursuit. Will you notify me if you will be prepared to join me at 11 o'clock, when I will arrive in a closed carriage? Again, our deepest gratitude for your assistance in securing our happiness, kindest of friends.

Yours,
Oliver

Esme had dispatched a note to his quarters, assuring him of her willingness to accompany the eloping pair, and had told Bessie to make a visit to her relatives so as to be unavailable if the Cranfords should take it in mind to quiz her. All seemed to be in train for this adventure. Although Esme regretted this secret elopement, she knew that her aunt and uncle would never allow Fannie to wed Oliver. And without her help she doubted her cousin would have the courage to make the effort to oppose her parents, no matter how miserable their plans made her. She smiled as she thought of Aunt Mildred's outrage. But it was no more than she warranted, forcing Fannie to wed that hateful Lord Moreton. Fannie deserved better and she would have it with Oliver, who would always be kind and supportive.

Gerald Beaumont spared no effort in charming Esme that evening. He complimented her effusively on her looks, presented her with a charming tuzzy-muzzy of roses to tie on her wrist. He had tenderly shepherded her into a bespoken box at the Theatre Royal, where they would see Jessica O'Neill star in a much heralded performance of "Romeo and Juliet."

Gerald's own tastes tended toward less respectable performances, but he knew that Esme enjoyed Shakespeare and he wanted to pave the way for the evening's climax with as little trouble as possible. As he had expected, she was thoroughly engrossed with the drama and watched the stage with an absorbed interest. This left Gerald free to savor what was to come. Neither of them noticed Hugo Carstairs entering his box halfway through the performance, nor were they aware of his studied glances in their direction.

Hugo had not invited any guests for the performance and was able to brood in silence over the sight of the pair opposite. His thoughts were not happy ones, and he had to concede that Esme seemed very pleased in her escort's company. The tender, selfless emotions of the dramatic lovers made little impact on Hugo's emotions. He ignored the players on stage and concentrated on an entirely different cast of characters.

# Chapter Twenty-Two

"Isn't this rather secluded," Esme asked of her escort as he ushered her into a private dining room in Clarendon's Hotel. The hostelry had a deserved reputation for serving the finest French cuisine at shocking prices. A bottle of Clarendon's claret or champagne cost at least a guinea. Gerald had spared no expense, Esme noticed, as she viewed the intimate table laid out for their after-theatre supper.

"I prefer to be alone with you, Esme, and this seemed the most suitable setting," he teased, but his glance was fiery and Esme had the first stirrings of uneasiness. She sat down to pick at the lobster patties and other delectables Gerald had ordered.

While the waiter was in the room, Gerald's attitude was most polite and gentlemanly, but Esme had few illusions about her newest beau. She suspected he was about to try to seduce her. Obviously he considered her fair game, a woman of dubious reputation living alone, whose name was linked with one of the most blatant libertines of the *ton*. Well, if he had expectations of that sort, she would soon depress his desires. But the frisson of mistrust dampened her appetite.

When the waiter had at last removed the covers, she awaited Gerald's next move with some trepidation. He rose and poured her another glass of champagne, despite her protests.

"Come, Esme, another glass of wine will surely not affect

you," he cajoled, smiling at her.

Esme demurred. She needed all her wits about her. She noticing his eyes ranging over her bosom with what she could only consider a possessive and searching gaze. Oh, dear, it really was the outside of enough—to have to cope with another amorous male, when all she wanted was to enjoy her supper in peace and then seek her chaste couch. How stupid she had been, not to be aware of his intentions. She remained obstinately silent. Let him make the next move.

She was thus quite unprepared for his sudden lunge as he dragged her into his arms and looked down at her with smoldering eyes.

"Esme, you have toyed with me long enough. I know you are not indifferent to me, and you must know that I feel deeply about you," he said, wine and passion suffusing his face with a dark flush.

After an initial struggle, Esme went rigid in his arms. She could not fight him, suspecting he would only enjoy subduing her, but his touch and his hot rancid breath repelled her. She looked at him cooly, hiding her disquiet.

"Gerald, if I have given you some cause to think you could make advances, I regret it deeply, but I feel nothing for you but friendship. You are an experienced man with many conquests to your credit, but I do not desire to be one of them," she insisted with a certain hauteur.

But her words fell on deaf ears. Gerald was so certain of his romantic prowess, so convinced that she would yield to his persuasive tactics, that he barely heard her protests. "Come, Esme, there is no need to play the coy temptress. I know you are not virtuous, and I am prepared to excuse any past lapses. After all, I am not without some knowledge of women. You crave a master, dear Esme, and I intend to be that man." He attempted to force her chin up and press a kiss on her tightened lips. "You were made for a man's bed, and if you please me, I am prepared to seal our relationship with wedding vows," he promised.

229

Aghast, Esme wrenched herself from his arms, and retreated behind a chair, her temper now thoroughly aroused by his condescending words. His touch revolted her, and she cursed herself for allowing such intimacies to be visited upon her body, for allowing herself to be placed in this compromising position. But she would not lose her temper. He might enjoy that, and she wisely decided that light ridicule was the best strategy.

"Really, Gerald," she said calmly. "Was that what this lavish supper was supposed to bring about? You set the scene for a seduction quite cleverly, but you have mistaken your victim. I am not available for any man's casual conquest."

Gad, she was an enticing piece, Gerald thought, so cool on the outside, but underneath a mass of emotions. He recognized the fury beneath her aloof facade, and it goaded him to ignore her words. He believed she was only making the obligatory objections, in order to whet his appetites.

"No need to play the prude with me. I know you too well."

Esme repressed a gasp at his effrontery. "You are obviously quite carried away by the evening and the wine. I have never thought of you in that way. Perhaps I was mistaken in allowing you so much freedom, but I had no idea you thought of me in this way."

"I want to marry you, Esme, but I do not believe in buying until I have sampled the wares," he said crudely, edging toward her. She could not stay ensconced behind that chair for the rest of the night.

"That is hardly the most inviting way to propose marriage," she pointed out. But she knew words would not be enough to stop him. Her hand went out to the table and she picked up a wine glass, smashing it so that its jagged edges would serve as an effective weapon if he succeeded in closing the distance between them. "If you intend to force yourself upon me, you would be wise to think again," she threatened, brandishing the glass.

"Damn it, Esme, you drive a man mad!" he groaned,

throwing all caution to the winds. But before he could fulfill his intention, the door sprang open with a crash and the two combatants looked up to see Hugo Carstairs on the threshold.

"I seem to be interrupting a most interesting scene," Hugo drawled, taking in Esme's defensive stance and the flushed countenance of her attacker.

Esme sighed with relief. Humiliating as it was to have Hugo catch her in such a compromising position, she could have embraced him with gratitude for coming to her rescue. Summoning all her pride, she carefully placed the broken glass on the table.

"How convenient of you, Hugo, to arrive so precipitously," Esme said. "I was just on the point of leaving myself. Could you escort me home? I fear Mr. Beaumont has taken a bit too much wine, and has forgotten his manners," she explained lightly. She could see the ugly light in Hugo's dark eyes and hoped to avoid any disaster.

"Your intrusion is unwelcome, sir," Gerald said, slurring his words. "Please take yourself off at once. Esme and I have some important unfinished business," he growled, appalled at this unlooked for contretemps. How had the fellow known of their whereabouts? And how dare he push himself upon them? By now in a fever of thwarted desire, Gerald was aware that he was in danger of losing all he had expected confidently to gain. He was beside himself with rage and frustration.

"Oh, come now, Beaumont," Hugo, responded sardonically. "The lady obviously welcomes my arrival with relief." He propped himself against the wall and viewed his opponent with infuriating composure. He knew that Esme, who had backed away from Gerald and edged up to him, was reluctant to let him know how frightened she really had been. For that, Beaumont would pay.

"Are you calling me a liar, Carstairs?" Gerald threatened, his fists clenched.

"No," Hugo replied silkily, not at all disturbed by Gerald's dangerous stance. "I am calling you a bounder and a cad. I'm

231

tempted to plant you a facer right now, or if you prefer, to offer you a challenge."

Gerald, losing all restraint, lunged at his enemy, determined to avenge the insults, but before he could land a blow, Hugo had thrown a punishing right hook to his chin and felled him to the floor. Turning his back on his recumbent foe, he took Esme by the hand. "Have you a cloak, my dear? I think we had best make our departure."

He appeared as cool as if he were discussing the merits of Turner's work, but Esme recognized he was holding his temper in check with great difficulty. She noticed a pulse beating in his temple, and he looked murderous. She took up her silk cloak, which was lying across a nearby chair, and allowed Hugo to help her with it, sparing a glance for Gerald who moaned and tried to struggle to his feet. Before he could gather his senses, Hugo had whisked her through the door, leaving the wretched spectacle of her predicament behind.

As they descended the stairs of the Clarendon, Esme was conscious, to her dismay, that several curious eyes watched their progress, but Hugo ruthlessly ignored the watchers and pushed her ahead of him with an iron hand. Much as she hated his arrogance, she could only be grateful for his protection, no matter what the gossips believed. He had rescued her from a horrid dilemma, and she must thank him for that, if for nothing else. Wisely she held her tongue until they were safely established in his curricle.

"Thank you, Hugo, for your timely interruption, for I had no idea . . ." Esme began, but he silenced her abruptly.

"Hold your tongue, my girl. We cannot talk here," he warned, indicating the presence of the stolid tiger perched behind them on the curricle.

They traveled down Bond Street at a spanking pace, then turned left into Grosvenor Street before she realized they were not going to St. John's Wood. Rousing herself to protest, Esme took one look at his intractable face, and bit back her words. Time enough to make her annoyance clear when they

232

reached his Grosvenor mansion. She was tired to death and in no mood to listen to his reproaches, nor to serve as a butt for his anger.

In this she wronged him, for Hugo's reaction, now that he had rescued her from Gerald's clutches, was primarily one of relief. He thanked providence that he had arrived in time. If he had not employed a man to watch Esme, he would not have known where the couple had gone after the theatre, for he had missed them in the crush of the departing audience at the Royal. His own feelings were a combination of satisfaction in flooring Beaumont, fury at Annabel Poole's schemes, for he believed she had urged Beaumont to pursue Esme, and an overwhelming desire to take Esme to bed and settle his frustration and her rejection of him once and for all. He was in no humor to listen to explanations or excuses, although for one dreadful moment he wondered if Esme really cared for that bounder who had intended to despoil her.

Ever since he had met the girl, she had disrupted his life, challenged his established conduct, insinuated herself into his senses. He loved her, incredible as it was to him, and he had finally admitted that he could not comtemplate going on without her by his side. But he doubted that she would be convinced of his sincerity, and he was not yet prepared to expose himself to her scorn. He knew of only one way to persuade her, and he could no longer wait for the legal sanction of his actions.

As they drew up before his mansion, Esme turned to Hugo, prepared to do battle. But the look on his face dissuaded her. He was holding on to his control by a whisker, and she knew that if she began to protest his treatment he would lose it. Somehow that prospect did not frighten her as it should. She felt exhilarated and challenged. Hugo Carstairs did not command her life and he would not cow her with force. He might want to rake her over the coals for her rendezvous, albeit innocent, with the rakish Gerald Beaumont, but she did not intend to give him the satisfaction of revealing how little that spurious gallant meant to her.

"Really, Hugo, need you behave in such a masterful fashion. I am quite grateful to you for rescuing me from Gerald, although I am sure I could have handled the situation in a less violent fashion," she offered as he extended his hand to help her dismount.

"Like you handled me, you termagant?" he growled, propelling her up the steps to the entrance of his imposing house. His butler threw open the door before she could answer, and she contented herself with smiling mysteriously, unreasonably pleased with his irascible reply.

Watching his dark face cautiously from beneath her eyelids, she concluded with some glee that Hugo was jealous. Why was it that only Hugo made her blood sing with excitement, oversetting all her best resolutions?

But before she could examine the state of her heart, her protagonist had ushered her smartly into the drawing room, ablaze with candles. He then gave curt orders to his servant for refreshments. She walked to the mirror over one of the pier tables and patted her hair, amazed to see that her recent encounter had left so little mark. Her eyes sparkled and her cheeks flushed as she prepared for the upbraiding she knew was due. Well, Hugo Carstairs would see he had some accounting of his own to do.

He stood staring somberly at her for a moment, considering his words. Then, as if forced to ask an unpalatable question, he blurted out, "Do you care for that rogue, Beaumont, Esme?"

"I have found Gerald a most pleasant companion, Hugo. Until tonight his conduct was most gentlemanly. I must confess, his intentions for this evening came as somewhat of a shock. I think perhaps he was in his cups."

"And if I had not interrupted the tender scene, would you have submitted?" he asked, his tone enigmatic, but his eyes locked on hers.

"Of course not, Hugo. I do not want to either marry or bed Gerald Beaumont. You quite mistook the situation," she said severely, conscious that she was waiting for some explosion.

"Just as well, for he would not have lived long enough to claim you," Hugo muttered, crossing the room to her and taking her in his arms. "You are a damned thorn in my side, giving me no peace, and I will no longer put up with your willful ways," he insisted, clasping her in a tight embrace and kissing her as if to enforce his mastery.

Before she could protest, they were interrupted by Hugo's servant with a tray of refreshments, Esme broke away from the duke in embarrassment. Affairs were not marching quite as she had expected. Hugo frowned and dismissed the man, and tardily remembered his duties as a host.

"Pray have some madeira or tea, although I believe a tot of brandy is more in order," he offered, his good humor restored, now that he had her where he wanted her, in his house and in his power.

"No, thank you. I have recently dined most richly," she demurred. Esme found it difficult to read his closed expression. Finally, when she could bear the taut silence between them no longer, she asked, "And now? Are you going to take me to task for my imprudent behaviour? Rather ironic, for you to play the model of propriety, Duke!"

"My conduct, reprehensible as it might be, is not the issue here. You deliberately court danger when you tangle with a man of Beaumont's stamp." Hugo came up to her again and raised her chin with a powerful hand.

Esme, mortified that he had put her at a disadvantage, tried to justify herself, although she saw no reason to explain her conduct to Hugo.

"I see nothing untoward in accepting some attentions from Gerald. Never before has he put a foot wrong. I cannot understand what made him behave in such an appalling fashion. He has always acted most respectably before." She wrinkled her brow, for in truth, Gerald's attack on her had surprised her more than it truly frightened her.

"My dear innocent. Despite your experience with me, you

235

retain a most surprising faith in your fellow man," Hugo said. "And would you have wed him if he had forced you?"

"I shall marry for one reason and one reason alone," she answered softly. Then, as if weary of this catechism, "If you have quite finished with your scolding perhaps I might be allowed to go home."

"Since when have I 'allowed' you anything? You have always held onto your damned independence. Far be it from me to keep you here against your will," Hugo ended this ironic speech by dragging her into his arms, and beginning a slow assault on her senses. "You are quite free to go," he murmured against her throat. "I won't lift a finger to stop you."

Esme opened her mouth to reply, which was a mistake. Hugo took that as his cue to crush her lips beneath his. His hands wandered down her back, pressing her close to his body so that she could feel his arousal, and her own limbs lost their rigidity under the compelling seduction of his hands and mouth.

Esme was helpless against the warmth rising unbidden under his expert touch. Hugo lifted her in his arms, and strode to the door, which he threw back in impatience. Esme, should have struggled, but she could not deny that she craved his lovemaking, welcomed the close clasp of his arms.

How it happened she did not quite understand but within moments they were in his bedroom, a vast cavern of a room, shrouded in darkness, and she was only dimly conscious of his lowering her to the bed, his hands roaming over her body and skillfully removing her clothes. He murmured her name under his breath as he continued his assault and she yearned for what was to follow. She watched, her eyes slumbrous, as he quickly threw off his own clothes, and came to her again.

What followed was a passionate coupling which robbed her of all her defences, as he continued to woo her with his passionate lovemaking. A languorous tide of emotion swept her body. She could no more have subdued the rising impatience for his possession than she could have halted a tempestuous flood. She had wanted him for so long, and at last she admitted to herself that only Hugo could induce this tremendous response. They came together in a panting silence. He made no professions of love, and she bit back her own gasps of delight. He had lost all control now, and the experienced lover was lost in a storm of physical urgency as he at last satisfied her pleas for the ultimate conquest. She fell back at last, breathless and satiated.

Hugo rested his dark head on her breast.

After some time had passed and Hugo had fallen asleep, Esme lay awake, unmoving but troubled. He had not made any claims of love, but possessed her with a tender savagery. He had overcome all her resistance, and she admitted ruefully she had yearned for his possession although she knew she was only storing up sorrow for herself. She edged gently away, but he stirred and his grip tightened. "You are mine now, and no other man shall have you," he muttered before falling back into a profound slumber.

What did he mean? Esme wondered. Was he so arrogant that he demanded her surrender without any commitment himself? She could not bear to be used so. Tears trickled down on her cheeks as she realized that his passion had not been inspired by any lasting emotion other than an undeniable desire not to be denied. He did not really love her as she had so briefly believed, but only lusted for satisfaction.

As darkness stole slowly toward dawn, she wrestled with her decision. She could not wait supinely for the morning and the sorrow she did not doubt awaited her. She must leave before he awoke and cruelly claimed her again.

Carefully, she inched her way from his demanding arms, waiting breathlessly as he muttered and tossed in his sleep. But then he settled down again and she made her escape, hurriedly donning her wrinkled dress, and creeping from the room, which had seen such pleasure and such pain. She must gain her sanctuary, remove herself from the temptation Hugo offered. If he insisted she return to him as a compliant mistress, she did not know if she could deny him. She knew she would hate herself and him if he forced her again into that loveless relationship.

She slipped warily down the stairs of the great house and across the marbled hall, hands fumbling at the bolts of the mahogany door. At last it opened and she walked trembling to the street, praying she could find a hackney to convey her to St. John Wood's before he woke and followed her. As she reached her house with the sun just breaking over the horizon, she suddenly remembered Fannie and Oliver's elopement and realized that this was just the respite she needed to escape Hugo.

## Chapter Twenty-Three

Esme could only be grateful that she had sent Bessie away, and that she could restore some order to her senses and person in privacy. She had no time to brood over the events of the past evening, for she must pack and ready herself for the appointment with Oliver and Fannie. Thank goodness she had the elopement to distract her, she thought, although she knew she could not keep the memories of Hugo's lovemaking at bay indefinitely. She repressed a sigh of longing as she wondered what her response would have been if he had confessed to caring for her. But he had been strangely silent for such a passionate seduction. She blamed herself for the outcome of the disastrous evening. Why had she allowed him to take her to bed? He had not renewed his offer of marriage. In fact, he had made nothing but a few muttered endearments as he conquered her again.

She gave little thought to Gerald Beaumont, for she was sure she would not see him again, and for that she felt nothing but relief. When would she learn not to trust men with their deception and their desire? Well, she could not idle here repenting the past. She must dress and pack for the expedition to Somerset. At least she would secure Fannie's happiness and for that she would sacrifice a good deal.

Hurriedly, she changed from her bedraggled evening dress,

giving a passing thought to what Bessie would say about its condition. She had previously bundled a few necessities for Fannie into a case, for her cousin would not be able to smuggle anything from the Cranford house before she left on her assignation.

Restored to some calm, she was ready for Oliver when he arrived to collect her, dressed soberly in a midnight blue silk redingote cut away in the front to reveal a simple cream underskirt, and a small straw bonnet faced in matching blue. Aside from the dark shadows under her haunting gray eyes, she showed little effect of her night's experience. But try as she might, she could not banish the memories and wondered wearily if she ever would. But she allowed none of her malaise to dampen Oliver's excitement. As he helped her into his closed carriage hitched to two sturdy chestnut horses behind a hired coachman, she hoped that her escort would be too absorbed in his own plans to notice her distraction. And so it proved. Oliver, as the horses trotted toward Picadilly, spoke worriedly about his arrangements.

"Do you think Fannie will be able to elude her maid and arrive at the appointment?" he asked as they turned into the avenue. Despite his initial wariness, he was now eager to claim his bride, Esme observed with satisfaction.

"Fannie is a resourceful girl, and she will do what is necessary. I believe her main concern is that you crave this union as much as she does," Esme replied, smiling a bit over Oliver's nervousness.

"Oh, yes, Esme. Have no doubt of that. Every time I think of her parents coercing her into that dreadful marriage, my blood boils," Oliver replied, his face set and determined.

"You will never regret claiming Fannie as a wife, Oliver. I have not lived in close companionship and affection with her all these years not to appreciate her true worth. You are a fortunate man. Have you notified your parents of your intention?" she asked, and listened with a wistful expression to Oliver's detailed explanations of his arrangements.

Before he could finish, they drew up in front of Hatchard's book store, where Esme had suggested that she meet Fannie. It would not do for any stray passers-by to notice Oliver escorting Fannie from the premises. Esme entered the shop and found Fannie fidgeting over some novels, her eyes straying constantly to the entrance. She greeted her cousin with sparkling eyes and a mischievous smile. As they left the shop together, Fannie confided that she had cleverly sent her tartar of a maid to the milliners for a promised bonnet, and they must be away before she returned. Her shy smile to Oliver as he helped her into the carriage was received with a reassuring hug. Within moments they were on their way.

"Oh, Esme, my heart has been in my mouth all morning! It was all I could do to swallow some chocolate and pretend to my abigail that all was as usual. If only I could have packed some clothes, but it was impossible. I shall look a rag when we finally reach Somerset!" she burbled, excitement giving her plain face an unaccustomed glow.

"I anticipated your problem, and have prepared for it. You will not be a paragon of fashion, but at least you will not disgrace us," Esme promised, her spirits lightening at Fannie's excitement. As London's streets began to thin behind them, she found herself caught up in their glowing plans for the future. They were both deserving of all the happiness she knew lay ahead. Fannie was a bit apprehensive about pursuit, and Esme set out to allay her fears.

"It will take some time for your abigail to realize that you have eluded her, and even more time for your parents to comprehend what has happened. You did not leave a note?" she asked with some fear that kind-hearted Fannie might have been unable to abandon her home without some announcement. That could threaten the outcome of this elopement.

"No, and I felt so hateful—causing such worry and trouble! They will be quite alarmed and may even set the Bow Street runners on us!"

Listening to Fannie's anxieties, Oliver applauded her good

sense and promised that the Cranfords would be notified of their daughter's safety, but not until after all threat of apprehension was out of court.

"The Cranfords may believe you have fled to Gretna, and will pursue us north, while we are going west. Have they any idea that you have not obeyed their strictures against meeting Oliver?" Esme asked, doubting that Fannie lacked the ability to act in a conspiratorial fashion.

"Oh, no, I have been very clever," Fannie twinkled, caught up in the devilment of the affair. "I even acquiesced in their invitation to Lord Moreton for dinner this evening." She chuckled, the threat of that horrid man fast fading with the miles lengthening behind them.

"I had no idea you were such a conniving girl, Fannie. It does not bode well for our married life," Oliver teased, seeing that Fannie needed approval and comfort. After all, she was trusting her life to an unknown fate.

Fannie, taking his words seriously, hurried to explain. "I am not usually so devious, Oliver, but I feared Mother's sharp eye. She is determined that I accept Lord Moreton, but she can have no reason to believe I would have any means of disobeying her. I have not been besieged by offers," she admitted candidly with a little moue.

"You have been besieged by me, dear Fannie, and I pray you will never regret trusting yourself to me." Oliver looked at her lovingly, giving both Fannie and Esme a warm glow of satisfaction. He continued. "I thought we would stop at Basingstoke tonight. I have bespoken a change of horses and rooms at the Bird and Bottle there," he explained.

"You did get the special license, Oliver?" Esme asked suddenly.

"Yes, I secured the license from the Bishop of London without much trouble. I am not such a sapskull as to leave it all to chance!" Oliver replied laughing at his companions' worried faces. "And my parents will be over the moon, making every effort to prepare for our arrival," he soothed. "They will love

Fannie as I do, I know."

Heartened by his enthusiasm and obvious happiness, the trio in the carriage relaxed and discussed the outcome of their journey with anticipation. As the journey continued at a good pace, Esme repressed a sigh of envy. If only her future were settled so comfortably.


Fannie had been quite correct in her assumption that her abigail, an elderly woman of uncertain temper, would take her time in notifying the Cranfords that their daughter had unaccountably disappeared. She had met a fellow servant at the milliner's and the two had chatted for some time about their employers and other matters while the milliner wrapped her promised bonnet. Then Horton, for that was the abigail's name, had not hurried to meet her mistress at Hatchard's. She suffered from sore feet and walking was agony for her so her progress was leisurely. On arriving at the book store to find Miss Fannie gone, she had at first not worried about her absence, for the haughty clerk had acknowledged that young Lady Cranford had left the shop with a friend. In a rare omission, the considerate Fannie had left no message for her maid. With some difficulty, Horton wrung a description of the lady from the clerk and guessed that Fannie's companion must have been Esme. Favoring her sore feet, she ambled back to Mount Street to be met by Lady Cranford. Mildred learned of her daughter's behavior from the disgruntled maid with more irritation than concern for her whereabouts.

Lady Cranford dismissed the maid with a warning that she should pay more attention to her duties. Feeling most ill-used, Horton protested with the familiarity of an old retainer and placed the blame squarely on Esme's shoulders.

Lady Cranford, although annoyed at her daughter, did not for a moment suspect that Fannie had done more than wander off at Esme's request on some rubbishy outing. Really, Fannie

243

had no sense, and her relationship with her cousin was spoiling all her chances. When Fannie had not returned by tea time, Lady Cranford's simmering anger came to a boil, and on the earl's appearance she lost no time in enlisting his aid.

"Really, Egbert, you must speak to Fannie," Lady Cranford complained to her much-tried husband. "She constantly defies us. Lord Moreton is expected for dinner and I believe will make his offer this evening. If he knew of Fannie's association with Esme, who is the butt of every gossip-monger in town, he would be disgusted, and possibly cry off!"

"You make too much of the matter, my dear. Fannie is devoted to Esme and your constant carping about their companionship does more harm than good. I must confess I feel we have been a bit harsh in our own treatment of our niece. Doesn't look well to have turned her from our door. Lord Cranford had conveniently forgotten his own part in the matter. He had endured some hard words from his cronies at White's about the family's treatment of their niece, and he wanted to put the fault where he believed it rightly belonged.

Still, the Cranfords were inwardly convinced they had acted out of the noblest of motives. Fannie had always been a disappointment and her latest jape just reinforced their opinion. But as dinner time approached and Fannie did not appear they became seriously worried at last.

Their notions of polite behavior were outraged and they dreaded telling the estimable Lord Moreton that his quarry had inexplicably flown. They could not comprehend that their insistence on a marriage between Fannie and the aging lecherous peer was at the root of her disappearance.

Finally Lord Cranford bestirred himself to ride out to St. John's Wood to challenge Esme. Disgruntled and guilty, he realized as he approached the small cottage that he had made little effort to understand Esme or her wish for independence. His guilt and anger were not assuaged to find the cottage closed and the futility of his furious demands for admittance increased his unease. Where could the cousins be? Had Esme lured Fannie into some embarrassing escapade?

He hurried back to Mount Street to give his wife the disquieting news that both Fannie and Esme seemed to have disappeared. At last his fatherly feeling rose to haunt him with the possibility that his and his wife's stern insistence on obedience might have produced dire results.

His temper was not improved by having to write a hurried message to Lord Moreton postponing the dinner, giving as an excuse that Fannie had taken a fever. At a loss for his next move, he spent the evening railing at his wife for her careless supervision of their recalcitrant daughter. He had no idea that as he and Lady Cranford exhanged bitter words of blame, Esme, Oliver and Fannie were enjoying a quiet supper in the inn at Basingbroke.

The day of Fannie's flight had been equally frustrating for Hugo Carstairs. He had awoken from a deep sleep, prepared to lull Esme's fury at his seduction, to confess his love and carry her off to the nearest church to seal their vows. But he found she had vanished. Knowing she had every reason for suspicion and anger, he cursed his hesitation in speaking of his love. He dressed hurriedly and rode off to St. John's Wood where he arrived within an hour of Esme's departure.

Unlike Lord Cranford, he wasted little time when he realized that Esme was not available. No servant answered his urgent knocking, but after some ferreting about the cottage, he was approached by the man he had left to watch Esme's movements.

"I was coming to report, governor, just waiting to see if the lady returned with the gentleman," the young man justified himself, not liking the ugly look in his master's eye.

"What gentleman?" Hugo barked, his fears rising.

"That military cove who hangs about here a lot. He arrived with a bang up outfit and took the lady off with him. She had several cases and looked prepared for a journey," the man reported, now thoroughly alarmed that the duke might cause him some harm, or at the very least, refuse to pay him.

"Why didn't you stop them, sirrah?" Hugo, now thoroughly alarmed, looked murderous. Had she eloped with that callow officer? He could not believe she would go from his bed, where their night of passionate lovemaking had been a mutual delight, to wed the first man who offered. She could not have been so vengeful and foolish to destroy her whole life because she wanted to punish Hugo. Putting his desperate hurt behind him, he dismissed the man with a curse, throwing him a gold coin and mounted his curricle, riding off in heedless fury. He must prevent this unhappy escapade from reaching any disastrous conclusion.

Within the hour, he was at the Chelsea barracks of Oliver's regiment, brooking no refusal from the corporal who tried to prevent his interruption of the commanding officer. Colonel Crichton had some knowledge of the duke, and received him politely, although Hugo extended him no such courtesy.

"To what do I owe this honor, Your Grace?" the colonel asked, as Hugo brusquely acknowledged his greeting.

"I want some information, Crichton, and you should be able to supply it. I must see one of your officers with whom I have some pressing private business," Hugo explained, his temper not soothed by having to waste time in observing the barest rules of etiquette.

Crichton, a stalwart, bluff army type unaccustomed to dealing with the nobility, was quite cowed by Hugo's manner, although he tried to disguise his reaction. On hearing that Lieutenant Wells was the man sought by the exigent duke, he tried to put a good face on the matter.

"Alas, Lieutenant Wells has resigned his commission and retired to his country estates. Illness in the family, I understand. He was an able officer and I am sorry to lose him," the colonel offered, hoping to cool Hugo's temper, but his hope was dimmed as he noticed the hard look of his interrogator. But Hugo had now some command of himself and suavely pursued his inquiries, demanding, with the utmost politeness, that the colonel reveal the address of his former officer. Within moments he had the information and with more circumspection, thanked the man for his cooperation.

The colonel's curiosity was aroused, but he hesitated to satisfy it, not wishing to incur another explosion from his august guest. In the end, Hugo left him flattered and calmed by his profuse apologies and gratitude, not reveling any information, but gaining much.

Hugo made his plans to follow Esme and her suitor, whom he feared were heading straight to the altar to solemnize a union both would regret.

# Chapter Twenty-Four

Oliver's parents welcomed the tired but jubilant travelers when they arrived at the Wells's small manor house a few miles from the market town of Shepton Mallet. The squire was a heavy-set man whose ruddy complexion had paled from the rigors of his arthritic condition, but his illness had in no way depressed his spirits. His wife, a small, dainty woman in her late forties, must have been a delicate beauty in her youth. They were both unpretentious, contented folk, delighted to welcome their only son, whose absence on his military duties had obviously been a great loss to them. Their reception of Fannie was all that the diffident girl could have hoped for, and she glowed in the obvious approval they displayed for their son's bride. To Esme, too, their greetings were warm and kindly. Their only concern seemed to be that Oliver, in marrying the daughter of a peer, might have earned the disappointment and disapproval of the Cranfords.

Fannie and Oliver, both too honest to dissemble, admitted the hurried match was due in part to Lord and Lady Cranford's efforts to prevent the relationship. Too polite to express their justified anger that anyone, even a peer of the realm, could take their son in disgust, they nevertheless voiced their dismay at the elopement. But Fannie, determined to secure her happiness, hurried to reassure them, with Esme's assistance.

Esme's optimistic view of the bond between Oliver and Fannie, and the pair's determination to secure their union, did much to allay the Wells' fears.

Later, after the first greetings were over, Fannie confided timidly to her future mother-in-law that her parents had preferred another match, to an odious widower whom she had taken in great dislike. Fannie's confidences won Mrs. Wells' heart and she conceded that the pair had no choice but to elope. Esme, by accompanying the couple, had signified her own approval, and the Wells were much impressed with Fannie's elegant cousin. Then, too, their natural inclination to receive any bride whom their son chose tended to increase the warmth of their reception. The quartet had a delightful supper to celebrate the event and agreed that the vows must be spoken immediately.

The next morning Oliver and Fannie visited the vicar of the small village, where they were received with much excitement. The vicar would perform the ceremony the next afternoon. Esme wished they had not postponed the day but, she could see that some preparations must be made. She had brought a simple white dimity dress for Fannie's nuptials, and Mrs. Wells eagerly offered her own veil, which had been packed away in lavender against just such an event. Riding with the affianced couple around the small estate, Esme could only conclude that Fannie's lines had fallen in pleasant places. She would be the perfect chatelaine for this tidy manor.

Fannie's bridal day dawned bright and sunny, an omen which Esme hailed with gratitude for she had spent a troubled night, beset by doubts at her interference in the lives of two people dear to her. Although neither Fannie nor Oliver appeared to have any last minute doubts or heart searchings, Esme craved to be convinced so she visited her cousin, who was merrily drinking her morning chocolate, looking relaxed and quite winsome in her cambric nightgown and wrap.

"Well, Fannie, you look contented and quite smug for a bride. Have you no fears or concerns about this precipitate match and your parents' reaction?" Esme asked, seating herself on her cousin's bed and smiling at the picture Fannie made.

"Oh, no, Esme. I am so happy! I know that Oliver will make me a wonderful husband," Fannie bubbled. "My only fear is that I am not quite the wife he wanted," she chided, a cloud passing over her spirits.

"You are too humble, Fannie. You will make a perfect wife, and I can see you are most fortunate in your in-laws. Oliver's parents are dear people. But will you not mind living here, so removed from the society you have been accustomed to meeting?"

"Society has not been too kind to me, and I have been miserable trying to fulfill my mother's unrealistic expectations. And her dislike of Oliver is so unfair, so unfounded! I will write them of my decision, but only after I am wed," she said with unusual spirit. Then abandoning the gloomy picture of her parents' displeasure, she continued. "He is the only man I have ever met who has treated me with affection and gentleness. I could not bear an arrogant, unfeeling brute, like the Duke of Milbourne for example," she said with a veiled look at Esme. But Esme was not be be drawn out, although the perceptive Fannie noticed her cousin turn her face away. Hugo Carstairs had made some impact on Esme's heart, Fannie romantically believed, and she craved her cousin's confidences, but respected her reticence. She owed her cousin a great debt and would do nothing to shatter Esme's calm by asking her for disturbing revelations.

"I suppose Oliver would have preferred you for a wife, Esme, and even if he has taken second choice I will see that he does not regret it," she vowed, for Fannie was too forthright not to face reality.

"Nonsense! He might have found me appealing in the beginning, but there was no real meeting of minds or hearts. I had nothing but friendship to offer," Esme replied cheerfully dispelling Fannie's last niggling doubt. Fannie's suggestion

250

that Hugo Carstairs may have captured Esme's heart was one she could not bear to entertain, at this point. The day was her cousin's, and Esme would not spoil it by confiding her own unhappiness.

"Mrs. Wells has sent the gown I brought for you to be pressed. I know you will make a lovely bride, so come now and get into your finery. I am here to help you," Esme said briskly.

The small company set off for the village church about one o'clock after a merry if frugal luncheon. Mrs. Wells had insisted that Oliver keep away, believing the old saw about a bridegroom not seeing his bride before they met at the altar. His father would escort Fannie down the aisle, and Oliver had invited the vicar's son, home from Oxford, to be his groomsman. Despite the haste, the simple ceremony was to be both memorable and bountiful, for Mrs. Wells was a master at arrangements. Although the wedding had come as a surprise to the villagers, they had eagerly set aside their chores to see the squire's son wed, enjoying this unexpected break in their routine lives.

As Esme, dressed in a simple gown of gray silk accented in crisp white, preceded her cousin down the aisle, she smiled serenely, causing several in the congregation to stare in wonder at this elegant, haunting stranger. As the time-worn words of ceremony, intoned by the vicar, began, Esme tried to banish her own dejection and think only of Fannie. The vicar a bit undone by the suddenness of the rites, for he had never married a couple by special license before, smiled beneficently at the pair before him, so radiant in their expectation. As the hallowed words flowed, Esme held her breath, fearing that even at this eleventh hour, some cloud would darken Fannie's happiness.

The vicar's deep melodious voice spoke the fateful words, "If either of you know any impediment why ye may not lawfully be joined together in matrimony, ye do now confess it: for be ye well assured that so many as are coupled together otherwise than as God's word doth allow, are not joined together by God, neither is their matrimony lawful." He paused, as was customary, and Esme had a sudden fear that Lord Cranford would materialize and forbid the vows. After all, Fannie was still a minor, and perhaps this could be a bar to the legality of the marriage.

But the voice that interrupted the ceremony did not come from Lord Cranford.

"This marriage cannot continue," a strong harsh voice interrupted, causing a shock of outrage to ripple through the assembly. Down the aisle strode the Duke of Milbourne, his boots dusty, his black hair falling in careless disarray and his every linement showing the effects of hard riding.

"What is the meaning of this disruption, sir?" the vicar gasped, for never in his long tenure had any ceremony been so rudely interrupted.

The Duke of Milbourne, giving a furious glance at Esme, and ignoring Oliver and Fannie, who stood mute and aghast at this untoward disturbance, said, in cool, haughty tones. "Let us step into the chancel and we will discuss the matter." He was behaving as if the whole affair was his to command, but Esme noticed the pulse beating erratically in his temple, and knew that he held his temper on a tight leash. What could he mean by his extravagant gesture? Why should he have ridden *ventre à terre* to prevent the nuptials? Was he the Cranford's emissary? No, that could not be. But before she could voice her objections, she was grasped in a ruthless hand and shepherded with Oliver, Fannie and the vicar into the chancel, trailed by the uncomprehending, worried Mr. and Mrs. Wells. Behind them in the nave, they left a veritable buzzing of conversation, for the villagers, witnesses to such a drama, were agog with speculation.

In the privacy of the small chancel Hugo glared at Oliver. "I will not have it. You cannot marry Esme. She is promised to me, and if you dare to continue with this devilish ceremony, she will be a widow before she is a bride," Hugo promised wrathfully, paying no attention to the shocked demurs of the company, who could not fully comprehend his words.

Esme, a sudden warmth rising, realized that Hugo had misunderstood.

"You are quite mad, Hugo. I am not marrying Oliver. It is Fannie who will be his bride, if you are not too ill-natured as to delay the ceremony further with your mistaken interference!" she protested, since no one else seemed able to answer his furious challenge.

"What do you mean, my girl? You dash off from London with this fellow, bound for the country, causing me all kinds of trouble, and then . . ." For once, Hugo was speechless as the meaning of Esme's words sank in.

"Don't make such a cake of yourself, Hugo! I accompanied Fannie to lend her support. After all, she could not travel two days in Oliver's company unchaperoned. Wherever did you get the idea that Oliver intended to marry *me?*" she chided gently.

"I . . ." Hugo began. "I don't know. You have got me so bedeviled . . . All that I do know is that I love you, Esme, and I cannot live without you."

Paying no heed to the aghast group huddled in the small chancel, he drew Esme into his arms and kissed her with a passion and urgency which completely undid her. Her arms crept around his shoulders and she returned his embrace with equal ardor. Then, suddenly remembering their audience, she gasped and drew away her eyes searching his face and seeing the arrogant lordly Duke of Milbourne regarding her with a tender quizzical air.

But Hugo quickly regained his aplomb. "Since I have a special license secured some weeks past from the Archbishop of Canterbury, I see no reason why these rites cannot continue with two brides, with your permission, sir," he added as an afterthought, turning to the confused vicar. "And yours, of course, my dear," he said, giving Esme a look that made her blush with the audacity of it.

And so it came about. Fannie and Oliver, too dazed at the

suddenness of events, agreed that it would please them above all things to share their day with Esme and the duke. So Esme became the Duchess of Milbourne and Fannie claimed the more humble title of Mrs. Wells before the congregation, who would mull over the exciting denouement for days to come. Later, the two couples partook of the collation, which Mrs. Wells had hurriedly arranged. The brides bid each other a happy but tearful farewell with many promises of future meetings. The duke was impatient to carry off his bride and before the sun had set they were on their way to his estates some leagues distant.

Several evenings later, Esme, still in a daze from the change in her circumstances, lay beside her lord in the vast canopied bed in the master bedroom at Milbourne Abbey, replete from lovemaking, so satisfying, so tender, so different from their previous encounters, looked across the room at *The Tyrant* which hung in a dominating position on the wall above the fireplace.

"Although it is probably my best work, I should never have painted that picture. You did deserve all the approbation it brought, I believe, but I regret it exceedingly," she submitted, distracted by His Grace's attentions. She tried to look disapproving, remembering their violent dueling in the past. He should not be allowed to think he could always have his own way.

But Hugo, recalled to his transgressions, gave a rueful grin. "I deserved it, true, and I cannot regret the painting. It is a provocative work quite worthy of its artist—and its subject," he mocked. Then, before she could protest, he raised her chin from its resting place on his bare shoulder and raked her body with a look that caused her heart to pound.

"I was a fool, Esme, not to appreciate you from the start, but past experience had made me wary. Still, you showed me that

254